OF SEA

THE GUARDIAN MOUNTAINS
REALM OF SKY
MUNINNS HOME
TUNDRA PROVINCE
DESERT PROVINCE
KIN
REA
REALM O
IN-BET
THE MOUND
WHISPERING WOODS
'ESIS'
VERDANTVALE
REALM OF LAND
JUNGLE PROVINCE
HILLS OF YOID
THE FOUR REALMS

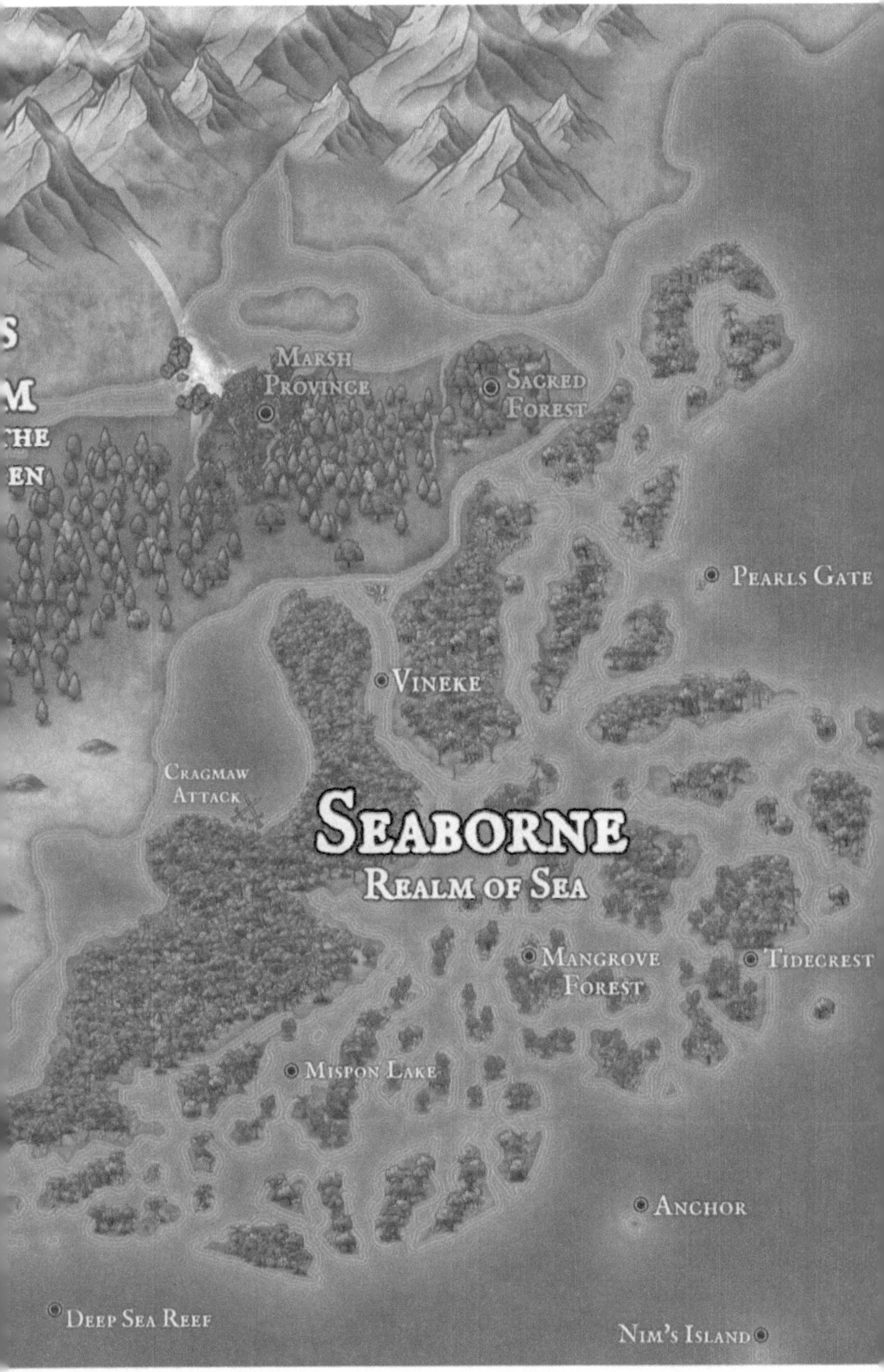
S
M
THE
EN
Marsh Province
Sacred Forest
Pearls Gate
Vineke
Cragmaw Attack
Seaborne
Realm of Sea
Mangrove Forest
Tidecrest
Mispon Lake
Anchor
Deep Sea Reef
Nim's Island

CONTENTS

To those who seek
To those who've found
To those whose journey is more than where they're bound.

"I will give unto him that is athirst of the fountain of the water
of life freely."
Revelation 21:6

OF SEA

S. J. GRAGG

These are not stories of the past
but prophecies of the future.

PROLOGUE

THE STORM RAGED ABOVE. Muffled thunder and bolts of light brightening the depths of the silent deep randomly. Lightning burst out in fits as it shot down from the vexed sky, illuminating the night sea to a darkened blue.

They sang their songs of melancholy and joy as they swam gently through the familiar abyss. Steadily, they dived further down into the serene darkness, looming over the past. Pieces of jutting metal stuck out of the seabed at uncomfortable angles. These creatures guarded the past and kept the history as they traveled the same paths throughout their generations.

As the traces of this long forgotten civilization disappeared from above, remnants remained below.

I

TRAPPED

ONLY ONE KIND OF FAUNANOID DARE
CROSS THE DEEP WATERS CURRENTS, THE
FOOLISH.

"Help!" she shouted, crying as she banged her fist on the rocky black stone.

"Someone! Please, *help!*" She turned around, running into all the walls that stood looming around her. Her face turned to the dark abyss above. The walls extended endlessly. Her knees buckled, and she fell to the floor in despair. A mixture of the sand and rock slid under her bare feet, creating patterns on the ground. This small enclosed area consumed most of her time. But occasionally, memories would resurface. She could recall being outside of the prison. The smell of salt on the ocean wind. The color of the tide. Most however was a blur, incohesive.

Images of what she recalled flashed through her mind. She shut her eyes. It had been so long since she had seen the sun dazzling on the waves above her as it shimmered through the coral city full of its pinks, purples and blues. Streaks of a majestic white castled marked by the sun crossed her mind, beckoning for her to remember as she sat huddled in the corner where two walls met and continued to cry. She thought of her home.

"He-hello?" A cautious voice came through clearly from the other side.

Her head jolted up. Her eyes wide and alert. She held her breath.

Was it my imagination?

"Hello?" she squeaked in a small, hopeful tone.

"Um, is... someone in there?" A young woman's voice asked unsteadily.

She jumped up. Her heart pounding against her chest.

"Yes! Yes! Please help me!" She cried out. Her hands ran mindlessly along the rough opaque wall as if she could reach her new companion on the other side.

"How... is this possible?" A hesitant voice spoke. "I'm so confused."

"No please! You must get me out of here! I've been trapped in here for so long." Panicked, she scrunched her nose in an attempt to hold back her tears and covered her mouth.

"Don't leave me here," she said in a small, defeated voice.

"I won't!" They exclaimed, surely. "I'll stay as long as I can, but I don't think you understand." The voice paused for a moment, then continued, "This- is my dream. You're *in* my dream."

"What?" Now it was her turn to be confused. "What are you talking about?" She stammered, as she tried to understand what the voice on the other side of the wall had said. She held her head steady with her hand.

"I don't know. I have never had this happen before. I could never talk to the people I see in here," there was shuffling as the woman came closer, "this is a first for me... sorry."

She tried to steady her emotions and squeezed her eyes closed, willing herself awake. The sound of her heartbeat drumming in her ears.

"Do you know why you're in there? Is there no way out?" She called from the other side.

"I've tried everything—there's no end, no escape."

She broke down into a full cry, falling back to the ground with a thud. The sound of her muffled sobs echoed through the barren chamber as she continued to weep, hiding her face in her hands and wrapping her arms around her legs for comfort. Her cheeks burned as tears welled up and fell in heavy drops, leaving a glistening path on her skin.

"Hey, it's ok, it's going to be *ok*. We will get you out, I promise. What's your name?" Her voice was smooth and calming.

She looked up through her hands and back at the wall.

"It's- Lyra." She responded, sniffling.

"It is nice to meet you, Lyra. I'm Sam."

Sam jolted awake, the boat rocking beneath her as the pieces of the dream slipped away.

She wiped her face with her hands, trying to force the foggy headache to disappear as she thought back to her dream. A scowl appeared on her face as she remembered how fast she had been pulled from it. Lyra's voice echoed in her mind as she woke, her heart racing. She hadn't even been able to say goodbye.

She looked around at the others sleeping as the boat's ferryman escorted them without strife through his known path towards the border city. They had been traveling by boat for a couple of days after they had reached the ocean and followed the coast. That is where they met the ferryman, who said he could take them the rest of the way towards the lake town, Vineke.

Sam waited for the others to wake as the sun rose over the ferns that decorated the sides of their river trail. It differed from the sunrises of the forest but was still solemnly beautiful as the beams silhouetted the grass, weeds, and ferns that stood tall against the sloshing water. She put her hand over the side of the sturdy boat and dipped it into the water, watching it ripple around its new obstacle. With the gentle rush of water against her fingers, she closed her eyes, focusing on the small current she had created. It soothed her the way the forest did, the crispness of the freshwater alerted her to her surroundings, waking her further.

The others stirred, from their slumbers. Sam watched Bram sleep. He still had not shifted back to his original form, and she was almost certain that he would be stuck as a human forever. Sam sighed and turned her attention to Cedar and Fin. They had been working hard to practice their fighting. Cedar had become stronger in her skills as a fire summoner while Fin worked on his hooked sword skills. She chuckled to herself as she thought back to him, slicing reeds on the shore from the boat in his dramatic tone.

She had also been trying to improve herself, but it was a battle through quicksand. Painstakingly slow and deteriorating her motivation to continue forward. Her thumb scratched at the boat's railing as she tried to move past it.

Looking back at the rising sun and the water, she waited for the others to wake so that she could give them the news about her newest dream.

"Havin' trouble sleepin'?" The older ferryman gruffed from behind her. She looked back at the amphibian man who pushed a long bamboo pole into the water and propelled them forward with the flowing current.

"I guess I am not used to sleeping in boats or on the water yet." She smiled at the gilled, light green man. He had no hair and gills on his neck that seamlessly merged with his skin and extended along his collarbones. He kept his finned feet free but wore a set of brown trousers. On his light green skin were two lines of blue that went up his neck and down his stomach. His eyes were an even lighter green accompanied with pupils that were long, vertical, and rounded at the ends. As Sam observed his features, she noted that he was the least human faunanoid she had met and wondered if all the fau from the Realm of the Sea were similar.

"Well miss, if y'er going to the water of the seas and rivers, y'er gonna have to get used to it." He looked at her, nodding. "It'll take a week 'er so, but you won't notice it after then," the ferryman said as he gave the pole another long steady push.

"Thanks, I'll have to keep that in mind." She smiled and heard more shuffling from the others. Cedar sat up, squinting groggily from her makeshift bed of pillows and blankets.

"When did you wake up?" She yawned. Bram sat up sleepily as well, stretching his arms and neck.

"Not that long ago, as the sun rose." Sam nodded toward the rays of the early morning as they continued to head that way to the lake town. Cedar swiveled her head in response towards the sunrise as she picked up and folded the blankets she had slept in.

"I had a dream last night," Sam added unhappily as her mind thought of the confusing conversation to come.

Cedars' eyes went wide eyed at that.

"You know who the next person we need is?"

Sam nodded.

Bram looked at both of them, his darkly tanned face molded into confusion.

"What are you talking about? The next person for the tournament thing you are doing?"

Fin sat up and scratched his head, shifting his bun around and replacing the ornamental pins in his hair.

"Well, someone catches on fast, don't they?" He tilted his head and raised an eyebrow in sarcasm toward Bram.

Bram shot him a look.

Fin smirked, content with the reaction. He laid back down, propping himself up with his arms.

Sam rolled her eyes but answered his question anyway. "I met a Wind Summoner before we left the village. Her name was Muninn. She is the keeper of dreams apparently and has been sending me dreams of the people that I need for the Journey of the King." She stopped to see if he was following, then she continued. "I first saw Cedar, then I had like two dreams about Fin."

The thief wooed in response.

Cedar snorted. Sam ignored him and kept talking. "Then, last night.... I had another dream, but this one was different-" she cut short. Her confidence dwindled at how to explain what had happened.

"Sam? What happened? How was it different?" Worry filled her voice. Eyes laid on her. Cedar packed away the blankets and now sat cross-legged in front of her, giving her full attention. Sam shifted uncomfortably on the balls of her feet.

"Ok, so, you know how in my dreams I have only seen darkened silhouettes of you two and I couldn't talk to them either? I didn't know who you were, but I was given clues about Fin."

They nodded.

"Well, I heard a woman crying for help, then I approached this massive wall made of rock and sand. After I got to it, I realized that the crying was behind the wall. So, I called out and.. she answered." Her brows knitting themselves together in confusion.

"Wait, you talked to someone- in your dream?" Fin sat up, becoming more focused on their conversation.

"What did she say?"

"Her name is Lyra, and she told me that she doesn't know how long she's been stuck in there. But she seemed so scared and I didn't want to leave, but I had no choice. When I woke up, I got pulled out of it." Sam rubbed her face in guilt and sunk down next to Cedar.

"So what does that mean?" Bram prompted, his hair morphing between black, gray, and brown through the different angles of sunlight.

"It means... our sea walker is trapped in my dreams."

A wave of scrutiny passed through the group at her response. Cedar spoke first. "How would that even be possible?"

"I have no clue, but she was there. We talked to each other like how we are right now." She motioned to the four of them. "I couldn't *see* her though." She laughed at her luck. "This will never be easy, will it?"

She met the eyes of pity from her friends. Sam turned away, upset with herself. She didn't want pity. She needed solutions.

"It'll be ok, we know her name and once we get to Vineke, we will begin our search for her." Cedar voiced confidence, trying to motivate the group.

"You're right, we aren't clueless. We have to work a little harder, that's all," Fin added in an attempt to cheer Sam up. Sam smiled.

"Thanks guys."

From behind her and Cedar, there was shuffling as the ferryman came up to the front of the boat, rocking it softly, and started rummaging through a pile of his things. A moment later, he pulled out a couple of fishing rods that had laid underneath a net and some twined rope. He held the items out to the four of them, his voice rising to address the group.

"This time of mornin' is good for fishin'. Who's hungry?"

They all looked at each other, a shy smile split apart Sam's face.

"You know, I don't think any of us know how to fish."

The quiet rustle of the water beneath the boat was the only sound as he paused, skeptically gazing at the group.

"So you're tellin' me you're headin' for a realm of mostly water and you don't even know how to fish?" He scoffed.

Then threw a pole at each of them. Sam caught hers off guard. "Y'er learnin today!" With a shake of his head, he scooped up another, much longer pole and a small box while beckoning them to join him.

A couple of hours had passed since they started fishing. The bobbers sat still in the water and the lines remained unmoving. They had caught nothing. Sam was beginning to sweat from the sun's beaming heat, with no trees to make shade and the water reflecting the sun's light. It was even hotter on the water than in the forest. Irritated, she shifted where she sat as she listened to Cedar grumble, annoyed with the idea of fishing all together.

"Your part fox Cedar, you should be good at this." Sam leaned in closer to antagonize her. Cedar didn't respond, she just made a face, mocking what Sam had said and put the pole down. Sam chuckled, looking back towards Bram and Fin who seemed to be enjoying themselves.

In her brief moment of distraction, her line began to tug gently. She snapped her head back to the now rippling water. In disbelief, she waited. She felt another tug. The bobber dipped into the water, disappearing for only a second. Excitedly, she slapped Cedar's arm to grab her attention. The ferryman came over and they watched as it completely ducked under the water and the line straightened out.

"Looks like you got one. Now pull the fishin' rod back and gather the string. Hurry now, you don't want it to snap."

Then looking at Bram, he added, "young fella, go grab my net. Quick, now!" Bram gave Fin his pole and scrambled up to find the net. Sam continued to struggle, dragging the line up, pulling the heavy fish to the surface. Her arms ached in the exciting battle between herself and their breakfast.

Bram returned with the net soon after and tried handing it to the ferryman.

"Nooo, no," he said waving his hand while he used the other one to help Sam, "you do it, you need to learn, now when the fish comes out, scoop'em up! Easy peasy!"

"I can see it!" Cedar squealed as she leaned over the side. "It's *huge*!" Sam gave another sharp tug, using her legs as she pushed against the side of the boat.

With a hectic splash, a slick, dark gray fish with black stripes and long whiskers came flying out of the water.

"Get'em in the net now!" The ferryman hollered. Unsure, Bram stiffly tried to catch the panicked fish, failing multiple times as it flopped around on the water's surface. Sam still gaining control of the line. After the third try, he succeeded and engulfed the thick fish wholly in the grass weaved net. He looked around triumphantly and held it up for the group to see. When he did, it flapped its fin and smacked Bram unexpectedly in the face with a wet thwack. Shocked, he dropped the net onto the boat and stepped back, holding his face. The rest of the group howled in laughter as the ferryman picked it up and chuckled along with them.

"You did good on your first try." He nodded to the two of them. "Now, who's ready for breakfast?"

Sam's stomach growled, and they all agreed eagerly.

"That... was... *hilarious*!" Fin got up and slapped his hand down on Bram's shoulder, laughing.

"Whatever." His face flushed as he slid Fin's hand off of his shoulder.

"Good job guys!" Cedar added.

Sam smiled as she got up. "You did great. Don't let him fool you," she reassured Bram. He rolled his eyes but cracked a smile as he followed the ferryman back to the small hutch where he cleaned the fish. A small bleating noise distracted Sam, and she peeked inside the deep hutch.

"Heyyy, I was wondering when you were going to get up, buddy." She laughed at Ajax, who laid in the shaded cabinet of the boat. He raised his head to look at her as he woke up more. He joined them on the deck, sprawling in the afternoon sun.

They spent the day fishing while learning to clean and gut the ones they caught. Sam's stomach flipped with the idea of scaling and gutting at first, but Bram caught on naturally.

"You're a little *too* good at that," she side eyed him sarcastically, watching him clean his hands from the previous fish. He stopped and looked at her.

"You know I used to *hunt* and *kill* my food before I became this mess," he gestured up and down himself, motioning to his now human body. "Right?"

Sam's mind flashed back to the night where he had fought Nakoia, Amos, and Uldous. Rain pattering on his monstrous face with the blood of her friends dripping from his mouth. The scars of his bite pulsed on her calf. She glanced down and could see they were visible but healing. A flash of blood gushed from her leg, as if it had happened only moments ago, then in a blink, it was gone. Her hand flew to her mouth, a cold sweat breaking out on her forehead as the room spun, threatening to swallow her.

"Sam, I-" Bram started, she put her hand stopping him from getting any closer and she left him there. The memories pressed in, suffocating her, and she frantically searched for an escape, a place where she could finally catch her breath.

Roughly, she sat down near the front of the boat, rocking it. She looked in the water. It was too deep to see the bottom, but swift specks of light darted around and past the boat.

"Way to go, doofus. I thought you wanted everyone to forget about that." Fin retorted at Bram's expense.

"I- I wasn't thinking, I'm sorry," he stammered. "I'll apologize."

"Give her a minute. Cedar can check on her. *You* can apologize later but *right now* we need to finish setting up dinner."

Bram must have agreed because there was no more conversation about what had happened, and Sam's mind split shamefully back toward the water.

She felt the boat rock again and heard light steps. The recognition of Cedar's presence sent a wave of heat through her, and she hastily covered her face, overwhelmed with embarrassment.

"I don't know what happened. I feel so bad. I started thinking about the fight we had with him in the hills and I couldn't get out of it. It was like I was back there," she sniffled. Cedar sat next to her, saying nothing but putting her hand on her back. Sam continued, "I am such a dummy. He has been trying so hard to fit in and I ruined all of our hard work with one stupid comment."

Cedar laughed. "You're being too hard on yourself Sam, the wounds from that are still relatively fresh, metaphorically and physically," her voice dripped with sarcasm, as she pointed to Sam's leg. "Of course, we are still going to be cautious around him. It is going to take time for him to earn our trust."

"Ya, ya I know, it's just...." Sam sighed, looking at the setting sun on the small grassy cliffs that now guided their trail. "He reminds me- of me."

"What do you mean?"

Sam looked at Cedar. "*I* was the monster. *I* was the hated one. *No one* trusted me, except for you and the family. Now look where I am. If you didn't give me that chance to prove myself, then I would probably be dead by now." She lifted her hands and let them fall back into her lap. "He is a kid and on top of that, he doesn't even seem to have a family or anybody." Sam looked back towards the boys, who were now fishing near the other end of the boat. With a glance back at Cedar, she added. "I'm going to give him that chance. The chance you gave me."

Cedar nodded, "And I'm with you the whole way, you know that!" She leaned in to Sam, nudging her with her shoulder and chuckling. Sam smiled, resolve blooming in her mind.

"I'll apologize to him tonight after dinner and be honest with him. I think that's the best thing to do."

The anchored boat sloshed quietly as it sat in the shallow waters. The fire cracked towards the sky and cooked the fish that had been caught earlier that day. Everyone sat around, watching with growling stomachs. Anticipation growing as the ferryman turned the pikes.

Cedar spoke up in the silence, "You know, we have been traveling with you for a couple of days now, sir, and we don't even know your name." A cluster of eyes turned to their guide.

"If you must know, it's Amphire Toad, but most just call me Amph," he said as he stripped the cooked fish from the hot metal pike.

Sam smiled to herself at the irony of his name matching his appearance.

"It's nice to meet you then, Amph," Cedar said, and the rest nodded in greetings. "This is Sam, Bram, Fin and my name is Cedar." Amph looked at them all gesturing at the formal greeting of the sea.

"Thank you for taking us to the border town, Amph," Sam added as she reached for the utensils and plates, then handed them out to everyone.

"Well, it's my job, y'er payin' me, so I wouldn't think too much of it." He chuckled and handed out dinner to each of them. "Now let's enjoy this dinner y'all worked so hard on. Eat up now." He ended the conversation with an enticing bite of his food.

Sam looked down at her own plate. The fish sat cooked, looking up at her with one dead eye. She grimaced and gingerly took a bite. Once the food was in her mouth, she closed her eyes and chewed. It was tender and with the spices they used, her stomach viciously growled for more. Quickly swallowing, she tore another piece off and ate vicariously.

They had finished eating and were dousing the fire when Bram walked up to Sam.

"Can we talk?" He asked reluctantly, pointing with his thumb away from the group for privacy. Sam met Cedar's eyes for a brief moment.

"Ya, I have to tell you something, too."

"Sam, I am sorry about earlier. I didn't think about what I was saying."

"No, I'm sorry. It was a whole thing for no reason. I need you to understand that I trust you and it *is* ok." She put her hand on his shoulder, Bram looked down at the ground, not saying anything.

She sighed.

"Did I ever tell you about when I woke up into this world?"

2

DOWN THE WAY A BIT

THE WAILING MAIDENS OF MISPON DO NOT
SING FOR THE LIVING.

"WE'LL BE AT VINEKE at some point today. But it depends on the water and the current," Amph called to the group from the back of the boat. "This canal can be dangerous, so mind yourself, and don't call any attention to us," he grumbled while pushing the long pole through the clouded water.

Sam noticed that they traveled close to the edge of the river canal and their guide used the bamboo pole to keep them under the shade of the trees and out of the open water. The canal was a large rounded area, the other side barely visible as the trees poked up on the water's horizon. It shimmered with the late morning sun and the sky painted pastels across itself with the few clouds that hung still over the land. She looked back at their ferryman, wondering what fears he would have on such a peaceful day. However, trusting his experience, she left the topic alone.

Fin had become fond of fishing and had used every opportunity to practice. He sat at the edge of the boat with Cedar. A fishing line bobbing in the water lazily following next to the boat and floating out into the deeper waters.

Sam joined them sitting cross-legged on the wooden board.

"Catch anything?"

"Fin said he saw something flicker, so he wanted to try to catch what was swimming under us," Cedar chuckled. "He won't be able to though. He is so bad at fishing, he didn't even put bait on the hook." Cedar pointed to the bob in the water.

"Masters don't need bait," Fin retorted. "Just skill and willpower."

Sam snorted back a laugh. "So you're calling yourself a master now? It hasn't even been two full days since you learned how to fish."

Fin rolled his eyes. "I am, and I will show you, once I catch the glorious fish I saw!"

"Hmm." Sam leaned over the edge and looked into the water. Cedar joined her. They stared into the murky brown, trying to catch glimpses of the lake bed or at least something that might be swimming by.

"Where did you see it?" Cedar asked.

Fin pointed behind them. "I saw it swim this way, and its bright scales vanished into that shaded patch up ahead."

Then he pointed forward to a shaded patch of water they were headed for. It had a fallen tree dipping into the water, with ferns and moss growing on its back. A big rock jutted out towards them, this gave them no way to stay close to the shoreline. Amph would have to go around it and away from the shallow waters.

"Hey Amph!" Sam called back to him. "Is there a reason you're staying close to the shore?" She looked at the trees and the tall grass that grazed against the boat. "Wouldn't it be faster to go straight through the middle?" She gestured a line with her hand.

He nodded, "I'spose, normally. But this part of the lake can be nasty to newcomers. It's a large and deep body of water. Big fish like large and deep bodies of water..." He stared at the three of them, not saying anymore as he continued to push them along.

Sam opened her mouth to respond, but Bram appeared from the back of the boat, silencing her.

He had been working on tying some rope for Amph. He greeted them as he sat down next to Cedar.

She thought back to the conversation they had the night before. He seemed surprised at how the village felt about her when she first arrived, covered in blood, sweat, and mud. She told him that she understood how he felt isolated and hated.

"But Sam, you haven't done anything. You took on the image of a monster. I have done terrible things as a shifter. I hunted, and fought, and destroyed people's lives so I could stay alive."

He said exasperated, "I am trying to right what I have done, and maybe in this human form I can, but as my actual self, the emotions and rage are too hard to control. It's like I was blinded for so long and then I woke up covered in the blood of everyone around me." He looked at his hands. His face shrouded in pain. "They don't feel clean, no matter how hard I scrub them."

Fear knotted in Sam's chest at the thought of him becoming that monster again. But the regret etched in his face made her heart ache too. She couldn't bring herself to voice her fears. He was dealing with the new thoughts of a human, contorting with the blind animal instincts he normally had.

Refocused now on her surroundings, she watched Bram in pity. He had so many new emotions and thoughts to understand that he didn't have as the shifter.

"Amph! What fish have blue scales?!" Fin called back to him. Amph leaned to the side, his brows furrowed. "Cedar is saying there aren't fish like the one I am describing."

"What color blue?-"

The expression on his face sent worry in Sam's heart.

"It wasn't dark or light... just blue. It went that way and disappeared in the shade." Fin answered his question hesitantly. "Why?"

Before Amph could answer, the water rippled violently, a dark shape rising right below the surface, sending chills through the group.

They stared in silence at the disturbance that came from the underside of the murky water. Deliberately, Amph took the pole out of the water and clipped it along the edge of the boat. Fin, in a swift motion, spun the reel, now the hook dangled above the water like a shining beacon.

Ajax, sensing the tension, bleated softly, his head poking cautiously out from the hutch.

"Go back down and stay silent," Sam hissed quietly to the young Qilin.

"I wouldn't do that if I were you," Amph grumbled. The three of them turned to see who he was talking to.

Bram was leaning over the edge.

"Bram!" Cedar grabbed his arm.

The water began to rise and ripple underneath him, he snapped his body back into the safety of the boat as a massive fish with glistening teeth and a long thin mouth jumped into the air, snapping its jaws shut where Bram's head would have been.

Sam stared on in horror at the creature as its blue horizontal split eye locked onto her. Chills ran through her body as she tried to stifle a cry of terror. Hurriedly, the four of them huddled in the middle of the boat in fear as it collided with the water, harshly rocking the boat back and forth. Water slushed in on both sides, soaking their feet.

"Amph! What *is* that?!" Cedar yelled. Lighting her hand that was closer to the edge of the boat on fire.

"That," he started as he picked up a metal tipped spear, "is the fish yer pal wanted to catch."

Amph grabbed hold of the hutch to steady himself and grimaced towards the water, trying to find his aquatic opponent. "I told you these parts 're dangerous, didn't I?"

He held a spear up.

Sam's jaw clenched, her eyes narrowed into a fierce glare at Fin.

"What?! How was I supposed to know that a *giant angry blue fish*, with sharp teeth was what he meant?!" He waved sporadically at the water.

Fin unlatched his hooked swords.

Sam responded by shooting him another look and snatching a spear up. Amph handed one of the metal tipped spears to Bram, whose previous choice in a weapon was no longer available. Then he placed his two webbed fingers in his mouth and whistled a tune of three high and low pitches.

"Why are you calling it back?!" Fin yelled desperately.

"The Cragmaw ain't leavin' anytime soon. I am callin' somethin' else. Be ready," Amph replied calmly.

They held their weapons, watching the water, waiting for it to attack again. A few moments passed with nothing. Sam anxiously studied the water for signs as she grew restless.

"Are you sur-" Cedar had started.

The boat lurched from the shore.

Sam fell back, knocked by the sudden movement of the boat. She caught herself on the bench and scrambled shakily upwards as they floated out towards the open water. The blue eyes and the jaws of the Cragmaw staring at them from the murkiness. Before anyone could react, Amph launched one spear towards it, spiking its side. Red drifting to the surface. Now the creature, in a fit of rage, flounced around in the water, trying to detach the weapon from its side. Amph pulled on the rope that was connected to the spear and yanked it out of its scaled side, releasing even more crimson blood. It dove deeper into the lake, away from the boat.

Once again, the vessel bounced with the waves, making anyone who was not used to it unsteady. Bram went and looked into the water, readying his spear. When he didn't see anything, he backed up.

"Maybe you killed it?" He looked at the ferryman hopefully. "There is a lot of blood."

Just then, the Cragmaw flew out of the water further this time. Its whole body flying over the passenger boat, and aimed itself downward towards them. The boat lurched again, but more violently now, a sickening crack echoing as a gaping hole appeared in the side of their vessel. Their opponent dragging the chunk with it into the unknown.

Sam and Fin, who were closest to that side, lost their balance and fell with the Cragmaw into the water. Sam fell, tumbling over the side, and splashed into the water back first. She surfaced, choking on both water and air. Simultaneously trying to breathe and swim for the boat. As she got back to the boat, she held onto the edge and searched for Fin. She saw him further out, waving his hands around and moving uncontrollably.

"I can't swim!" He struggled and yelled as his head dipped under the water and resurfaced, like the bobber on his fishing line.

"Are you kidding me, Fin?!" Cedar yelled out as she shot a fireball into the water near him.

Fin yelled again, "It touched me! It's so *slimy*!"

Sam looked at Cedar in desperation, who let out another fire ball towards the water.

"It's going to figure out that it's safe in the water soon! Someone get him!" Cedar shouted angrily.

Sam turned to Bram. Their eyes met as she wordlessly pleaded, and he groaned in annoyance.

"I am going to kill him." Bram snapped as he dived into the water towards their drowning friend.

Amph shot another spear as Bram reached him.

"Stop moving, you're making this harder than it should be! Hold on to my back." Bram grumbled.

Fin grabbed on and they swam back to the boat as Cedar continued to shoot off small fire balls behind them.

Amph pulled Sam up, and then the two of them helped Bram and Fin. When they got out of the water, Fin flopped onto the boat in exhaustion.

"The first thing I will do... if we live through this... is learn how to *swim*," Fin said, exhausted. Amph shook his head. Sam looked away as she tried to stifle a laugh, his wet orange fur clinging to him and the boat.

"Keep a lookout. A Cragmaw only stops when *it's* dead or *you're* dead." Amph grabbed the rope attached to his spear and began pulling it back on board.

Bram scrambled to his feet and copied Amph. Sam and Cedar kept an eye on the eerily still water.

"How do you even kill one of these?!" Fin sighed exasperatedly, he got up and shook the water from his fur.

Amph scoffed. "We don't have the manpower to kill this fish. Hopefully, our friend will be here soon. She'll kill it."

Before anyone could react, the Cragmaw jumped half on the boat. The other half of its scaly body hung in the water. As Amph went to grab the spear from the water, it latched its long horizontal mouth onto his arm. He cried out in pain as the monster dug it's teeth in more and tried to drag him into the lake.

"Amph?!"

Everyone panicked, rushing over to help. Fin wrapped his hooked swords around one of the Cragmaw's fins, slicing it off with ease. The long translucent blue fin flopped to the bottom of the boat. At the same time, Cedar put her hand on the giant monster's eye, catching her fingers on fire and searing it, sending the smell of burnt fish into the air. The massive beast let off a horrific screech, releasing the ferryman's arm and receding back into the water. As it fell, Bram attacked the flank of the Cragmaw with the second spear. They turned to see Amph clenching his arm as thick blood spurted from his deep wound. Cedar got to work instantly with some poultice she had already made to stop the bleeding.

Sam hadn't noticed that the rope connected to the second spear raced out of the boat and wrapped itself around her ankle as it sank into the depths of the lake canal with their wounded foe. She felt something tight around her foot and once she realized what had happened, it was too late.

"Cedar!" she cried as her right leg gave way from underneath her. She braced her fall with her hands but hit her head on the side of the boat as the unaware fish dragged her overboard. The last thing she saw before she sunk into the water was her friends grasping for her hand.

With the spear still lodged in its side, the Cragmaw descended, pulling her out into the immense lake. She struggled to unwrap the burly twined rope from around her ankle. The water rushing past her at a speed that made it almost impossible to move. Sam worked to manage her panic as water rushed into her nose.

It slowed. Then stopped. Frenzied for air, she swam towards the surface, hoping that the rope was long enough to reach. Upwards she went. The rope tightened. The Cragmaw swam further away, dragging Sam with it.

Once again, she worked with the rope, untangling and twisting it. Unsuccessfully trying to keep her panic from skyrocketing. Need for air growing. Her lungs aching. The rope loosened, and she pulled free from her trap. Hopeful and frantic, she took towards the surface where the water met the sky. She could see the sun and the clouds on the waves of water as it rippled above her. As her lungs begged for air, she watched the bubbles escaping her nostrils. The surface was within her grasp.

Sam froze in horror.

Two glowing blue eyes of the Cragmaw locked onto her, its gnarly teeth gleamed in the dark water.

The moment the Cragmaw had noticed she had seen it, it swam towards her in a persistent ferocity. She braced. Terrified, crossing her arms in front of her face for the sense of protection. Her mind raced—her friends, her quest, the countless things she'd never get to see. Her heart pounded, she took the chance. Her body moving on its own to the surface.

A noise shattered the thickness of the silence in the water.

It sounded like a whale call echoing through the lake. The Cragmaw stopped only feet from her death. It now looked to its side at something else. Sam looked too. At that moment, from the darkness came a light. The light of an outline of a large mass swimming towards them at an incredible speed. It was a giant creature with two front flippers, two back flippers, an incredibly long neck, and a tail equal in length. It glowed a green on some patches of its smooth looking skin.

It called out again, and the Cragmaw, accepting the challenge, darted straight towards it with its jaws open. Sam, not being able to hold her breath anymore, swam back to the surface. As she reached the edge where the sky and the water meet, she gasped for breath, choking out the water that had made its way in.

"Sam! You're ok!" Cedar cried out as she hung over the boat, grabbing onto her. She had tears in her eyes as she hugged her. Sam nodded, dazed. She looked up at Cedar, speechless, not knowing how to explain what happened. Baffled, Sam took a breath and pushed off the boat back into the water. Cedar yelled out as she went back under, but she needed to see the new creature that had emerged to rescue them.

It was hard to make out, but she could see two silhouettes circling each other. They merged and split multiple times, but after the quarrel, she watched as the glowing savior bit the neck of the Cragmaw and dragged it in their direction and downwards. It kept a tight lock on the Cragmaw as it spun around in the dark and sped up, making its way to the surface.

Sam went up for air again. She clung to the side of the boat as the majestic creature breached the water and flew high into the air with the defeated Cragmaw in its mouth. It jumped in an arch and gave off another one of its soothing calls as the sprinkle of water sent droplets of fire to sparkle in the afternoon sun. It dived back into the water, releasing the Cragmaw from its grip to let it float on the water with the waves as a semblance to their safety.

"Wha-what was that?" Fin stumbled for his words, and Sam looked up towards the baffled faces of her friends. She laughed in response to their reactions. Which rapidly morphed into vexation when she felt the water shift around her.

Sam turned to look out at the direction of the shift and in front of her emerged the long neck and the head of the green and purple creature staring at her. Her eyes widened as she mushed herself against the boat, trying to appear as small as possible, but it had already noticed her and put its giant nose against her face, smelling her.

Its heavy head pushed against her and its nostrils flared open and closed as it loudly sniffed her.

Her body trembled. Unsure what to do, she closed her eyes and put her hand out. A wave of warmth and delight washed over her as she stroked the creature's slimy skin, its rhythmic heartbeat bringing a soft, comforting chuckle to her lips.

"It's alright there girly, this is the one I called for." Amph came to the edge, still keeping his arm close to his chest, blood dripping down onto his stomach and staining his pants. He patted the neck of the creature.

"This is Tarati Tui, which means purple water lily, she is named after the iridescence on her body, she is a Ness." He nodded as he stroked the front of her face down to her nose, she closed her eyes and let out a deep breath that rippled the water. Cedar, Bram, and Fin helped Sam out of the water. She spoke up with a question once she was standing stable on the destroyed boat.

"Ness, like Nessi- *the Nessi?*" Sam asked, glancing between Amph and Tarati Tui.

"I'm not sure, but their species has been called the Ness since the Elementals brought them here. They have been our companions and protectors since the beginning."

Sam took a sharp breath in and let out a baffled laugh.

Looking at her, Cedar smiled, her eyes full of curiosity. "What?"

"Nothing," she shook her head but smiled to herself at the irony of her past once again revealing itself in an odd way.

"Tui, bring over the Cragmaw. That'll be good eaten and we can sell the scales." He gestured to the lifeless fish that now floated in circles. "Since you guys did most of the work, I'll give you the scales to sell and rations of the meat for your journey. Cragmaw meat is delicious if cooked the right way."

"Thank you, but we should probably get you to someone who can look at that wound." Fin frowned as he saw the ferryman's arm.

"I'spose," He studied the fresh wound. "I can't row anymore, so Tui will have to pull us the rest of the way, if she is alright with it." He nodded towards her. She let out another short pulse that came from the back of her throat.

"Thank you for the assistance, Tui. You'll get yourself a mighty portion of the Maw for doing the heavy liftin'." Amph smiled and patted her neck again as she came back to the boat.

Sam gasped and turned towards the hutch.

"Ajax!"

Bram stood next to the wooden board. He kneeled down quickly to open it. Sam rushed over to look inside. Hearing a scared bleat and seeing his horned head pop out, she let out a sigh of relief.

"I completely forgot you were here!" She exclaimed.

He bleated once more and emerged fully from his hiding hole and shakily walked up to the edge of the boat to examine their new friend. Ajax bleated happily and Tui gave out a couple of short, cheerful squeaks.

"That's.. adorable." Fin responded.

"Help me tie this to the front of the boat and toss it in the water for her when you're done." Amph tossed another twine rope towards Fin, who awkwardly caught it in surprise but nodded. He and Bram headed to the front and began arguing about how to tie the rope. Tui softly dipped back into the water, disappearing from sight.

"You two, can you grab the rope that's connected to the spear still lodged in the Maw? Drag it towards the boat and I'll clean the beast once my arms bandaged more." Amph pointed towards the other end of the boat. Looking back towards Fin and Bram, he yelled.

"Today boys! Or we're gonna have to deal with another one soon!"

After he said that, they got quiet. Then began mumbling, and nudging each other as they worked.

Sam laughed and made her way towards the back. She looked in the water for the rope and saw it floating close to the boat. Cedar handed her one of the spears, she nodded in understanding, and used the edge of the tip as she hooked the rope and brought it on board. Cedar grabbed it, pulled the Cragmaw closer and tied the rope around the wooden cleat.

"Wow, they're already done and *you're still arguin'!*" Amph called towards the other two. They looked back and glared at Sam and Cedar, who couldn't help but snicker. Fin pushed Bram out of the way and finished tying the rope to the front cleat. Proud of his work, he smiled. Bram rolled his eyes and tossed the rope into the water.

Tui emerged and grabbed it. With a mournful creak, the boat jutted forward, Fin stumbled again. The group chuckled as he got up and sat down, not looking at them. Cedar patted his shoulder, still laughing as she sat down next to Bram and Sam joined them. They watched in silence as Tui pulled them slowly toward the distant lake city of Vineke, the tension of the battle fading with each rolling wave of the water.

3

WHERE THE FIREFLIES GO

THE LAKE CITY EXPANDED and followed the course of the water. It was a common belief among the people that the areas where the river formed pathways were sacred, and rather than forcing their own route through the land, they adapted to it. There were three main sections within the city.

Sam and the others arrived through the first area where many waterways snaked off of the central river producing passages for the Nessi to travel through, and giving homes for those who could not breathe underwater but still lived in sync with it. Smooth river stone, wood, and mud were used to construct their homes and shops. Inside each of the homes sat a regular entrance and an underwater entrance carved into the side wall for the smaller Nessi or for any other gilled creature to come through.

In the second section, a series of three interconnected levels of many small pools served as dams. People took advantage of the pools for fishing, cleaning, and cultivating floating farms for vegetation. While the waterfalls created irrigation, it also led to the third and the last section of the lake city.

The deepest and widest part of the lake was under the falls. The underwater homes of the residents were located there. River stones were used to build these homes, with each stone strategically stacked and positioned to maintain balance. With a keystone placed at the entrance to ensure the structure's security. The houses were designed with intentional small holes in the walls to allow for unobstructed water flow, preventing any damage to the structure. The koimaids and other fau that spent their lives under the water farmed the kelp and plant life that grew there. They caught the fish that was sold and looked over the sea cows that roamed the underwater meadows of their homes.

The Nessi used connecting waterways to travel on both sides since they couldn't go over the waterfalls. Sam learned the female Nessi grew larger and were fewer than the males, so they roamed the lake, keeping away predators, and protecting the city. The males being smaller, were the carriers of goods and faus. Often they were kept as honored pets or guests to each household. As pups, they start out with the name of Tui, which means water lily for the females or lily pad for the males. But once their colors came in with maturity, they were given their second title, that represented the color that showed through.

To the travelers, the city was known as the border between Verdantvale and the Seaborne. However, to the people that lived there, they called their home Firefly Grove. They see themselves as guardians of their environment, responsible for the well-being of plants, and animals that reside there. The fau had a celebration each summer called the First Sighting, where they would celebrate the fireflies return at the beginning of the warm season, and watch them light up the night sky with the stars all summer long.

Sam and the others had stayed with Amph, who had attentively asked them to join him and his family after the attack. He lived in one waterway in the first section of the lake with his wife, Lorelei, and their Nessi, Ban Tui, who was named after his tan scales that had come in only a couple years ago. They had no children. When Cedar asked, Amph's wife wistfully told her that she could not bear any. So they dedicated themselves to taking care of the others around them. Lorelei resembled Amph, wearing gardening clothes with purple skin and long brown hair tied in a messy bun most of the time. She was kind hearted and soft-spoken to all.

It had been a couple of days since they had arrived. Lorelei took them and showed them around with Ban Tui as Amph stayed at the house healing with Ajax for company. She explained the culture of the river and how the people worked with it. Sam had been eager to continue exploring after Atlon, but she was baffled at the sight of Vineke the Firefly Grove. The people recognized the value of water and chose to partner with it, rather than destroying what they didn't want in order to access what they needed. Lorelei explained that the only change they had made to the lake was the connecting waterways for the Nessi to move around effortlessly.

After the first couple of days of exploring and asking around for the sea walker named Lyra, the group grew anxious.

"What if we are wasting our time here?" Fin asked Sam, "What if she isn't here? Or we aren't able to find out which Province she is from?"

"Reefs and Lakes," Lorelei interrupted.

"We call them Reefs for salt and Lakes for fresh, dear. Please don't stress about it. I'm sure you will find her." She smiled as she put out a salad on the table for lunch.

"I didn't know the other realms called them something different," Cedar said.

"I haven't had any more dreams about her either. I am getting worried about losing time on our travels. We still need to get to the Realm of Sky and find our flier." Sam hopped back to Fin's previous comment as she twisted the bead in her hair.

"Stop that," Cedar hissed, smacking Sam's hand away from the restless movements. "You're going to pull your hair out," she said sternly, side-eyeing Sam. In response, she returned the look but stopped and fiddled with the water style carvings on the stone table.

"Why don't we give ourselves a couple more days, and then decide what we want to do," Bram spoke up. "We can see if you will have another one of your dreams, and in the meantime, we can keep looking and get ready to make our way to the next Reef or Lake." As he finished speaking, he stuffed a wad of salad into his mouth. Bram wrinkled his nose in disgust as he chewed on the leaves, but he swallowed them anyway.

"I agree with the boy," Amph added, gesturing to Bram. "You need to be sure on your next move, and in the meantime, if you need a distraction, you are welcome to help with the sea cows or the floating farms."

"O! I call manatees!" Cedar raised her hand. "I've wanted to see them since Lorelei mentioned them!"

"I wouldn't mind seeing how you farm on the water, back in our village. I was interested in gardening," Sam said.

"I was thinking the same thing. I wouldn't mind learning how it works. Maybe we can figure out how to do it in Atlon too," Fin nodded.

"I guess I can go with Cedar," Bram shrugged, "the sea cows sound cool."

Fin snorted and stifled a laugh at his response, Bram shot him a look but didn't continue the conversation.

"Alright, then it's settled. Stay for the rest of the week! We will decide what to do then!" The conversation came to an end, and the aroma of their midday meal filled the room as they ate, all in agreement.

As Sam ate, she watched Ban Tui swim through the underwater entrance of their home, and come up through the small pool in their eating area where Ajax sat. Additionally, the floor of the small pool was adorned with a large semicircle of river stones, and on the wall where the pool opened. Her eyes sparkled with delight as she rested her chin on her hand, a playful smile forming on her lips, awaiting the lively interaction between the two. As Ajax approached, she gave a subtle smile and patted Cedar to get her attention.

He sniffed the water, making his way towards the Nessi but keeping as far away as possible from Ban Tui. He stuck his neck out to sniff the lazy creature. Ban Tui had his head on the floor and laid there as he side-eyed Ajax coolly. After a moment, Ajax decided that there was no threat, he licked the top of Ban Tui's leathery head and laid on the floor on his side with his head closest to the Nessi. Sam and Cedar chuckled at the exchange and continued their lunch.

"Fin and I will go check out the pools and you guys will be with the sea cows at the bottom," Sam said as the four of them stood outside the house. "Then we can meet back here at sundown." She added.

"Yes, that works. But I think you should wear the mask, just to be safe..." Fin put in.

He scrutinized Bram. "We should probably get him one, too."

Sam grew quiet. She didn't want to, but understood why she needed to. She and Bram locked eyes, and he murmured an agreement as well.

"On our way, Lorelei and Ban Tui can take us to the market to look for something like hers." He gestured towards the blue and silver fox mask that Sam had pulled from her pack.

She put it on and felt the familiar curves of the clay. She hadn't needed her mask, staff, or armor yet. They had met Amph by accident and he didn't seem to take notice of them, and the city had been so overcrowded they thought no one would have noticed her either. However, now they headed to the middle section where the farming happened, and it was bound to be less hectic and more noticeable.

"That sounds like a good idea," Cedar beamed, "and we can go shopping!" She jumped in excitement at the idea.

"I have never gone shopping before." Bram said.

Fin sighed and slapped his hand down on Bram's shoulder. "You're gonna hate it, good luck, buddy." Fin saluted him with his first two fingers. Sam laughed as they set off, while the other two waited for Lorelei.

"I didn't know you were into farming?" Sam spoke up on their walk to the waterfall pools.

"Ya, I guess," he shrugged as he continued, "I helped my aunt with the spirals and gardening back when my mom died."

He looked down as he kicked a small rock along with them. "It helped me put my mind away, and it became something I grew quite fond of. So, I'm sure she would also find this elusive aquatic farming thing pretty interesting." He wiggled his fingers mysteriously. Sam rolled her eyes but couldn't help but smile at the thought of the thief gardening with his warrior aunt.

As they walked across stone arched bridges, she couldn't help but gaze at the serene city around her. It hid in the foliage's greenery and trees. Each house had moss and other plants growing in the mud plaster they used to hold the stones together. This gave the homes an ancient look of tranquility and kept the air suitable for hot days. Giant stone arches connected to both sides of the river banks, acting as bridges and gated archways over the river. There were hanging glass lanterns in the shapes of ovals that also accompanied the homes and archways. Upon closer inspection, she realized though that they were empty, confused she continued to admire them.

"Hey... what's with the empty glass lanterns?" Sam asked Amph, as she pointed to them.

He looked up, "Those are lanterns alright, but we use the fireflies as the lights during the summer. At night they are caught, then in the morning we let them out. We also use the different colors of firefly lights to communicate. There are four colors; yellow, orange, blue and green." He counted them out on his fingers. "Yellow's normal, orange means dangerous animal or fuas, blue's hazardous weather, and green is really too close to yellow so we just use both colors for everythin's fine."

"What? I didn't know that there were that many colors of fireflies," Sam said.

"Mmmhmmm, when I was younger, my cousin told me that one time, he saw a purple one. We spent most of our summers looking for another'n. To this day, he still tries to convince us he saw it." Amph chuckled and looked up towards the sky.

Fin oohed and squatted on the stone pathway. Sam stopped and kneeled over him. He picked up a shimmering rock, examined it, then stuffed it in his pocket for safekeeping. She looked at him flatly and he just shrugged as he continued walking.

"It's pretty." Fin added as he walked ahead. Sam snorted in response, but ran to catch up with the other two.

Bram, Cedar and Lorelei walked through the lined stalls and stores that decorated both sides of the river's boardwalk. Merchants could even sell wares and food from their boats that were tied to the planks. Vineke seemed to be a larger city than Bram had thought it would have been. He looked around nervously at the people walking past to the talking and interactions that happened around him. Turning back to the planked walkway, he realized he had never been in such a crowded space before. Even though he was used to the wilds of the forests, he remembered a time when he had traveled through the other realms trying to find somewhere to live. He side-eyed Cedar anxiously, wondering if he should tell them about his childhood and where his family was. She skipped happily looking through the stalls and windows of the stores unaware of the strife he was mucking through. He took a deep breath and shook his head. That was a conversation for another time.

"Bram! Wow! Look at all the stuff! I have never been to a place that sold so much clothing!" Cedar squealed as she ran ahead to another shop window.

He laughed, "I have never been to a place that sold stuff. So ya, this is pretty crazy!" He smiled and Cedar looked back at him. For a moment, he saw in her eyes the shadow of his monster.

"Sorry, ugh, didn't mean to bring that up." He said, flushing and looking towards the ground.

"Is it too much?" Cedar asked, coming up next to him.

"What?"

"Is this all too much?" She gestured to everything around them. "I know when I went to Atlon, I was definitely excited but also nervous about all the stuff around me." She looked at him and put her hand on his reassuringly. "So, I can see this being overwhelming for you, too."

He looked down and stammered. Her hand was soft and gentle, while his were stained with the blood of her family. Blushing again, he didn't know how to respond. He took his arms and crossed them behind his back, instantly regretting the absence of her warmth.

"Hey kids! I found a clothing shop that sells some festival masks like your friends. Come and see if these are what we are looking for!" Lorelei yelled from the doorway to a small shop a little way down to their right. Cedar smiled happily at Bram. He smiled back, relieved of the escape.

They went inside the small rectangular shop that sold small trinkets and other items to decorate one's home. On the right wall hung a cluster of festival masks. As they approached, they examined them, trying to find one that would suit him.

Cedar held up a tiger mask, a red one with a long nose, a white fox, and another one with long tusks with its mouth in a snarl. Bram shook his head at each of them. He couldn't seem to find one that he liked.

Then a glint caught his eye. He moved through the pile on the shelf. It was an all black dog mask with gold painted inside the ears, eyelashes, and golden fangs sticking out of its calm face. The mask ended where the jaw should have been, just as Sam's blue fox spirit mask. He picked it up and stared at it. He could feel the rage behind its calm expression.

Looking over at Cedar he smiled sadly, "kind of ironic isn't it?"

She was silent for a moment as she looked between him and the mask. "I like it," she said without emotion. "I think it suits you, *silent but secretly dangerous*." She let out a smirk, and they snickered together. Content, they walked over to the merchant that sat behind a desk of jewelry near the door.

"Good afternoon," Cedar said politely, drumming her hands on the wooden desk. "We would like to buy one dog mask, please."

The merchant looked up. She was an older woman with blue tinted skin and gills hidden under her long black graying hair and she wore a baggy dark pink dress. "Oooo yes!" She touched the mask that now laid in front of her. "I see you found the demon dog mask from the Sky Realm. Very good. This mask helps to ward off evil spirits and other demons!" She picked it up and examined the mask dramatically.

"Did you hear that Cedar? It's a *demon dog* mask! It's perfect for me!" Bram looked at her, his mouth curving into a coy grin.

She shook her head at the bad joke, pointing to the mask she replied, "But! It wards off evil spirits. We are going to need that." She raised her eyebrow sarcastically back at him.

The merchant lady continued, now clearly upset at the two. "Do not push aside the lore behind this mask! It is said that he is the god of the dead, and that is not something to take lightly!" To make her point, she firmly but gently placed the mask down back onto the desk. "That would be 20 copper bits, then."

"Man, I don't think we have that much... we gave a lot of it to Amph." Cedar groaned as she rustled through her pack, "What about this fish scale thing? Amph said it cost money," She placed one of the Cragmaw scales on the counter. "It comes from the cragmaw lake monster."

The merchant behind the counter's eyes grew wide for a moment, but just as quickly returned to normal. As she went to snatch it up, Lorelei smacked her hand over the iridescent scale. Bram and Cedar turned and looked at her, and saw her eying the merchant with no emotion. They said nothing. Keeping her hand over it, Lorelei grabbed a handful of her own coins and tossed them towards the lady while simultaneously scooping up the scale from the counter.

The merchant grumbled, waved her hand, dismissing them, and turned without saying another word. Bram grabbed the mask, and they walked back outside into the warm breeze before speaking again.

"Lorelei, what was that?" Cedar asked once they were clear from the store.

She took a deep breath. "You need to be careful showing people you have these. They are extremely valuable and worth a lot more than a mask." She handed the scale back to Cedar. "Make sure to only trade them when you need bits or for something equally rare. And above all else, don't let anyone in this realm know you have them," she hissed quietly in a stern voice while meeting their eyes.

"Understood. I am sorry, I didn't know they were that rare," Cedar said, frowning as she put the scale safely back in its velvet sack.

"It's not your fault," she said, "I am just letting you know that people have killed over those."

Bram and Cedar nodded in response. His breath caught at the thought of killing for even one of the scales that Cedar carried a sack of on her side.

"Now let's take a look at this new mask you bought." Lorelei added in, in a more cheerful tone.

Bram blinked away the thought and held it up, putting it on his face. It felt snug and warm, as if it had been sitting in the sun baking for a time. He touched the cheeks of the smooth mask to readjust it, but the fit felt correct. Putting his hood over his head to add effect, he said in a spooky voice.

"What do you think? Do I look like I ward away bad luck and demons?" He crossed his arms and puffed out his chest to make himself look bigger. Lorelei laughed, and Cedar chuckled as she shook her head.

"Scary indeed." A woman's soft voice chuckled behind him.

A chill ran up his spine and his neck hair bristled. He looked at the other two and, seeing their shocked faces, he swung around.

It was a koimaid.

She was the color of magnolias that bloomed in the middle of summer, and her upper body was splotched with an orange red and as it went down, the orange red covered her whole tail with small splotches of the magnolia white. She had black hair that was longer than he had seen on anyone before. It danced in the water with the bottom of her fins as she sat on the edge of the boardwalk, letting her lower half cascade into the deep river water. Her arms were crossed neatly into her lap. As she looked up at them, Bram saw that she had black makeup around her eyes accompanied by a deep red lipstick.

Not sure how to reply, he backed away. The koi mermaid's sudden appearance left him stunned. He had only laid eyes on a few in real life, but being younger, he couldn't recall what they looked like.

"Hanako," Lorelei interrupted the silence with a deep bow. Bram slid in next to Cedar and they copied her movements.

"Please allow me to introduce our guests who have been staying with us. This is Bram and Cedar. They are... personal friends traveling through." She looked at both of them in order. "Thank you for taking your time and stopping by Oracle." Lorelei looked at them and added, "this is our Oracle, our *leader* of Vineke."

Understanding that, they perked up and bowed again, saying their thanks.

"Your name is lovely, Oracle Hanako. It is so nice to meet you. Vineke is the most beautiful place I have seen," Cedar responded respectfully.

Oracle Hanako chuckled again and bowed her head slightly in thanks. "I am glad you and your friends find it welcoming, and I am happy to hear the Ness have taken a liking to you, this... is a good sign." She looked at Bram. Her eyes that were the same color of the orange red that adorned her skin seemed to hold an all knowing wisdom behind them and his breath was taken away when they made eye contact.

Looking away, he added in the same tone as Cedar, "We are grateful for the shelter and food your people have provided in our time of need."

"There are four of you and a Qilin, yes?" She said as she picked a lily from the water. "I have still not met the other two and was planning on heading down to the falls to speak with them when I saw you here. It was very nice to meet you, but I shall be going now." She lifted the light pink lily and gave it to Cedar. Her hair fell into her face as she bowed and gently dipped back into the water, disappearing underneath. Cedar crouched on the edge and looked over into the flow of water.

"Thank you!" She said, holding up the flower in awe. "Look Bram." She said, looking back at him in excitement. He came to the edge and followed her finger to where she was pointing. He saw a streak of white and red swimming gracefully through the current with a group of other koimaids of various colors.

"Woah," he said, looking after her. "That was-" He couldn't find the words to express how he felt. "Unexpected?"

"Hanako is a beautiful koi and her kindness does not fall short either. The faunanoids of Vineke see her as our symbol of serenity, she *is* Vineke to us," Lorelei added, looking on towards her as they began walking towards the deep lake. "Let's head to the meadows now, before the sea cows get tired and leave for a nap," she chuckled. Cedar beamed with excitement as Lorelei helped to adjust the lily in her hair.

4

GOOD COMPANY

THE HEARTS OF THE NESSI BEAT AS ONE WITH
THE LAKE.

THE POOLS OF WATER lay in front of Sam crisp and clear. Copying Amph, she stepped down into the one that was closest to the bridge after taking her shoes and socks off. As she looked ahead to the many pools that jetted to the other side of the now vast riverbed, she counted a multitude of them having gardens occupying them. Some, she noticed, had three small gardens, two medium-sized gardens, or one large garden that took up the majority of the pooling water.

They walked closer to the nearest one, her eyes followed the flowing water as it cascaded downward into the next layer of the falls. She watched it and looked out towards the deep lake where Cedar and Bram had said they would be heading.

Wondering if she could see them, she walked to the edge and peered out.

"I'd be careful doin' that. The water's current can be unpredictable and strong at times." Amph said, as he kept walking.

Sam's eyes widened at the thought of falling over. And her sight scoured the falls to where she might end up if she lost her balance. She nodded, slowly refocusing on the task at hand as she waded through the water, feeling the gentle current push against her legs as she moved toward the others. The ground underneath her was sand. She could feel the graininess in between her toes and she would sink a little with each step she took.

Even though the water was barely above her knees, she noticed that the lake water around her was immensely clear and that she could see to the bottom.

Fin and Amph had already made it to the closest one when she caught up. It was one with two medium-sized beds floating in the pool closest to the bridge. Chopped trees were used to build the sides of the platforms. Sam touched the border of the garden. The container was solid and overflowing with rich, dark soil. The vegetation growing on the two platforms appeared to be some kind of blue beans and pale yellow squash.

"It is the middle of the summer, so the plants are plentiful right now." Amph said as he picked one bean from the lush green stalk and popped it into his mouth.

Fin copied him, "These taste so fresh! Is it because of the aquaponics or because of something else?" He dipped his head under the water to peek underneath. Amph and Sam followed.

She gripped the edge to steady herself against the soft current, then knelt down and dipped her head underwater to inspect the floating farm from below.

On the bottom was a small forest of roots and algae. They were able to safely grow out of a thin mesh twine rope. Keeping the structure in place were a couple of supports that went into the sand. As well as loose ropes tied to each corner that shot further out into the pool, giving them room to float a bit.

Something light brushed by her foot, a small brightly colored fish, no longer than one of her fingers examined her feet. Smiling, she wiggled her toes and the bright purple fish darted away and back under the garden. She watched it swim and disappear into the dense roots. At that, she began to notice a flicker of color here and there. She saw greens, blues, pinks, purples, oranges, and reds all darting back and forth in a lively manner. Once in a while, one of the small vibrant fish would dart out mistakenly but hastily swim back into its home and continue its work of eating and cleaning. She patted Fin and pointed to the small community of fish and they went back up for air.

"What type of fish are those? Do you know? I have never seen ones so colorful," Sam asked, wiping the excess water from her face.

"I think some look like little goldfish, but I'm not sure about the others," Fin responded, his rough orange hair stuck in awkward positions on his face.

"Those would be betas," Amph spoke up, "very aggressive little buggers, but effective, nonetheless."

"These are aggressive?!" Sam laughed and held out her hand to a light pink and white beta that had made its way out from the safety of the roots.

"Not to us. They are to each other, but with the roots being so dense, it's harder for them to fight. Once winter comes, though, it'll be a bloodbath." He shook his head as he stood up. Sam raised her eyebrows in disbelief as she looked at the small fish fluttering around her fingers and then back into its home.

She stood up as well and looked at each of the farms. "Do they all have the little fish in each pool underneath the roots?"

Amph nodded.

"So, then, how does this work exactly? I am kind of new to farming and gardening." Sam motioned with her hands to the garden.

"Well," Amph scratched his head, "it's like any other gardens I'spose, except it's on the water."

A look passed between Fin and Sam and they exhale a quiet laugh behind Amph. Sam had thought that he would understand the gardens, but she realized now that he was the ferryman, so he must spend little time in the area.

"What do the goldfish and bettas do then?" She asked out loud, trying to think her way through to the answer.

"They clean and maintain a healthy plant," Amph responded.

"Ok, then what about the water? What is the difference between planting in the ground or letting the roots dangle in the water?" Fin asked, putting his hands on his knees and looking back into the water at the roots.

"I don't believe there is a right or wrong way. I think it's just different from you land folk," Amph answered. "But the flowing water helps irrigate and keeps the plant roots from getting rotten."

"Ok, ya, I can see how that might help the roots grow. Can we go check out the other ones too?" Sam motioned towards the other gardens and the workers who maintained them.

Amph nodded, "Let's try to stay out of the way of the farmers though, we don't want to be too much of a distraction from their work."

They crossed over the pool and set about their way, examining each of the different gardens. The layouts to each were the same, but the sizes of the plot varied along with what was growing there. Sam and Fin saw beans, squash, corn, pumpkins and vibrant summer flowers all being harvested. Some of the shallow pools of water were empty of a farm, but contained a large net that extended the width of it.

"What are the nets for?" Sam asked, looking at Amph. "Fish?"

"Yes, they are how we catch the salmon we eat and sell to other Reefs or Lakes." He pointed towards the nets and Sam realized they had formed an on and off pattern. "We catch only what we need. The nets stay but fishers come out when a run of salmon are seen further down at the beginning of the village. They travel through to the sea where they go for some years and will come back this way again, back to where they were born." He motioned towards the sea and then back again while he talked. "Since it is summer now, we might have time to see some while you are still with us."

"I didn't know there were fish that were both salt and freshwater. Is that true for sea faunanoids too?" Fin poked in.

"A rare gift, those who carry the trait are important to our society and keep the divided waters together with it." Amph responded.

Sam opened her mouth, but something tickled her leg again.

"Hey!" She chuckled and looked down into the crystal water. A sea foam colored beta swam intertwining her legs. She ducked into the water next to the floating garden of beautifully colored flowers to watch the beta swim up and through her hair that was floating around her.

She chuckled. It came close to her face and saw its back fin was large and spread wide from top to bottom, almost like a peacock with its open feathers. It had sparkling green spots on its body and swam gracefully around as if it wanted to show its dress of fins off.

She felt a tap, which brought her back to her surroundings. Lifting up, she looked at Fin, who had poked her.

"Do you hear that?" He asked.

Once he brought attention to it, Sam realized that she could hear the faint noise of a horn being blown. It blew three times, then third lasted longer than the first two.

"Well, there ya go," Amph put his hands on his hips, "looks like y'all will get to see a salmon run after all." He turned and started wading back to where they had come. Sam got up, her clothes sticking to her. The wind causing a chill to run up her spine on the warm summer day.

"Wait, there are salmon swimming to us?" Sam asked, getting excited.

"Yep, and if I were you, I wouldn't stand there in the way unless you wanna get hurt." He looked back at the two of them and tilted his head while raising his eyebrows.

They looked at each other for a moment and then looked to where the salmon would come from.

"O..." Fin said, the realization hit him. "O! We are in the middle of where they would swim!"

Sam drew in a sharp breath, glancing at the knee-deep water and then at Amph, as a wave of clarity washed over her. He was nearly back at the stone bridge and was signaling for them to hurry. Her eyes turned towards Vineke's entrance, where she spotted people standing on the sides, witnessing fish jump out of the water and swim towards the farms and towards her from afar.

She swallowed and motioned for Fin to go. Looking around, she realized that the other farmers had left the waters as well and only those with nets stood on the edges of specific pools. As she trudged through the waters, she could feel the relentless current pushing against her, making each step a struggle.

Sam had almost made it back to the first garden when something big and gray buzzed past her, zipping through the water. Quickly she followed the colors and watched as a fish as large as her thigh jumped into the air and down into the pools below. Glancing back, she could see a sparse of the same fish joining it over the edge. She took a deep breath and closed her eyes.

Great.

She quickened her pace, pushing her feet into the sand and using the force to propel herself forward more. Fin had made it to the last pool when she saw, in the corner of her eye, one of the gray glimpses in the water gliding towards him.

"Fin!" Sam shouted. He turned and as they locked eyes, the salmon unknowingly knocked into his legs. His knees buckled and he crashed into the water. A look of terror twisted across his face as he helplessly fell with a splash. Amph jumped back in to help him. Sam continued her way forward, praying that the same wouldn't happen to her. She adjusted her mask as it began to slip off her face.

"Sam! Look out!" Amph yelled as he helped Fin out of the water. A sudden weight slammed into Sam's calves, knocking her off balance and sending her plunging downward. Pain coursed through her knees. They turned at a awkward angle. She fell hard but caught herself with her hands in time. Now surrounded by a flurry of fish, passing by her one after another. Sam scrambled to pull herself up, still disoriented from the sudden hit.

As if on cue, a salmon lept from the water, colliding with Sam and slapping her face with its body. Her mask slammed into her face, and it slid off. Salmon taking it away with them. The moment her mask was knocked off, a surge of searing agony overcame her as she abruptly plunged beneath the water's surface. Salmon now whizzed past her left and right. She tried to snap out of the daze. Frantically grabbing for her mask that she watched swim away with the horde of fish around her. Another one hit her. Then another. And another. Panicked, she forced herself to sit up in the water, focusing on breathing rather than rescuing her mask. The dread filled Sam as she understood the trouble she was in with the rush of salmon pushing past her.

She forced her hair out of her face, gasping to take deep breaths. One hit the back of her head and she tumbled back into the water. Her mouth and nose filled with lake water. They burned, as they tried to reject what she just engulfed. She was shoved closer to the waterfalls that they were so eager to jump from.

"Sam!"

She could hear Fin yelling her name through the rushing water, but wasn't able to respond. The lingering panic causing her fear of the situation to rise. Her energy gone. Body bruised and muscles aching. She tumbled in the water further. Exasperated, her fingers clawed into the sand. Grasping for something. Anything. To stop from moving any closer.

In response, she threw herself upward, in a last attempt. Becoming unafraid by the torment of the run. She forced herself to get what was most important to her at the moment. Air. She surfaced once again and gulped down air as she coughed out the water she took in only a moment ago. Her back, the unfortunate sacrifice to any harm that might come her way. She continued to focus on breathing. Her hands and arms became shields to block any more hits to her face. Sam made herself small in the water.

A firm hand grabbed her shoulder, and a body wrapped protectively around hers. Her eyes glimpsed a long golden tail with red, white, and black spots. She tried to look up to see who was guarding her from the run, but as she tilted her head upward, their other hand pushed her head back down.

"Keep your head where it was, unless you want to get hit again," a man's stern voice spoke from behind her. She flushed.

"Can you move?" He asked.

"I think so." She braced herself and stood wobbly. Her head, back, and legs throbbed painfully in tune with her heartbeat. She looked behind her to find a koiman with a long shield that blocked the both of them from the rushing salmon. His face was soft and elegant that partnered perfectly with his long glossy black hair braided into a ponytail. His body was splattered with the same spotted colors from his tail, and he had fish fins on the tips of his ears accompanied with gills on his neck.

He moved with Sam at her slower pace and used the shield to guard them from getting hit again. She flinched at each of the thumps the salmon made against the shield, but the koiman gripped her shoulder tighter to reassure her as they proceeded. She looked up to see Fin, Amph, and a group of mysterious koimaids waiting for them.

"Thank you," Sam groaned. She rested her head in her hand, caressing the pain, as they got closer to the others.

"It's my job to keep everyone in Vineke safe. You're lucky we were passing by when we did," he responded.

At that moment, Sam remembered watching her mask float away in the water. "My mask!" She called out, looking behind them at the falls where she dropped it to see if she could spot its blue.

"The Oracle has your mask. Try not to stress yourself." The man said, pointing to the group that were at the edge of the bridge now. One woman held her mask as she spoke with Amph. The koimaid had long black hair, the same as the man's and an orange red body. The rest of the koi were similar in color, a couple were gray black, while the others were mostly red, orange, and white.

As they got closer, Fin joined them and helped Sam out of the water. Holding on to her, he examined the now forming bruises.

"I think you'll live," he said sarcastically, "we should get Cedar to check out your head though. That looks pretty nasty."

Sam nodded through her headache. "It's hard to focus right now. I feel like I got hit with..." she faltered, trying to think of a comparison, but gave up halfway through, "something *really* dense."

"Thank you for finding my mask ma'am, it means a lot to me," she gripped Fin's arm as she reached out to receive her mask from the beautiful koimaid.

"You are most welcome indeed. I was on my way to introduce myself to you when we saw what was happening. I am glad we were able to assist you." She bowed her head. Amph motioned for them to do the same, so they bowed. As she did, her body throbbed again. Grimacing, she stood up and leaned on Fin for support.

"You should rest. I will visit you in a couple days for tea and we will talk properly then." She spoke softly and with a wave of her hand, the others slid into the water and made their way back into the deeper lake while waiting for her to join them.

"Thank you again." Sam added more firmly towards both the one who saved her and the one who saved her mask.

They nodded and slipped into the water, swimming upstream back towards the marketplace and disappearing into the lake. Once they were gone, the formality vanished with them. Sam slumped further into Fin and held onto her head once again.

"Everything hurts," she groaned while massaging her temple.

"Ya, my legs feel like they got run over by a horse, good thing I tucked my tail around my stomach or it might have been ripped off," Fin snorted.

"Let's head back and get y'all situated." Amph walked over to Sam's side, gently placing his arm around hers to assist on the remainder of their journey back.

"Sam!" Cedar gasped and ran to her as she entered the main room of Amph and Lorelei's home. Bram soon followed, surprised as well to see Sam injured and sitting in the pooled entrance next to Ban Tui.

Running up to Sam, she threw herself around her and held on tight. Sam's body repelled at the touch, and her face scrunched through the pain.

"Ahhh Cedar, please let go," Sam groaned, "I hurt, just... *so* much."

Cedar backed up in shock. "I'm sorry, I wasn't thinking." She smiled stiffly and looked down at Sam sitting in the chilly lake water.

"Why- are you sitting in the water?" She hesitated. "With your clothes on?"

Sam splashed her hand around in the water.

"Lorelei said I needed to keep my bruises cold and that this would help with the pain and headaches," she shrugged. "And I don't have a swimsuit or water clothes."

"O-k, well, if it's working, that's good. I should just examine your head and make sure there isn't any serious damage. I have some herbs that can help with the pain. We can make tea!" Cedar got up quickly and pounced into the girls' room, to find her satchel full of the herbs she had packed before they left.

"I'm fine!" Fin leaned back to shout towards Cedar, "my legs don't hurt at all, I was probably too strong for the puny salmon that hit me anyway," Fin added smugly as he shot a cocky smile at Sam. She rolled her eyes at him but cracked a smile.

"That's perfect, then I can save my herbs." She came back into the room, grinning. Fin straightened up.

"Well, I mean, a little wouldn't hurt the inventory, would it?" he asked, "just to- you know, make sure I won't be in pain later."

Cedar laughed. "Sure, I think I can spare a couple of leaves for you, strong man."

Fin sighed in relief, sinking deeper into the lake. Despite the twinges of discomfort, Sam couldn't help but chuckle softly. She copied Fin, and sank deeper into the water, feeling the chill dampen her hair and numb the aching.

As Cedar got the tea ready, Amph and Lorelei sat at the table chatting about their day. Bram came over and showed the two his new dog mask. He laid it next to Sam's. She propped her arm on the edge and laid her head on it, examining the smooth black snout and its calm eyes guilded with gold. It was similar to hers but held a different type of emotion in its figure. For a brief moment, she gazed at Bram, trying to understand what she couldn't fully comprehend.

"It's got a quiet ferocity to it, like you," Sam said, touching the mask to see if it felt as glossy as it looked.

"I thought it was ironic, too. Once I saw it, I didn't care for any of the others. The merchant lady told us that it's the demon dog who wards off bad spirits and other demons," Bram said.

"It would have been nice if it warded off salmon too, but-" Fin raised his hands dramatically.

"It *needs* to ward off stupidity." Bram retorted back.

"Hey-" Fin started.

Ban Tui swam through the entrance and landed in between Fin and Sam. He shot out of the water like a missile, splashing both of them in his wake.

Annoyed and almost completely wet now, Sam dipped herself all the way into the water. Patting Ban Tui on the side to say hello, she emerged and pushed the hair out of her face.

"Thanks for that," she said flatly.

Fin groaned, which grabbed Sam's attention. She leaned around Ban Tui, who had happily joined them, and saw Fin's hair smeared across his face. He held out his arms in disdain and looked down at himself dramatically.

"Don't be a baby, go underwater." Sam held back a laugh.

He held his breath and dunked himself under the water and popped back up, still soaking wet but looking less uncomfortable.

"Here are the teas." Cedar brought back two black stone cups with steam drifting lazily into the air.

"Thank you!" Sam and Fin said in unison as they took their cups from her.

Sam slowly took in the smell of the steam that wafted against her face. It was pungent and hit her nose hard. A soft hue of orange and a small purple feathery flower floated in the tea water.

"It has a sharp taste to it, but I added some honey, courtesy of Lorelei to... soften the blow," Cedar added.

Sam nodded looking down to her cup she held with both hands and waited for it to cool off.

"Why don't we go outside and watch the fireflies while the sun sets," Lorelei spoke up as she stood from her seat. Amph rose and joined her as she walked outside.

It took a moment, but Sam and Fin were able to gradually stand and joined the others on the planks that made up the front of their home's walkway. The planks laid over the lake that ran underneath it and they sat on the edge, sticking their feet into the water.

Sam could hear the frogs croaking the songs of the night, along with the crickets and cicadas joining in tune. The air, thick and musty with humidity, blended perfectly with the warmth of the setting sun.

As she delicately sipped her tangy tea, memories of the cottage in the Whispering Woods flooded her mind - the place she and Cedar called home. The sun shone through the silhouettes of the trees and reflected off of the lake, giving them the light of a double sunset. Sam watched the pink and purple colors bounce off the rippling water, and she smiled to herself.

The water was alive, just like the forest.

Cedar cut through her thoughts, "So, can you pleeassee tell me what happened? I mean, I know it was the salmon run but like... what happened?!"

Sam groaned in contempt of the subject. "Ok, but first you *must* tell me about these sea cows that I keep hearing about," she put in, trying to change the subject.

Cedar's eyes lit up, and Sam smiled in delight at the success of her plan.

"Sam! They were so cute, they were huge and floated around in the water like giant weightless flowers! And they would munch on the kelp and other plants that were growing in the lake meadow in the middle of the deep end. They remind me of the cows from the village!" She squealed in excitement.

"They were pretty cool," Bram added, "we also met Hanako the Oracle."

"We met her too. She was the one that saved helpless over there." Fin pointed his thumb in Sam's direction and she shot him back with a dirty look.

Cedar looked wide eyed at Sam. "Yaa, I guess that's what happened." She sucked in a deep breath, and let out a heavy sigh.

At that, Sam, as hastily and painlessly as possible, caught them up on what happened at the floating farms.

"I don't want to keep talking about it though. It's *physically* a sore subject." Sam made a discomforted face.

"So, Amph told us there is an illusive firefly that his cousin found once. It's purple and I bet you I will spot one tonight." Fin spoke up as he took a sip of his tea.

"Purple?" Cedar asked, sounding interested.

The group watched the fireflies grow denser as they blinked in and out of existence and danced through the night, imitating the stars.

5

CALM WATERS

A ROUGE NESSI IS A DANGEROUS THING.

THE NEXT FEW DAYS passed Sam as she rested and let her bruises heal. She found herself excited and buzzing to leave to see the lake glade and the sea cows. Cedar continued to talk about the experience with them, leaving Sam to her imagination and boredom.

She still hadn't had another dream with Lyra either.

Lost in thought, she picked at her nails, contemplating the reasons behind their prolonged lack of communication. The search continued on with no luck in Vineke. In the next few days, they would be packing and heading to the next village, with or without the help of her dreams.

Lorelei hectically ran back and forth in her kitchen cleaning and tidying the house as Amph went to the floating gardens to get food to make for lunch with Oracle Hanako. Sam could tell that the two were nervous to have the leader of their lake visit them.

"These are looking better," Cedar said as she walked up. "They are changing color, which is good. It seems to be healing fine."

"My muscle pain isn't as intense now. But they are still a bit sore," Sam responded with an uncomfortable face as she moved her body to test its boundaries.

"I was hoping I could maybe see the glade in the lake today. I feel better and can move around much more." She looked hopefully at Cedar.

Cedar added, glancing doubtfully back at her. "Well, I guess it wouldn't hurt. I'll come with you to make sure you don't overdo anything."

"Grrreaattttt..." Fin walked in with Bram. They both held woven baskets for picking food. "You get to play with the sea cows, and we get stuck picking vegetables," Fin scoffed. Bram shook his head at Fin, glancing at him, but didn't respond.

"You can always stay here and help me tidy up," Lorelei yelled from the other room.

"Actually, I think we should drop these off to Amph... sorry!" Fin yelled back hesitantly. Wide-eyed, he nudged Bram, and they made their way to the door quietly as Sam snorted, trying to hold back a smirk. Fin looked back at them, threw his head back and sighed in over dramatics as he dragged himself out the door behind Bram.

Once she heard the door close, Lorelei popped her head around the corner, giving the girls a mischievous grin and a wink.

"Best be off then. Oracle Hanako will be here in the evening." She waved them off and ducked back into the room to continue scurrying around.

After thanking her, Sam grabbed her mask, while Cedar went to collect her satchel. They headed out into the morning mist of the lake and set off to the underwater glade.

"I'm going to miss them when we leave." Cedar started as they walked over one of the moon bridges.

"They have been accommodating. Especially with tolerating everything we've put them through," Sam said as she kicked a small pebble with them across the stone bridge. "We should do something for them, in return for their hospitality."

The smiling faces of Lin and Amos flashed through her mind. Thinking about them and wondering what they would do in this situation.

Cedar murmured in agreement.

As they strolled down the lake, following the current, they saw many of the faunanoid beginning their day as well. Merchants had been open since the sunrise and the koi folk traveled up and down the lake busy with errands and the chores of the day.

Once across the bridge, they trekked through dewy grass on a small dirt trail. They looked out and saw the gardens and floating farms as they passed.

"O, hey! There's Amph and the boys!" Sam said excitedly as she pointed toward the three, who seemed to be picking tomatoes from the garden that floated closest to them.

In the distance, Bram stood and waved. Cedar and Sam waved back as they continued on their way.

Sam's jitteriness grew as they followed a downward set of stepping stones to the lower parts of the lake. She had never been this far before. While looking up, she could see the opposite end of the falls and the water cascading over it. She thought back to a couple of days ago and gently caressed the bruises on her back, grimacing as she thought about the salmon run and the koiman who had saved her.

Cedar linked arms with Sam, grabbing her attention. She looked over and saw the soft excitement pass over Cedar's face as she pointed to something in front of them. Following her gaze, Sam saw the large calm body of water before them that lay under the falls.

The water was crystal clear which gave sight to the emerald sea grass and kale that were anchored to the lake floor but floated upward and gracefully around in the water's movements. She could also see turtles sprawled and fighting for room across logs that stuck out of the water. Velvety moss decorated rocks on the outskirts of the water's edge, and tall grass sprouted in random places while massive lily pads swayed on the water near the lapping shore.

Sam gasped in delight when she noticed them. Bumps of land bobbed up and down all across the lake in the form of gray or brown masses. Cedar walked into the water knee high, beckoning for Sam to follow. With another glance stolen at the intriguing blobs, she took off her shoes and mask and proceeded into the water cautiously. Standing on a stone in the water, Sam saw that the platform went down much further. Cedar plucked a clump of kale from the bed and motioned to place some of the droopy plants in Sam's hand.

Sam shivered at the squishy textures in her hand, but didn't complain.

"Are you ready?" Cedar leaned in, grinning from ear to ear.

"Let's do this," Sam nodded in avid anticipation.

Cedar let out a long whistle. The silence afterwards cut deep as they listened to the echo slid across the glass of water.

Slowly, the mass of blobs meandered their way towards the call.

A thick head popped out of the water to Sam's other side. It faintly bellowed out to her, and she stepped back in surprise. The sea cows were bigger than she had expected.

It moved closer to her as it examined the food, beckoning for a treat. Reluctantly she held out her hand and opened her palm. The massive creature leaned in and licked the plant up into its sandpaper tongue, leaving no trace of the morsel only saliva in its wake.

Sam laughed uneasily as she looked into the water for more of the plants that Cedar had given her. She could see that more of them were drawing near and Cedar was already feeding a smaller one that had reached her first.

"Why is its tongue so rough?" Sam asked as the underwater cow licked another plant out of her hand and scraped her palm with its long tongue.

Cedar shrugged and laughed as more showed up to be fed.

"You know-" she looked over at Sam, "the other day, I saw someone swimming in the lake with them." She glanced at the creatures waiting impatiently, then back at Sam.

Sam ran her fingers through her hair, unsure of the idea of swimming in the middle of a deep lake with them. Even if they were gentle. Doubtfully, she looked at Cedar. Her confidence in the thought dwindling, as she continued to grab more plants from the water to satiate the hunger of the four sea cows who crowded them.

Cedar waded deeper, patting them on their backs as she pushed past them.

"Cedar-" Sam stammered fearfully.

"Come on!" She responded, gesturing for her to follow.

Reluctantly, Sam walked the same path as Cedar. Deeper into the clear water. Her heart beat pounded as she looked at her feet and felt the rocky earth beneath her turn to moss, then mud. Now she was chest deep when she swam out deeper after Cedar. The sea cows lumbered behind, interested in the commotion.

They made it into the center of the lake when Cedar dunked herself under the water. Sam's fear rose but she followed. With a deep breath, she pushed herself under the crisp surface. The sea cows seemed even bigger when fully submerged. One nudged itself against her curiously, as she watched a couple more float down to the bed and nibble on some of the tall grass and kelp. As she felt her fears ebb away, she allowed herself to sink deeper, relaxing her muscles and sensing her hair floating around her in its own form of freedom. All at once the dense water engulfed her, enclosed her, suffocated her, but still she felt safe, hugged by the water.

She propelled herself upward for a breath of air. She breached the surface and floated on her back for a time, taking in the morning sun's rays that were emerging from behind the trees and finally reaching the water's reflection. The fog had lifted. Only pieces of the mist laid over the land and water now. By angling herself down, she swam backwards and watched the ripples above as they enveloped her, trying to bring a sense of peace. Air bubbles escaped, spiraling upwards back to where they belonged. Spinning in a circle, she managed to push herself further underwater. Constant force pushed against her the deeper she went with the gentle creatures around her.

When she could almost grasp the tall grass and seaweed that reached upwards with her fingertips, she stopped and relaxed her body again. Immersed in the slow motion of the smothered tranquil sounds in the underwater glade. She felt the life around her, serene like the forest, but lively in its own way. The water always flowed elsewhere, never stopping, moving along on its journey forward, forever mobile.

She opened her eyes to see Cedar floating above her on the surface. In front of her, a sea cow drifted cautiously her way.

Sam reached out and touched its snout as it drew near. A smile spread across her face as she ran her fingers over its whiskers. The last of her air bubbles out as she waved goodbye and paddled her feet, propelling to the surface. Their backs in the water and their eyes toward the sky. Cedar and Sam spent the rest of the morning swimming in the meadow.

Oracle Hanako sat on a thin, deep red cushion near the lake entrance of Amph and Lorelei's home. Delicately, she sipped her tea as the others watched nervously, not knowing how to begin the conversation.

"Thank you again for saving me the other day." She admiringly looked at her and at the koiman who sat next to her.

"Once again, you don't need to thank me for completing my job. I merely did what I was supposed to," he responded but bowed his head anyway to receive the thanks.

Sam nodded, asking, "What is your name? I don't think I heard it."

"I am Ta-an, protector of the Oracle and of Vineke," he said in a dignified tone. "I am also Oracle Hanako's brother," he added.

She raised her eyebrows in surprise. The small similarities started to show between the two.

"Yes, I'm fortunate enough to have someone I trust deeply to be my appointed protector," Hanako replied, shooting her brother a playful smile. Afterwards, she turned her attention to Sam and her group of friends.

"How are you feeling, by the way? From the incident with the salmon run," She added, putting down her teacup and looking at both Fin and Sam.

"Much better, still a bit sore, but nothing like how it was." Sam moved her shoulders around and stretched out her back to feel the aching pain of the large bruises that still resided there.

"This isn't anything I can't handle," Fin stated, "I've dealt with worse, believe me." He smiled smugly and Hanako chuckled in response.

"You mean like the time you ran with your tail tucked in between your legs when Bram chased you out of the woods?" Cedar retorted, sarcasm filled from her tone as she dared Fin to respond.

He opened his mouth, but closed it and shrunk back into the wall that he leaned on.

Oracle Hanako's eyes swept the group, and they seemed to lie on Bram longer than the rest. Sam glanced his way, grasping for his thoughts but his face remained unreadable.

"And have you been enjoying the town so far? It is quite uncommon for us to get travelers from the Realm of Land, so I am curious to see what you think of our lake."

"We love it so much." Cedar's eyes beamed. "Amph and Lorelei have helped us tremendously. The gardens are amazing and we all have enjoyed being around the sea cows too." She said, nodding as she finished speaking.

"I'm glad you have enjoyed it. How have you liked the market so far?"

"It reminds me a lot of Atlon's," Fin added. "That is where I am from, the Twin City."

"Ahh yes, the Deep Forest Province," she said thoughtfully, "What about the rest of you? Are you also from there?"

"Cedar and I are from the Whispering Woods. And-" Sam stopped herself, glancing at Bram. She wasn't exactly sure how to respond. So she waited to see if he would say anything. He turned his head down towards the stone floor.

"And you?" Ta-an spoke up.

Everyone waited, silently. Sam swallowed, a cough struggling itself out. It was not long ago that she also felt the intense stares of the others around her, making her feel like an outsider.

"He is also from the woo-" She tried to rescue him from the situation, but as she spoke, he turned to look at Hanako.

"I am an Ascerian of the Outer Realms. I joined them to make my way home through the mountains' pass."

Ta-an and Hanako tensed.

Sam's eyes darted in a mix of surprise and confusion, first to Cedar, then to Fin, her mouth agape. They returned the same looks back to her. No one knew until now that his idea was to leave once they reached the Guardian Mountains.

"You're leaving? You can't leave." Hurt spread across Cedar's face. "When were you going to tell us?"

He crossed his arms and opened his mouth to speak, but Ta-an interrupted him.

"There was a shifter who traveled through here when we were children. Our parents aided it. They were severely injured. Was that you?" he asked.

Brams' eyes widened. "Your parents-" His jaw clenched. "Are- are they here?"

Hanako shook her head remorsefully. "They passed years ago, into the great lake." She put her hand on her heart and pulled it away from her chest in a symbol of respect.

"I'm sorry." He closed his eyes and looked away, stricken with regret.

Sam frowned. "Bram, you came through here before? And they said you were injured..." Not finishing her question, they all looked at him, expectant for an explanation.

"I- I don't want to talk about this." He heaved an anxious sigh, running his hands through his hair. Bram began walking towards the entrance of their home. When he opened the door, he turned back towards the onlookers and stared at the floor.

Not being able to meet their eyes, he turned his head with uncertainty towards Ta-an and Hanako. "Thank you," he said flatly. "I appreciate you telling me." And with a look filled with regret and sorrow, he turned to Sam, Cedar, and Fin. Then finally shut the door as he left.

"Bram." Cedar and Fin stood in unison to go after him.

"Wait." She knew this feeling of helplessness all too well.

They looked back at her in retaliation, but stopped short when she met their eyes.

"Give him some time. He needs to be alone now," she replied, trying to comfort her friends. "We can talk to him when he has had time to breathe."

Fin let his hands go limp, but sat back down. Cedar bit her lip to hold back her tears. Despite her obvious distress, Sam made an effort to mask her emotions and plastered a smile on her face.

"I am sorry, that was- unexpected for everyone." Ta-an spoke up.

"I apologize as well. We meant no harm. Our parents used to tell us the story of them looking after an injured shifter boy and then he disappeared. We never thought he would return. So, we were caught by surprise when he said that." Hanako ran her fingers through her long, silky black hair. Her appearance remained calm, but Sam sensed the anxiousness in her words now.

"No," Sam paused. "No, it's ok, we were taken by surprise too. We knew he was a shifter, but he hasn't told us much of his past. I didn't even know his species was called the Ascerian."

"I wish to speak with him again before you leave. I want him to know that our parents looked for him for many years after he left," Ta-an said, "he deserves to know they cared for him."

"I am sure he would like that," Cedar responded softly.

Oracle Hanako sighed heavily. "I think we have overstayed our welcome, brother." She smiled. "We should be off."

Lorelei, who had remained quiet for the entire conversation, spoke up. "Are you sure, my Oracle? We have food if you are hungry." She gestured to a plate of snacks that sat on the table.

Hanako shook her head. "We are filled with your hospitality and by the tea we've shared. I will visit again, but for now I believe the young travelers need rest and time to think, but thank you again for inviting us into your home and sharing your time with us."

Lorelei bowed in thanks as she tried to hide her disappointment. Oracle Hanako bowed in return to each of them and sunk into the water, disappearing into the depths. Ta-an looked at Sam solemnly for a moment before bowing and vanishing as well.

Once they were gone, the house breathed a sigh of relief and they slumped deeper into their seats. With Sam's elbows on her knees, she leaned over and buried her face in her hands.

"What a mess."

A hand graced her back. She looked up to see Cedar staring down at her with the same expression. Sam and Fin looked at each other and smiled in disbelief. She cracked a smile as she shook her head, laughing, trying to find the humor in the cascading of unfortunate events that had just occurred. Cedar chuckled as well at their misfortune and the group's anxiousness lightened.

"I'll go see how Bram is doing in a little bit," Cedar said as she walked over to the table with the midday snacks decorating it. "We can figure out what's going to happen to him later. For now, let's eat something. Then after that I'm sure we will feel much better."

Fin picked up a handful of cheese and bread.

"Agreed." He said through a mouthful of food.

Sam laughed in disgust as she got up from her seat and joined them.

"Lorelei, I am sorry we ruined your lunch. You took so much time preparing for her." She gave her a sympathetic look.

"But can you believe she was here? The Oracle in *my* home" Shaking her head in astonishment, she handed the plates out to each of them. Cedar and Sam glanced at each other. Relieved as they put food on their plates.

"And she even said that she was going to visit again." Amph spoke up as he wrapped his arm around Lorelei's waist caringly. She beamed even more at the comment.

"The thought of having the Oracle as a regular guest in our household is enough to make me faint," she said, waving herself. The group laughed in response.

They sat and ate the food Lorelei had prepared for lunch as they chatted about the events that had transpired. Cedar told them about their time at the lake glade with the sea cows.

As they ate and talked, Sam's mind harped on the few days they had left and the lack of direction they had for the next part of their journey. She looked at the door in hopes of seeing Bram walk through. He seemed to have a more interesting past than he originally let on.

She took another bite of her slice of bread with cheese and tomato and ran plans through in her head. Scouring her brain for ideas that could be the solution to their problems.

Sam stood once again in the vast emptiness, her hair floating around her as she watched dream bubbles float upward to an imaginary surface. She searched diligently. Hoping to find any clue that would lead her to Lyra's whereabouts.

"Lyra!" Sam cupped her mouth and bellowed from her chest, turning in a circle. She listened to her voice echo and waited for a response.

"Sam?" a muffled voice called back.

She turned towards it. As she did, a new dark wall loomed over her that had not been there moments ago. She rushed over to it, calling out for her again.

"Lyra, I'm here. I am so, so sorry I haven't been able to reach you," she exasperated as she examined the wall again for any signs of weaknesses or clues.

"It's ok, I understand-" Lyra cut short, her words brimming with emotion that cut into Sam.

"Do you know where your body might be? Do you have any consciousness when you're awake?" Sam asked, drawing closer to where she thought Lyra might have been.

"No, I- I can't remember Sam. I'm sorry, I feel so useless," she said as she began to cry.

"What? You're not useless. We are going to get you outta here and everything will be *ok,*" Sam said, facing the wall as she crouched on the balls of her feet. Her attention now focused on the sobs of the girl behind the barrier.

"We?" Lyra sniffed through her tears.

"O ya, I haven't even told you the best part." Sam sat on the ground cross-legged as she spoke. "There are four of us looking for you right now. Me and my friends are on a mission to find you. There is me, of course, and Cedar." Sam counted on her fingers as she went through the list. "She is a Flame Summoner. Then there is Fin. He is our land runner. He thinks he is funny, but he can be more obnoxious than anything." She smiled to herself as she continued, "Then there's Bram. He joined our crew last, but he is a shifter who is having some trouble right now. He is sweet and quiet." Sam frowned as she thought about what Bram had told them at the lunch, but took herself out of the thought and continued.

"Umm, so ya, we are trying to find you because we were going to ask you to help us on our quest," she said sadly as she finished.

Lyra was silent.

"Lyra?" Sam said, growing worried she had over shared.

"I don't know what to say. There is an entire group of random people trying to find me." She sniffed again. "Why? I'm not special."

"Well, clearly you are, you're in this dream- my dream. That's not what happened when I saw Cedar or Fin and you wouldn't even be here if you weren't a little bit special. You're meant to be our sea walker for the sea portion of the King's Journey," Sam said determined.

"You want me to be a part of your team?" She asked.

"I want you to be our friend," Sam responded. "If I can get you out of here, will you join us on our adventure?"

"I- I don't know. I can't even remember where I am, let alone if I have friends or family who are also in trouble. Can I think about it?"

Sam sighed to herself and stood. Upset that she said the wrong thing and shouldn't have pushed so hard. Lyra was still trapped and scared.

"Of course. Take the time you need. We will continue looking for you." Sam put her hand on the rough wall.

As she did, the wall glowed a bright neon pink underneath her hand. She pulled away and a bright pink coral revealed itself, then gradually dimmed back to black. She looked at her hand. It glowed as well in the bright color, copying the wall and faded back to its normal color.

Curiously, she studied the wall. Then swiped her hand in an arch on the rough texture. When she did, the coral reacted and erupted into bright colors of green, blue, pinks, and oranges. Her eyes shone bright as she witnessed the beauty of the luminescence.

"Lyra, I think you're in a reef, this wall is made of coral."

Sam smiled and touched the wall again to watch the coral react to her handprint.

Before Lyra could respond, the world around them shook. Sam's excitement vanished within a moment.

"Sam, what's happening?!" Lyra cried out.

"I- I don't know," Sam yelled back as she tried to keep her balance.

She moved backwards, back into the void, and away from Lyra. Frantically, she looked back at the wall.

"Lyra! I am waking up! But I think I know where you are!"

As she was lifted, Sam's body became horizontal with the ground.

"Sam!" Lyra called out, her voice pleading for her to stay.

"We will find you!" Sam yelled louder, hoping she heard her as the wall grew smaller and smaller in the distance. "I promise."

"Sam," someone hissed in her ear quietly. "Saammmmm."

They let out a small desperate cry.

Sam grumbled in annoyance as she forced herself awake through the confusion and grogginess. Cedar was kneeling by her bed, shaking her. She rubbed her eyes with her palms and ran her hand through her hair.

Sam jolted up and brought herself back to her surroundings. She could hear the faint noises of quiet footsteps drawing near to their room. Alert, she looked at Cedar, her hazel eyes held fear as she whispered.

"There is someone in the house."

6

IN THE LIGHT OF THE FLAMES

"CONNECTION WITH FIRE SHOWS REBIRTH."-TENZIN OF THE MOUNTAIN CITY

ADRENALINE AND FEAR PUSHED through Sam. Waking her and sending her out of her bed quietly. She and Cedar stayed low. Sam grabbed her staff as she looked back at Cedar, and they crept to the door. While listening to the noises outside, they could detect whispers and the shuffling of items in unwanted hands.

"Do you think anyone else can hear them?" Cedar whispered close to Sam.

She shrugged in response, not wanting to alert them of their presence. She put her finger to her mouth, signaling Cedar to stay quiet. Cedar nodded. Her attention promptly back to the door.

They could now see the flickering of a dim flame as it grew brighter, nearing the rooms of the home. Sam caught her breath. The heartbeat in her chest growing harsher and louder as the light grew towards them. They stared at the crevice where the wooden door met the floor.

Sam stiffened, and motioned for Cedar to follow her to the side where the door would open on them and give them cover in the shadows before the fight.

The handle of the door turned such a small amount, Sam almost thought it was a trick of the eyes. But then, faintly, she heard a quiet man curse with dissatisfaction behind the door. They're trying to pick the lock.

She tightened her jaw and gripped her spear, locking eyes with Cedar. They readied for the pounce.

The *'hoo'* of a particularly large owl made Sam jolt and caught the girl's attention towards the window. A wave of goosebumps flared through Sam's body as she looked and saw the face of a person staring in at the two of them. Her hair stood on end. She put an arm in front of Cedar protectively as her eyes adjusted to the black silhouette.

Ruffled orange hair and a twitching tail gave Sam a sigh of relief as Fin motioned firmly with his head for them to join him outside. She pushed Cedar to go in front of her as she watched the door.

"How did you know there was someone inside the house?" hissed Cedar as Fin helped her down from the ledge.

"You think I didn't hear them clomping around? What a bunch of amateurs," Fin scoffed as he rolled his eyes.

Once Cedar was out and down in the reeds hiding, Sam backed out the window as she watched the handle begin to turn softly again. With haste, she landed as quietly as possible and hid in the dense reeds near the side of the house with Fin and Cedar.

"Where's Bram?" Fin asked as they saw the lantern light brighten the room that they previously slept in.

"I thought he was with you?" Sam shot him a worried look.

A hushed breath escaped the group as they observed a thin man, his face concealed by a ragged beard and his eyes hidden under a hat, cautiously scanning the night through the window, hoping to catch sight of another person. Cedar lowered herself more, making herself smaller as she watched, terrified. Sam squeezed Cedar's hand to comfort her. Her own breath shallow, and ragged with worry.

What about Lorelei and Amph? Where's Bram?

She chewed on the inside of her lip.

The man ducked back in. The light faded as it travelled to the other rooms of the house. Fin shouldered them slightly and jabbed his thumb towards the window. Cedar and Sam nodded. All three slunk back into the room. Fin went first. He crept towards the now open door and checked to see if it was clear before motioning for them to come inside. Sam helped Cedar in and she followed last.

"We need to do something about these guys," Fin said as they crouched together. "I know there are at least two. I could hear them talking to one another," he whispered.

Sam nodded, "They are going to head to Lorelei and Amph's room soon, if they haven't already." A flush of anger ran through her at the thought of something happening to either of them.

"I am going to go around and come back in through the front door. Can you two be a distraction and keep their backs turned to me?" Fin asked expectantly.

Cedar and Sam made eye contact, understanding what needed to be done. They looked back at Fin and nodded.

"Ok, hang tight for a moment, then see if you can keep them talking while I sneak around." Fin hopped out the window again and headed for the entrance. They waited.

"Sam," Cedar whispered, "I'm scared. What if... something happened to them? What if something happens to us?" She looked at her with pained eyes.

Sam looked at her, trying to conjure the correct words.

"I- don't know Cedar. But I'll protect you. I promise." Sam shot her a smile that she hoped was convincing. "Besides, I thought *you* were the all powerful Flame Summoner?"

Cedar scrunched her nose and rolled her eyes sarcastically.

"I guess we have fought worse things, like Bram and the Cragmaw," she whispered.

Sam thought back to the battles that they have struggled through and wondered how this was any different.

A piercing scream erupted from the depths.

The girls snapped their heads towards it. Wide eyed, they looked at each other again when the silence was broken by the cries and yells of two familiar voices.

"Lorelei." Sam stood and frantically made her way out of the room quietly, Cedar close behind.

"Where is it?" A rough voice demanded. A thud and grunt accompanied his question. Sam peeked around the corner to see four men dressed in dull colored clothes surrounding Lorelei and Amph. Two held them as the other two interrogated them, destroying the kitchen in the search of something.

Amph lay crumpled on the floor from a blow the bigger man dealt. The slim man that Sam recognized from the window held Lorelei with her hands behind her back.

"Where are the scales? Don't make me ask again." The man prowled above him with a short-bladed knife in his hand. Amph glared up at him through a pained face. He spat on the man's finned feet.

Sam's heart skipped a beat. She closed her eyes while backing away from the scene.

They're there because of them.

She looked at Cedar, who stared at her with the same dread across her face. Both looked back to the room and imagined her satchel sitting neatly on the stand with the velvet bag of scales hidden in it.

"This is our fault." Cedar covered her mouth as she began crying. "We need to do something." She scrutinized Sam with a deep anger in her eyes. Sam could see the fire building inside of her and her hair beginning to sizzle. She nodded and without giving herself time to hesitate or overthink, she turned the corner, gripping her staff.

The man had Amph in the air now, holding him by his shirt collar. He threatened him with the knife.

"Hey!" Sam yelled, catching them off guard. He dropped Amph in surprise. They turned towards them.

The one holding Lorelei snorted. "You here for a fight?"

"We are if you don't leave." Sam pointed her staff towards the intruders.

"No, girls get out of here!" Lorelei's face scrunched as she closed her eyes, pleading.

"We're aren't leaving until we get those scales. We know you have them." He put a knife up to Lorelei's throat.

"That's a shame," a voice emerged from the shadows behind the man who held Lorelei captive. Before they could turn in response, he slid his hooked swords up to the culprit's throat.

"Fin!" Cedar cried out.

Confidence burned through Sam as she saw the four men's now unsure faces. By elbowing Cedar, she signaled to the one in the middle closer to Fin and glanced in his direction. She nodded understanding, and Sam went to face the other two who had Amph.

"Where did he come from?" the stout one grumbled, "I thought you said you checked the rooms." He glared at his friend.

"I-I did, none of them were there..." he stammered as he shifted his gaze between the other intruders and the people they held hostage.

"Idiot," he hissed turning and fixing his gaze on Sam and Cedar.

Sam widened her stance and braced herself.

This was it.

Cedar brought her fists close to her face. All eyes turned to her as they brightened the darkness of the night with the warm glow of flames.

"You best be careful missy, you don't want to catch these nice faus home on fire," the tall lanky one who hadn't spoken yet said in a slimy tone as he grinned.

Sam glanced at Cedar. She could feel her shift at the thought of losing control. Her flame flickered and dulled itself in response.

Sam responded before Cedar had the chance. "If this house burns, you'll burn with it," she growled. Sam nodded to her Summoner, trying to give her the confidence she needed to get through the fight that was building by the second.

The leader of the group pulled out his sword and stared down Sam while the other two faced Cedar. Fin held tight to the one who had a knife to Lorelei. Sam's heart beat in her ears. A bead of sweat fell down her determined face. She could feel her arms trembling as she kept her staff in front of her, creating a barrier between herself and the sword that was gleaming in the light of the flames.

He moved first. Dashing left and in an upward motion with his sword. She moved her staff towards the blow, blocking his slice with the middle of her staff. A sickening scrape rang out at the collision between the two metals. Sam's body jarred at the reverberation of the strike. Backing up in alarm as she tried to catch herself.

Without a moment's notice, he swung again. Now downward from where his sword ended from the last swing. Alarmed, she barely had a chance to block with her staff at the second attack.

She couldn't keep up. He was too fast.

The second swing hit the staff. Sam fell backwards and fell the stone wall from the force. Her breath knocked from her lungs as she fell to the ground. Her breathing rapid and uncollected with fear.

When she locked eyes with her rival, she could see a smirk grin aimed at her. In a quick motion, her eyes darted around the room. Cedar fended off her opponents by shooting out tiny fireballs and burning them with her hands. Sam could see she was scared, and struggling to concentrate.

Sam scowled and stared up to face her attacker again. However, he had another idea. The tip of his sword glinted only inches from her chest, catching her off guard. She fell back and pushed herself into the wall, trying to merge into it. A shocked cry escaped her lips.

"Sam!" Fin yelled. He pushed his swords closer to his thief's neck. "Let her go or I will end him!" He spat. The man cried out as a thin streak of blood ran down his neck. He released Lorelei. She collapsed to her knees.

His body shaking, Amph pushed himself up and dragged himself closer to his wife to shield her with his body.

While Cedar was distracted, the attacker on her left seized the chance and lunged forward. He swung his fist back, and with full force aimed for her stomach. Grunting from the impact, they watched as she fell, crumpling to the floor.

"Cedar!" Sam and Fin cried out. She moved to protect her, but stopped in her tracks once again by the blade now to her throat. Helplessly, she looked toward her sister as she lay on the stone flooring. Her eyes stung. Hatred and anger fumed through her. Sam locked eyes with the man across from her as tears streaked down her face.

"Is this what you enjoy? Beating the crap out of children?" she asked, spitting her trapped hatred at them.

He looked down at her as the other two picked up Cedar and held her arms apart. "What I enjoy... is money." He paused. "Now, where are my scales?" The man replied heinously.

Sam stared up at him with defiance burning in her eyes. He frowned and turned towards the others.

"Kill the girl."

Ajax and Ban Tui followed Bram when he stormed out that day, and stayed with him as he hated himself into the night.

"I shouldn't have said anything to them. I *knew* this was going to be a problem." He covered his eyes with his hand and shook his head as he thought back to earlier when the Oracle and Ta-an had told him about their parents' death.

"I just got caught up in the conversation," he sighed, frustrated. The two of them seemed to be listening intently. They had insisted on staying with him, and Bram was reminded of his curious pull with animals.

Trying to bring his thoughts back from the past and into the present, he forced his gaze down to the rippling, flowing water under the wooden bridge they rested on. After he had stormed off, they wandered the city of Vineke until he tired out and found himself here.

The small wooden bridge isolated from the rest of the city, had enough room for the three of them to sit on. Covered in moss, ferns, and other wild plants as the water flowed crisp with algae sticking to the rocks and small pieces of kelp stayed stuck in place as it tried unsuccessfully to follow the current.

As he laid back, he dipped his feet into the water and felt it trickle past him at a hurried rate, while looking up at the stars that dappled the sky through the covered tree line. He stared up at them, trying to make out constellations and letting his mind wander again to places he did not wish to remember. His eyes grew heavy and he could feel his breathing calm as the nature around him pushed him to slumber. Closing his eyes, he fell into the sleep of memories.

The world shifted around him as he woke and tried to pry open his sore, tired eyes. His mind rejected it, but his body forced him awake to a soft pain on his arm. He moved to swat it away, but hit a friend instead.

"Wha-" he tiredly forced his head up and saw Ajax nibbling at his arm. Ajax bleated aloud and pushed his wet nose into Bram's face, licking him awake.

"Ajax, come on dude, what are yo-" Bram stopped, he began to notice that Ajax and Ban Tui were acting strange.

Ajax bounded back and forth while Ban Tui barked at Bram and looked towards the city.

Confused, Bram stood. He made a face and shook his head at the two of them. Ajax stopped and bleated at him. Goosebumps ran up his arms.

Cautiously, he squatted to make himself low and examined his surroundings. He didn't sense anything. Ban Tui and Ajax wouldn't act up for no reason.

His breath caught. Another wave of goosebumps ran through his body.

"Something's wrong." He stared wide-eyed at the two when he made the connection.

With a splash through the creek, he bounded off towards their home on the water. Off the pathway and into the forest, he could feel that Ajax was with him trotting by his side. Glancing back quickly he saw Ban Tui following at a slow pace.

"Meet us at the house," he yelled back and continued forward with surging speed. He felt bad for leaving him behind but knew he couldn't slow down.

"I swear if something happened." He grumbled.

He could feel his body propelling itself forward, magnetizing to its destination as he jumped mindlessly through his obstacles. Even though he wasn't in his true form, he had not lost his other abilities that he gained through experience. His heartbeat steady and driven with purpose. He could feel his lungs calmly expanding and contracting with the fresh air.

His eyes snapped towards the light as he jumped over a dead tree covered in long golden capped mushrooms. Bram slowed as he neared, and noticed the dim light was the flickering of a flame from the kitchen. The door was pushed open slightly, making the hair on his neck stand. He looked at Ajax, who was crouched next to him and staring intently towards the house.

They made their way towards it covertly through tall grass and reeds, and stepped silently in the water trickling over the rocks so as to not make a sound.

As Bram neared the house, muffled sounds of a struggle reached his ears. His chest tightened. He pushed the door open, stepping cautiously inside.

"Kill the girl," a sinister voice growled.

His blood turned to ice.

Cedar? Or maybe Sam!?

Their faces flashed through his mind. Without thinking, he lunged forward, gripping the edge of the wall to steady himself before plunging into chaos.

The scene hit him like a fist. Four intruders, their backs to him. One had a sword pressed against Sam's chest, her face streaked with tears. Fin stood behind another, blade to his throat, rage etched across his face.

But it was Cedar who stole Bram's focus. Two men held her. Her head hung low, arms pinned, bruises blooming on her pale skin.

Something inside Bram shattered. A terrible, searing fury surged through him.

He roared and charged the man gripping Cedar's left arm. They collided with a sickening crunch, and Bram sank his teeth into the man's neck, primal and unthinking. Warm blood filled his mouth, and he tore deeper, the metallic tang igniting a sharp disgust. The intruder screamed as they hit the floor. Bram barely noticed.

When it was over, Bram staggered to his feet, blood dripping from his lips and soaking his clothes. His vision blurred as he turned to the second man holding Cedar. The sight of her battered face ignited the fury all over again.

"Bram." Sam's trembling voice broke through the haze, but he didn't respond.

The second intruder released Cedar, shoving her away as Bram advanced. She crumpled to the floor, her ragged breaths the only sound he could hear. He growled low, his teeth bared.

Before he could strike, Ajax leapt from the shadows. The Qilin glided, slamming into the intruder's back. The man cried out, stumbling into the wall before sliding to the ground, unconscious.

Bram turned toward the fau holding Sam at sword-point, but a sharp thud interrupted him. Fin struck his captive, knocking him out cold.

The final intruder's gaze darted between the unconscious bodies and Bram, whose bloodied figure loomed menacingly. Fear overtook him. He dropped his sword, backing away with hands raised.

Bram moved to pursue him, but something grabbed his ankle. In a flash, he twisted, teeth bared—

"Bram, *stop!*" Fin's voice pierced through the fog.

Bram froze, his fist raised. It was Cedar. She clung to his leg, her battered face tilted up to meet his gaze.

All the anger drained from him in an instant. He dropped to his knees, trembling.

"Cedar," he whispered, his voice cracking. "I'm so sorry." He gathered her into his arms, clutching her against his chest.

Her fiery hair, now streaked with blood, brushed his face as he buried his head in her shoulder. "I'm so sorry."

"You're squishing me," she grunted, her voice hoarse but steady.

He pulled back immediately, his face flushed. "S-sorry."

Fin and Sam moved to help Cedar stand. Bram staggered to his feet, staring at the unconscious intruders and the lifeless body on the bloodied floor. The weight of what he'd done crushed him.

"I'm sorry," he murmured, "I'll leave." His fists clenched as he turned for the door. They wouldn't trust him after this. They couldn't.

"Bram," Sam called, stopping him in his tracks. He froze, daring to hope.

She approached, brushing past the fallen intruders to stand beside him. Her voice broke as she spoke. "They were going to kill Cedar. We couldn't stop them. You saved her."

Bram's breath hitched as Sam pulled him into a fierce hug, her tears wetting his bloodied shirt. He stood frozen, until Cedar limped over with Fin's help and joined them, leaning into Sam's shoulder.

Finally, Fin wrapped his arms around them all, chuckling. "I can't believe we're alive."

Bram let out a shaky laugh, his tears mingling with theirs. For the first time, the crushing weight began to lift.

7

THE CHOICES WE BEAR

SEABORNE HOLDS THE MOST DIVERSE
GROUP OF FAUNANOID.

They struggled to find rest after the unsettling events from earlier that night. Amph went to notify Ta-an, and they gathered the ones that were unconscious and he took them away after dealing with the man that Bram had killed. Lorelei told them to get some sleep even though they all knew that it would not be something that was had that night.

"Bram- are you ok?" Sam asked hesitantly.

He looked down at the floor, not wanting to meet her or anyone else's eyes.

"You know this isn't the first time I have killed something, right?" He asked, pressing his lips together as he crossed his arms securely over his body. Sam could still see some dried blood on his neck and arms. She opened her mouth to respond.

"Yes," Cedar interrupted. "but, is this the first time you have killed a fau? Not just an animal for food."

Sam could see the pleading expression on her face, hoping to know what the answer was and what the answer wasn't. They all looked at Bram, waiting for a response.

He sighed, frustrated and ruffled his hair in annoyance. "I don't know what you want me to say, guys." He looked at the three of them one by one, then continued. "I have been by myself for *years*... a lot has happened in that time. And I don't expect you to understand what I went through. But I want you to know when I changed into *this*." He motioned towards his human form. "That's when I started to be able to control my aggressive behavior."

"Bram." Sam walked closer to him. "As long as you don't do *that* to us or any of our family, I think we will be fine." She motioned towards the floor where the blood stained the stone and mud.

"You did what you were supposed to do. You protected us," Cedar added and put a hand on his shoulder.

"Ya, you know, it was terrifying, of course," Fin shrugged. "But it did help us out. I felt like I had it handled, though. You kind of ruined my plan." He shot him a sarcastic look that Bram returned.

Sam shook her head.

Lorelei re-entered the room in a new sleeping dress that was decorated in greens of the lake images of kelp and with hints of blue.

"No one can sleep, hmm?" She asked as she sat down at the table after getting a piece of bread and cheese from the cabinet.

"No," Sam started. "Well, we tried, but ended up back out here after a couple of hours." She rubbed her face.

"It's hard to sleep when you close your eyes and all you can see is a sword at your throat." Lorelei nodded as she spoke.

"It will be fine. Give it time," Amph said as he entered the room. "You only have a day or two left, so you should try to rest during that time."

Just then, Sam remembered the dream she had been woken up from right before the break in. She stood, her mouth open as it creaked into a mischievous smile.

"Guys," she said as she looked from one person to the other.

They waited in anticipation, looking confused.

"Well, spit it out Sammi. What's going on?" Cedar furrowed her brow.

"Ppft, Sammi?" Fin said, mocking her nickname. Both Cedar and Sam shot him a look.

"I had a dream. Before Cedar woke me up-" she started. "I spoke to Lyra, and I think I know where she is."

Shock and relief mingled on everyone's faces as they stared.

"Well, what happened? What did she say? Where is she?" Fin spoke at a hurried rate as he tried to spit out as many questions as possible.

Sam cracked a smile at the sight and sat back down. As she got comfortable, she added.

"So she is stuck behind a *huge* wall. I can't see her, only hear her, right?" She looked around to see the agreeing head nods, Sam nodded in response and kept going.

"Well, I was telling her about you guys, our plan, and how she is involved. And I went to touch the wall." Sam held her hand up and pretended to touch the imaginary wall in front of her as she recalled what happened.

"Then, it lit up in all these beautiful colors, and they were corals. A giant wall made of bioluminescent corals." She looked in wonder around her friends' awed faces. "That's when I realized that Lyra was trapped in a Reef. She needs our help. We *have* to find her."

The room was silent as they drew themselves away from the images of bioluminescent coral under the sea. Amph broke the silence first.

"You're going to want to go to the third Reef. I'll take you," he said.

The atmosphere shifted uncomfortably and the four of them drew quiet. Sam knew they needed help, but she didn't want to make him do more than what he needed to do. Especially after what happened.

"Amph... we can't ask you to do that for us." Cedar said sadly. "It's just- too much to ask of someone."

Fin nodded and stepped forward. "Yes, you have done plenty. It is time for you to rest. We can find our own way, or maybe someone else to take us, but you should stay here with Lorelei."

At that Lorelei shook her head. "No, he will take you. And while you sail to the city on the water, he will teach you how to fend for yourselves in Seaborne. We will not abandon you kids and that's *final.*" She stood and wrapped her arms around her waist for warmth and comfort. "Now I expect everyone to get a good amount of rest in the next coming day because the day after tomorrow you will be leaving Vineke."

Sam opened her mouth to respond, but she didn't know what to say.

Her and Amph walked out of the kitchen towards their room.

"Lorelei," she called out.

"Thank you," Sam said, a tired smile played on her lips. Lorelei gave a nod of understanding and left.

Sam cleared her throat as she blinked and took a deep breath of determination. She stood, looking from Fin, to Bram, then finally Cedar, who waited for her to make the next move.

"Well, you heard the lady. It's time to get some rest. We will be leaving in two days."

Cedar lay awake in bed as she listened to Ajax snore lightly in the bed next to her. She shifted. He and Sam slept together, barely fitting in the small bed. She could see Ajax growing and becoming more prominent in his adolescence through the days.

Restlessly sighing, she turned back over to gaze out the window that her bed was up against. Her eyes scrunched together. The fight replayed in her mind. Imagining a way it could have gone differently. The different paths, the different moves she could have done to protect herself and her friends showed themselves, but vanished rapidly with excuse after excuse.

Cedar could feel it, the flame, in her. It coursed through her veins. She looked at her clawed fingers, her palm, then last her arm.

But why couldn't she at least be strong enough to protect herself? She should have used as much of the flame as she wanted, not holding back. Angrily, Cedar grimaced, balling her fist into the air.

No. No she could've hurt them. Cedar laid her balled fist on her forehead as the images of her friends, Amph, and Lorelei flashed through her mind. She turned over towards Sam and Ajax, whose faces were serene in sleep.

Cedar had power now, like she wanted, but was still not strong enough to control it.

She bit the inside of her lip, sitting up and silently hopping out the window.

She was going to be strong enough to protect her friends. To use this power to its fullest.

After a moment of wandering around for the right spot, she sat cross-legged on the ground, close to the singing brook and the swaying reeds. She took a breath and steadied her breathing as she ignited her hand. Mesmerized, the young girl watched as it danced. A small circle of flames around her. As it did, she practiced the ways her mother, Lin, had taught her to grow stronger.

Cedar thought back to what her mom had said to her before they left the Whispering Woods.

"Every new flame caller should go to the Temple of the Sun once they gain their powers to learn to harness them. I did too. But since you are going with Sam now, I will show you some meditational practices to mute your mind and grow the strength of the fire within. Once you have quieted your soul, then you will be able to truly master the art of summoning."

While dimming the one on her right, she drew herself back to her surroundings and focused, raising the flames on her left palm. Cedar watched as neither responded but continued to dance negligently, furrowing her brow. She continued this practice until sweat beaded on her forehead and the rays of the morning sun dappled the tips of the trees.

Rejuvenated by the sun's warm bask, she continued to focus on her task as the water flowed and the birds began to sing with the soft wind.

A light chuckle next to her broke her concentration.

"How long have you been at that?" Bram spoke up.

Cedar blinked as she looked up at Bram, and the fire from her palm and the circle dissipated.

"Long enough to have seen some progress," she grumbled and stood. "How long were you watching me?" She dusted the dirt off her.

"Well... I saw you when I went to sleep, and then I saw you again when I woke up," Bram said, "so does that count as the whole time?" There was a playful smile in his eyes as she shook her head.

"I'm too tired for this," Cedar laughed, heading back to her bedroom window.

"I think it's pretty neat, by the way... that you can do that," Bram said slowly, trying to find the right words. "I haven't met any summoners in the inner realms before."

Her heart skipped a beat. "What?" Cedar turned to face him, her brow furrowed. "The inner realms? There are Summoners *outside* of the valley?"

Bram nodded.

She shook her head, trying to process it. "I thought... there were only Summoners and Elementals here, in the four realms."

Bram's gaze shifted toward the horizon. "No, there are elementals outside these realms, too. From our territory, we have a clear view of their temple."

"They have a temple?" Cedar's voice rose in disbelief, hands on her hips. "Except for the guardian of the tree, no one's seen them in hundreds of years! And you're telling me the Ascerian live next to them?"

Bram shrugged, clearly caught off guard. "They keep to themselves, I guess. I was really young when we left, but my parents told me about it."

Cedar stopped staring at him and started pacing as she struggled to process the information.

Bram winced, his voice softening, "sorry. I didn't mean to upset you."

"No, you didn't," Cedar sighed, running a hand through her hair. "I'm just exhausted."

From behind her, a voice broke in. "Ya, Cedar, that was... weird."

She spun around to see Fin leaning against the porch railing, a peach in one hand, an amused look on his face. The warmth in Cedar's cheeks spread quickly.

Her eyes darted between Bram, who was scowling at Fin, and Fin, who seemed to find it all highly entertaining.

"I—I'm going to bed," she muttered, turning abruptly. Without another word, she stomped off, her face flushed.

As she jumped onto her bed through the window, she found Sam sitting there, an amused smile tugging at the corners of her lips.

Cedar flopped onto the mattress, hiding her face in the pillow.

Sam cleared her throat, trying to suppress a laugh.

Cedar groaned, pulling the pillow over her head. "Please, don't start."

Sam grinned, her eyes sparkling. "I mean, it was just a *little* awkward, right?"

"Sam, not you too! Can't I get any peace around here?" Cedar picked up an extra pillow that was next to her and tossed it at her friend, who dodged with a laugh before slipping out the door.

Cedar buried herself under the covers, muffling a groan as she let the weight of the day settle in.

"I can't believe we are finally leaving Vineke after a week of being here! How are supplies? Do you think we should go shopping while Cedar sleeps?" Sam pressed Fin anxiously.

He shrugged in response, unworried about the departure. "I am sure we have what we need. We have been here long enough to get ready."

Silently, she nodded in agreement. Her expression showing Fin that she had other things on her mind.

"Are you still worried about Bram?" He asked, glancing over to her. He cut the stem of the pinkish gourd and dropped it in the basket of food they planned on taking back to the small river home.

This time, Sam shrugged in response, and after a moment added, "I thought I understood him because he turned human, but I feel like there is so much he isn't telling us or- I guess- doesn't want to tell us." She sighed, tossing a couple of carrots into her basket.

"I just-" she stopped and looked at Fin, "want him to trust us." She shook her head as if disagreeing with her own words. Wiping the beaded sweat from her forehead, she bent back down to continue grabbing at a stubbornly hidden gourd.

"I mean- I'm surprised you trusted *me* that easily," Fin snorted in response.

"I literally stole from *you,*" he emphasized, "-you trust people too easily."

Fin had only known her for a little while but could tell she was able to open up to most people more easily than most he had met. She seemed to open her mouth to deny what he had said, but quickly closed it and quietly went back to work. He smiled and rolled his eyes at the fact that she couldn't argue.

"Give him some more time, he'll come around," Fin added more sympathetically, "I think this is enough for dinner, don't you?"

"I think so. Let's head back then," Sam answered as she and Fin picked up the baskets and began wading their way through the knee high pooled water and past the other gardens.

As they reached the shallow water where it met the bridged walkway, Sam turned to him.

"Do you think Bram will actually leave when we get to the mountains?" she asked, her eyebrows knitted together in concern.

Fin laughed, "Sam, you are so worried about him. You're going to smother him if you're not careful."

At that, she made a face, "I care about you guys and I thought he was going to stay... At least until after the tournament."

"I wouldn't worry about it right now. We have so much traveling ahead. Let's focus on dinner and getting ready for right now instead of what's going to happen in the future." He scratched the back of his head and ruffled his coarse orange hair.

Sam sighed again. "Yeah, yeah, I know—focus on the present."

Fin stopped walking. Hearing those words made something stir inside him. His mind drifted to his mother, who used to say something of the same thing. He hadn't thought about her in... awhile, but now, with Sam's voice echoing those words, the memory surfaced, vivid and sharp. For a fleeting moment, he could almost see her again.

A solemn smile touched his lips, followed by a quiet chuckle. The irony wasn't lost on him: here he was, telling Sam not to dwell on things, while he carried the weight of old sorrows every step of the way.

"You good?" Sam turned back, her gray eyes catching the afternoon light, sharp and inquisitive.

Fin shook the memory off and forced a grin. "Yeah, just thinking about Cedar and Bram earlier. Those two have *absolutely* no clue how to talk to each other."

Sam joined him, laughing and continued her way on the stone road. "I think she was exhausted from practicing her summoning."

"Sure, sure." Fin put his hand up defensively as he shuffled the basket in his arm to sit it more comfortably.

Sam shot him a doubtful look, but didn't say anything else.

They meandered back, enjoying the sun that fell on them. Fin could feel the heat of summer growing as the humidity of the river picked up around him, making his hair and fur stick to his skin uncomfortably.

"I might join you guys while you shop for stuff and get some more suitable sea clothing," he said, making a face as he pulled on his collar and the sleeves of his shirt.

"Well, let's make some dinner and then we can go pick up stuff for the journey and pack," Sam said, content with the plans.

As the sun rose to its peak and fell on their last day in the city of fireflies, Sam walked through the mass of merchant stalls and vendors that lined the river.

While Cedar perused the stalls that held the medicinal herbs and creams for healing, Lorelei and Amph split off to shop for food and other items for Amph's trip.

"I am *sooOOoo* bored," Fin groaned as Cedar paid for a bundle of dried green plants that were wrapped together with a twined ribbon.

Sam rolled her eyes at him. "Well, why don't you go somewhere *else*, then?"

Fin smacked his lips. "Come on, Bram, let's try to find you a weapon or something."

"Why?-" He started in protest.

"Buddy, you can't bite your way through all your problems. It's time for a sword or anything other than your teeth." Fin said as he beckoned him towards one of the stone bridges that cross over to the market on the other side of the river.

Bram groaned in protest as he unwillingly followed Fin in between the other shoppers and out of sight.

"He can be so demanding sometimes." Cedar looked at Sam and then back after the two of them who just disappeared.

"O, for sure."

"Do you want to-" Cedar started but stopped suddenly.

Sam stopped a moment later, noticing that Cedar had stopped walking too and was staring into a shop.

"Why'd you stop?" Sam asked, looking in the same direction to see a wall of masks.

"This is where we bought Bram's mask, the one he is wearing," she answered gradually, as if she was still lost in thought.

At the thought of the masks, Sam touched her own and felt the familiarity of the glossiness. She had worn it for so long that it felt as if it had become a part of her.

"And-" Sam prodded for more information.

"This is where that lady saw the scales. Lorelei had to stop her from taking one of them." As she spoke, she got quieter and quieter, turning into a whisper. Sam could almost see her thoughts as they both stared at her satchel and she brought out the small bag that held the illustrious scales.

"You don't think..." Sam started, but couldn't finish her question. She looked into the shaded store and saw a woman at the counter wearing a pink dress, fanning herself with a large grass leaf to escape the summer's heat.

"Yes, I do." Cedar said, shoving the small bag into its hiding place and starting towards the store and its merchant.

8

REFLECTIONS

WHEN AN ELEMENTAL OR SUMMONER
BECOMES NOTABLE THEY ARE ADORNED
WITH THE MYTHOLOGICAL TITLE OF THEIR
REALM AND ELEMENT.

A WAVE OF EMOTIONS passed through the woman's scaled face. She watched in dread as Sam and Cedar walked through the entrance. Uncomfortably shifting in her stool, she smoothed out her dress.

"You seem to remember me.. from the other day." Cedar said flatly. Without looking away from the merchant she added, "This is my sister, Samihanee."

The merchant locked eyes with her behind the mask.

"What a lovely fox spirit you wear?" Nervous laughter escaped her lips.

Sam stared back, and the woman shrunk.

"Y-Yes, I remember you. Do you need something?" she stammered.

"We do, yes." Cedar leaned on the counter and drummed her fingers on the corner of the wood. "You see, our friend's place was broken into the other night. You wouldn't know anything about that... would you?" Her voice was dark and cold, robbed of any form of pleasantries as the woman shifted under their stares.

The merchant stammered, not saying anything coherent as she turned away again.

Cedar's fingertips sizzled on the wood, and she burned a mindless pattern into it. "See, that's funny, because you're the *only one* who knew we even had the scales to begin with. So-" She stopped tracing her finger on the wood, looking up. She leaned in. "How did they find out about them?" she whispered.

The woman's eyes grew wide as she glanced back and forth between the girls and the entrance. Sam slid between her and her only escape.

Infuriated, she slammed her staff into the stone and exclaimed, "You're not helping your cause! I would speak up."

"Ok ok ok," she put her hands up, "I knew them. They came into town from the nearest Reef. They said that I could get some scales since I told them about it." She fumbled over her words. Making herself smaller by the moment.

Cedar let out a deep aggravated sigh, "Where is the one that got away? Is he here?!" She banged her fist on the counter, and Sam stepped forward.

"*No!* No, he's not." She covered her face as she cried out. "He left back to the Reef. He works for someone there. I don't know anything else."

Sam's face contorted with a mix of anger and hatred; her cheeks flushed with heat. Her heart raced as she saw the rage burning in Cedar's eyes. Trembling with energy, she clenched her fists.

"What's his name?" Sam growled.

"Toba," she wailed between tears.

"Ladies, I think that's *quite* enough."

Sam's eyes widened in surprise, and she stumbled backward. Heart pounding in her chest, startled by an unexpected presence.

"O-Oracle?"

The Oracle, Ta-an, Lorelei, and Amph were in the street, studying the encounter. Sam flushed, losing the confidence in her actions by the second. Cedar, however, seemed to grow only more irritated.

"How could you say that?" Cedar exclaimed. "She is the reason those men came into their home and tried to kill us!" She gestured to the woman who flinched away from her crimes. Tears brimmed in Cedars pleading eyes.

"And treating this woman like those awful men is going to make it better?" the Oracle responded tenderly.

Cedar's voice cracked with desperation as she opened her mouth to retaliate, only to be overwhelmed by uncontrollable sobs. Her hand urgently covering her mouth to stifle her anguish. Lorelei rushed over and wrapped her in her arms, walking her to the side and out of the main conversation as she tried to calm her down.

"Ta-an, brother, arrest her. We will question her further girls, do not worry." Oracle Hanako's gaze calmly fell to the merchant.

Ta-an motioned with his spear for her to come out. Other guards that Sam hadn't noticed earlier walked up, taking her away down the street wailing as onlookers stopped to stare.

Once Ta-an, the guards, and the woman were gone, Cedar had calmed down as she sniffled and caught her breath.

"I'm sorry." Her eyes drooped towards the ground, ashamed.

"Don't be sorry. You have a right to be upset and angry, but it's best to stop yourself before you act solely on your emotions." Oracle Hanako replied.

Cedar nodded quietly, accepting her words as she calmed more.

Sam looked at Amph. "She said that they are from the Reef closest to here. Is that where we are headed?"

"Yes."

Sam and Cedar looked at each other with the same thought. This wasn't over.

"Thank you, Lorelei, for *also* remembering the merchant. We came at a good time." Oracle Hanako bowed her head. "I also wanted to say goodbye before you leave tomorrow. So, I will leave you with this." She lowered herself into the water, dipping under, then coming back up.

"You will see him again, I have no doubt about that, but when the time comes, you have to decide if you want your emotions or your morals to be your guide. The choices we make will be only ours to bear, not others. I trust you will think about this and make the right decision when the time comes. Don't do something that is not in character because of how you are feeling in the moment."

Sam bowed her head lightly in thanks. "Thank you, Oracle. We will think about it."

"Yes, thank you for the wisdom." Lorelei said, releasing Cedar from her firm hug.

"Not wisdom... experience." Oracle Hanako said as her wistful eyes looked at them for a moment, "You will be missed Samihanee and Cedar. Give my best to the boys, and I hope to see you again someday. You'll have to tell me about the rest of your travels."

At that, she sank into the water and became nothing but a rippling mass of color that traveled upstream the way Ta-an and the guards went with the crying woman.

Cedar let out a sigh and wiped her eyes. "That was... *a lot*."

"I think it is time to head home for the night." Amph responded.

"We have everything we came for. If not, we can get it tomorrow on our way out," Sam agreed. "Let's get the guys and go."

The small boat rocked against the current of the gradually shrinking river. They'd been traveling since before sunrise, and now the sun hung high in the sky, casting a bright, relentless heat upon them. Sam covered her eyes as she looked upwards towards it and then outwards toward the water it reflected on. Causing it to become a mirror of heat and blinding light.

"Can it be any hotter?" she asked, fanning herself dreadfully.

"Don't tempt it." Fin waved the thought away as he laid on the boat in heated exhaustion.

"We will get more shade once we reach the dotted mangroves." Amph walked up from the back and looked out at the sea in their direction. "We should be there soon and maybe reach the Reef after nightfall if we don't get caught in any misdirection's." He walked back to the back and pushed the boat away from the right shoreline with his long pole.

"Dotted mangroves?" Bram's interest seemed to spark as he sat up.

"Wait, misdirections?" Cedar also seemed to catch something of what Amph said. She wiped her forehead with a cloth.

"The dotted mangroves are a chain of mangrove trees that've created small islands at the end of the river." He pointed out as if he could see the trees there. "We'll be at the salt water then but not the Reef, and these trees have made a maze for any sorry sap who doesn't know how to handle 'em," he grumbled.

"That's *fantastic,*" Fin added in a sarcastic tone. "And I am hoping that you are not a *sorry sap?*"

Amph looked at him for a moment, then back towards the river's horizon as he gave the boat another push.

"I'm gonna take that as a no."

Sam shot him a look. He laughed awkwardly. "What?"

Out of nowhere, Ajax's bleat pierced the air, grabbing Sam's attention. She looked down at him, his body protruding from the small storage shed on the floor of the boat. With a chuckle at his goofy posture, she squatted next to him and ruffled his head in a familiar way.

"Ajax, you won't stop growing, will you? You fit in there when we arrived in Vineke." She felt his horns and moved his head to the side to look at the patterns on his fur that had changed even more. "And look at this buddy, your spots are almost all gone and your horns have gotten *much* bigger!" Sam grinned at him as he bleated with pride.

"I want to see!" Cedar squealed excitedly as she scurried around items on the boat and over to admire the foals' attributes. "Ooo, you're getting so big, you gotta stop growing!" She laughed, sitting down on her knees and running her hands over his fur.

Ajax bleated again as he shook his head, beaming proudly.

"You're gonna give him an enormous head. He isn't *that* cute," Fin said.

Both girls shot him a glare. He chuckled and raised his hands innocently. "I'm just saying."

Ajax stood and pushed past the two of them. In a swift, simple movement, he jumped into the air and locked onto Fin's stomach. Before he could react or respond, Fin was already in the water and splashing about.

Sam and Cedar gasped in surprise and laughed as they watched Fin struggle to understand what happened and grab the side of the boat at the same time.

He cursed under his breath, grumbling in annoyance.

"Well, that's what you get for insulting him." Cedar responded matter of factly as she and Sam grabbed his arms.

"O ya?" Fin raised a mischievous eyebrow and gripped tighter onto them.

"You better no-" she started and then felt a rush of adrenaline as he pushed off the boat and backwards into the water, bringing them with him. The last thing she heard was the sound of water as it rushed around her, slapping her face.

The water was nice on the hot day. It cooled her off as annoyance dredged through her. She swam for the surface. As she breached the water's edge, she gasped for the air she wasn't able to get when she was pulled in. Sam splashed him as he crawled up the side of the boat. Laughing, he shook off the dripping water. Sam looked over at Cedar, who seemed to dread the fact that she was in the water at that moment. She grabbed at her hair, which was now lopsided and drenched. Her makeup was running, giving her raccoon eyes.

"My makeup..." she whimpered quietly.

The boat stopped now. Bram and Amph leaned over the boat and stared into the water.

Sam swam up to the side and pulled herself out with their help, then grabbed Cedars' arm.

"Rude." Cedar stood on the boat dripping both water and makeup.

Fin smirked.

Cedar shot him a hate filled glare but then waddled off toward the front of the boat and to her satchel full of supplies that would help mend the situation.

"That wasn't nice. You know she is sensitive about her makeup and stuff." Sam crossed her arms disapprovingly.

"Psh, I was playing, y'all shouldn't be such stiffs." Fin responded, waving them off as he walked off the other way to the back of the boat.

"He's such a butthead," Bram spoke up from behind her.

"We're all buttheads," she said, chuckling as she went to help calm Cedar down.

"Mangroves ahead!" Amph called to the tired and sun beaten group. Sam jolted up, standing and looking out towards the new formation of trees that drew closer by the second. She looked backwards to where they came and saw the trees and vegetation she knew on the river's edge. However, in front of them was a fresh sight all together. There was no grass or ferns that hugged the water, just thin roots jutting out attached to a taller tree with its deep green leaves on the top.

She looked on in admiration as the others joined her and they watched as they became surrounded by a mass of brown and green. The reflection in the water matched perfectly to what she saw. It was almost as the vision continued, making it appear like the trees were longer than they were. The mangroves guided them into their maze, leaving only backwards and forwards to pursue. Every once in a while, they passed a dip in the formation on both their left and right sides. Amph, however, did not falter or seem concerned about where to go. He pushed them on with unwavering confidence, easing the group's mind of the new terrain.

"This place is amazing!" Sam said in astonishment as she gazed at the tips of the trees and its leaves brushing through the soft breeze.

"Are you not worried about getting lost, Amph?" She spoke as she walked to the back of the barge. Standing next to him and admiring her surroundings.

"No. I've done this enough to have its route carved into my heart," he responded, nodding to himself as he looked onward towards the horizon of trees and gentle river water.

"So then, you enjoy ferrying people?" she asked.

"Yes, I didn't at first. It was just a way of collecting money for the house and Lorelei, but now it's somethin' I couldn't live without."

"Was it difficult at first? When you were learning all the ways to travel, I mean."

"Anythin' worth startin' afresh is hard at first. It took patience, years of mistakes, and experience to reach where I am today," he said, exerting a push that steered them from the mangrove roots into the river's heart.

Sam remained silent, grappling with his words. They resonated with her, awakening thoughts on what it truly meant to master something. As she glanced around the boat, her staff glinted in the afternoon sun.

"It'll take time for us to master anything," she sighed. "Were you... angry with yourself when you made mistakes?" Memories flooded her—times she fell short of her aspirations or failed to protect those she cared for.

Amph chuckled softly. "Yes, and I still get mad at myself when I slip up today." He lifted the bamboo pole, water dripping as it swung over the boat to the other side.

"But looking back, you know what I do now?" His gaze met hers briefly before drifting away.

"I laugh," he admitted with a faint smile. "at myself, at my mistakes. Even the ones that once seemed so monumental. I can't even recall what they were about."

Sam struggled to contain her emotions, a lump formed in her throat. "Even the big, terrible mistakes that felt irreversible?"

Amph's voice softened. "Those mistakes become a part of you, Sam. But it's what you choose to do next that defines who you are."

Bram, sitting quietly nearby, spoke up for the first time. "Even if you've killed someone?"

"It's up to you and you alone."

Sam closed her eyes, overwhelmed. "How can I move forward? How can *anyone* move forward?"

Silence enveloped them, broken only by Cedar's soft humming and the gentle ripples as Amph propelled them forward. Sam tried to find words again, but confusion clouded her thoughts more deeply than before.

"Look! Guys!" Cedar yelled to the back of the boat, creating a welcomed distraction among the uncomfortable group. "How pretty," she cooed.

Sam lifted her weary gaze to see Cedar peering over the boat and into the water. She walked over to her and followed her eyes below them to see a mass of vividly bright fish of all manners of colors darting here and there among the roots and sand of the river bed.

"Are these betas?" Sam gasped as she dipped down to get a closer look.

"No, the mangrove roots are home to the cichlids, tetras, and guppies. Colorful, but aggressive," Amph said as he slowed the boat down to a halt and propped the pole up as he joined them in watching the fish swim underneath. At that point, Bram and Fin were also leaning over the side, causing the boat to dip closer and closer into the water.

"How 'bout we spread out a bit, so we don't take a dive like earlier, hmm?" Sam said, eyeing Fin. In return, he rolled his eyes, but moved over to the other side.

"You know, you can swim with them if you want. We can take a break for now to eat." Amph motioned towards the small creatures, flittering back and forth beneath them.

"I thought you said they were aggressive?" Cedar asked.

"Yes, but they're more busy bodies than anythin'," he said as he stood and stretched towards the sky. "Besides, these old scales are gettin' dried up." At that, he dove into the water, leaving the four of them baffled and chuckling while looking after their ferryman. Sam looked up, laughing towards her friends. Bram met her eyes. With a shrug, he took one leap and cannonballed into the water. Soon after, Fin jumped in close to the boat.

"I was *almost* done with my eyeliner." Cedar said with a shocked expression. Sam raised her eyebrow and shot a mischievous look as she dove into the water, too. She didn't realize how truly deep the river was until she was in it. The others swamdown to the bottom to look at the fish and their small community.

Sam swam back up, piercing the water and smiling at the desperation on Cedar's face.

"Come on Cedar! Who are you trying to be cute for anyway?!" Sam yelled at her from the water and made a point to look in Brams' direction, then back at her. Cedar blushed and turned away.

"Makeup isn't free, you know," she said, but didn't argue further as she jumped into the water as close to Sam as possible, causing a small wave to push her underwater.

She breached for air. Cedar came up simultaneously. Then they both dived to see the fish that lived in the roots of the mangrove trees.

They seemed to not notice any of the group swimming around them or even watching them. The fish went about their business eating small pieces of grass or algae growing from the roots, going in and out of the small dark maze that lay before them.

Sam noticed that they differed from betas in size, color, and shape. Most of the beta she had seen in Vineke were just different variations of colors. When she looked at these, however, she could not see a resemblance in any of them.

They swam a ways away from the boat, going up for air when they needed it. After a while, Amph caught up with them on the boat, his scales looking brighter than before. As he caught up, Sam noticed that they had a group of followers.

A pack of river otters swam around the boat, playfully diving in and out of the water at fast speeds.

"It's alright girls." Amph called down. Sam could see that Cedar was uncomfortable. The otters swam to them and brushed up against them gently, giving them small shells or fish bones as gifts. Bram swam underneath them with two other otters playfully circling him. Sam dunked under, pushing herself further down, and swimming with the otters that decided to stay with her.

She even swam down further with them and watched as they scavenged the muddy bed for scraps of oysters and other bits of food they could find. She poked through the sand with them, creating small bursts of clouds. Once she had found what she was looking for, she picked it up, holding it in front of her. Looking at the shell full of food. One of the larger otters saw it and swam over to her. She held it out as a gift.

Once it accepted the offering, the small creature snatched the shell and swam merrily around her chirping. After that, many other otters noticed and began bombarding Sam for shells as they swam around her wildly. Cedar joined in as she became more comfortable with the boisterous creatures, and the group spent the afternoon feeding the group of river otters as they traveled further into the islands of mangroves.

9

FROM BEYOND THE MANGROVE TREES

SOME SAY THAT PEARLS GATE WAS BUILT ON
A REEF THAT HAS LIVED SINCE ANCIENT
TIMES.

"HOW DID YOU BECOME friends with the otters?" Sam asked, exhausted from her afternoon of swimming through the maze of trees. She kicked her legs back and forth in the water from the back of the boat where Amph stood as he pushed them along.

"Mmmm, they've been around for many years. I remember them from when I first started as a ferryman. But the best way to make a friend of any creature is to feed 'em." He winked at Sam. The otters flipped and glided in the water gracefully, trying to convince her to give them more food.

Sam smiled, laughing at their light-hearted behavior. Five had stayed behind. The others swam off earlier. Among the otters, one stood out as the largest, with a magnificent, dark brown coat that contrasted with his white front paws. Two of them, both around a medium size, swam side by side. Their white heads ombre against the lighter brown of their bodies. The two shortest ones were a whirlwind of energy, small white bodies varying with the patches of brown on their tails and feet.

"What are their names?" Sam asked, inspecting the differences so that she could try to tell the similar ones apart.

Amph set down the pole and focused his attention on them. "Let's see here." He cleared his throat. "This one is Oteo. He is their protector, of sorts."

As the otters danced excitedly at their feet, he singled out the biggest one and pointed to it.

"These two small ones are Ngram and Hammin. They are the youngest. And then the two closest to identical ones are siblings. Their names are Yvoir and Yvan."

"Wait, did you name them or someone else?" Sam grinned mischievously at the thought of Amph taking his time to name his otter friends.

"No, the mangrove folks told me," he said, bending over to pick up his pole and continue them along their path.

"Mangrove folk?" Her smile morphed into curiosity as she repeated him. Her imagination running wild as she pictured what exactly a mangrove fau could be.

He nodded, "The mermen and maids of the mangroves, you will see them soon. We will stop there for the night to rest."

"We're stopping?" Cedar came into the conversation as she walked to the back.

Sam smiled to see her join them. "How are you feeling?"

"Much better," she said with a relieved sigh. "The water takes it out of me. But I thought we were traveling through to the next Reef?"

Amph shook his head. "No, it would be best to stop for the night and get there on the morrow."

Cedar nodded with a thoughtful expression as she sat next to Sam. "You're the boss, boss man," she said and stuck her feet in the water.

They continued to flow with the river towards their destination. Sam echoed the names of the otters to Cedar and told her about the mangrove faus that Amph had mentioned. The sun sank in the sky, giving the clouds brighter, more vibrant colors than before. It changed into a more beautiful hue as it peaked out at them from behind the mangrove's leaves.

The sun hit the tree line as they saw mangroves that stood relatively bigger than the others. Homes were carved into the thick clumps of roots. Waking up Bram and Fin, they all gathered in anticipation when the boat made its way into the small, almost hidden village.

The roots were more condensed and stood taller than the ones they had seen previously. The island homes jumbled together, but still gave way to different pathways for Amph to choose from. Sam squinted, focusing her attention past the water and at the roots underneath. She could see that it created a protective wall of sorts. Forming a circular home with a gap for someone to swim in and small windows to look out. She glimpsed the inside of the homes and could see furniture made from wood and seagrass decorating the inside. As she scoured the sight, she noticed that the floors of the homes and the riverbed sprouted with dense seagrass. Its gentle sway mirroring the calm current.

There. A flash of color. Here, then gone. Another color. These were the residents of the village.

She drew a quick breath in and whispered to Cedar, "They're tiny!"

Their eyes sparkled with wonder at the new village before them and they both watched the mermaids and mermen as they swam around or stopped to look up at the boat of strangers going over them.

One even smaller mermaid, poked her head out of the water and looked at them, smiling. She had long brown hair and a seagrass shirt dyed purple. Her tail was pink and orange, with blue spots completely covering it. A pink dorsal fin trimmed with blue on the front and back of her tail.

"Hello!" she chirped in a bright child's voice.

Surprised, they waved back. Almost instantly a bigger mermaid poked through the water. She looked similar to the girl who was in front of them, except she wore a plain green bralette and had much darker blue spots.

"Sorry haha, we're trying to teach her not to talk to strangers," she said, flashing a polite but tight smile. The mermaid shot the small girl with a stern look as she dragged her back underwater and out of sight.

Sam and Cedar moved to the front of the boat to get a better look at the underwater village. The otters followed, waving their paws as they said goodbye and swam down one dip, disappearing from sight as well.

"I guess they wanted to take us here?" Sam shrugged, unsure.

"Probably," Fin jumped into the conversation with Bram. "But, hey! Did you see these people? They're so small!"

"They remind me of the fish we've seen on our way here. The ones who also live in the roots," Bram put in.

"Their tail's are the same," Sam added, looking at the vibrant multitude of colors of the few sea faunanoid still out and about.

"Amph, I didn't know merpeople could be different sizes." Cedar leaned back to look at him.

"We can grow to be much bigger, too. Most of those folk live in the ocean, though," He said as he tied the boat against one mangrove that was not a living space.

"Like Chief." Cedar looked at Sam as they thought back to the massive moose in the Whispering Woods. Sam exhaled in awe, her mind filled with vivid memories of the extraordinary creatures she had encountered on her voyage.

"We will rest here for the night and continue on our way at first light," Amph called to the group.

"Is it safe for us to sleep out in the open here?" Fin asked with concern evident in his voice.

"They are more afraid of you than you are of them," he stated as he finished tying the second rope on the boat's front to a jumble of roots clustered next to them.

Unsettled still, he looked at Sam for confirmation. She shrugged and nodded in response. Fin rolled his eyes.

The group gathered in the center of the boat around Ajax and ate dinner with the setting sun and dwindling light. As they munched on the breads, cheeses, and cooked fish they packed, lights underneath them glowed. It was the bioluminescent lights of underwater mushrooms that lit the homes. The brightness grew as it got darker, and it showed its beauty to the group as the currents rippled and flowed above the white, blue glow. They listened to the calm night as they settled in. Sam stared at the trees and the stars just beyond them. She drifted off to sleep when she heard the soft snoring of Cedar next to her and the rustling of Ajax as he moved closer to them. She looked up one last time to see the moon shine on her friends. Bram and Fin sleeping further to the back of the boat, and Amph who slept sitting up at the tail end.

Sam laid back down in between the boat's beams and back onto the plush sleeping pallet they unfurled after dinner.

Looking back up at the stars, she closed her eyes as she faintly rocked back and forth with the boat.

Sam blinked her eyes open into the dazzling sun, covering her eyes with the back of her hand. She sat up and rubbed her face awake. Her head ached on the humid morning. Sam pushed the blanket that covered her from the sun's light off of her and stretched out.

"O! You're awake now. I was wondering how long you would sleep till," Cedar said.

Feeling grungy, she nodded in response. "Did you put the covers over the beams for me?" She asked, wondering how long she slept for.

"Yes, I did. You were out of it when I tried to wake you, so we let you sleep longer."

"You seem chipper." Sam ran her finger through her ratted hair, trying to comb out the tangles as she wobbled up to Cedar.

"Do I?" Her cheeks bloomed into a soft red, and she smiled to herself for a moment, then looked back up to Sam. "I got a good sleep last night. It's been awhile."

Sam raised her eyebrow, curious to why she was acting strange, but pushed it off.

"You think you can braid my hair like that one time in the woods? It's getting unmanageable again." Sam groaned as she sat down in front of her, not giving Cedar much of a choice.

"Sure!" She grabbed a clump of hair and started sorting through it. Cheerfully, she hummed to herself. Sam furrowed her brows. Again caught off guard by the sudden mood change in her.

"Wait," she said, becoming aware of their surroundings. The village was gone. They were now in calm, open water.

"Where are we? How long was I asleep for?!..."

"You were asleep for a couple of hours after we got moving again. Amph wanted to get an early start for the Reef."

Surprised, Sam looked around at the tranquil, sparse nothingness in front of them. She turned and looked back to see the mangroves in the far distance with the leaves barely showing as a clump on the horizon.

"I can't believe how far we have gotten out to sea already," Sam said anxiously.

"Mhmm." Cedar put a couple of bands in her mouth and continued to sort through Sam's hair.

After much yanking, pulling, and pain, she could feel Cedar finishing the braids.

"There, all done. Now it looks much better. I didn't do it like the one last time, though. I thought you might like this one instead," she said, motioning to the water. They both peered over the boat and looked at the calm sheet reflecting as a mirror would.

Her hair was now neatly braided from the top to the middle, securing it out of her face, while the rest of her hair cascaded freely down her back. A few braids delicately framed her shoulders. She looked into the water and could see her reflection staring back at her. Her eyes weren't her own. When she looked into the water, her gaze met a strangers. As she touched her cheek, she could feel the gritty texture of dirt against her skin, urging her to wash her face. Carefully, she cupped the water in her hands, bringing it up to her face and feeling the droplets trickle down her skin. Sam leaned back in the boat and sighed, reminiscent of her reflection.

"What? You don't like your hair?" Cedar asked, concerned.

"No, no, it's not that." Sam gave her a soft smile as she wiped the excess of salted water from her eyebrows and mouth.

"When I see myself, it feels like there is something off." Her gaze fell to the scars on her arm from Bram and the other obstacles she faced in the new world as she tried to explain what she meant. Irritated, she turned to the side.

"I don't know how to explain it." She shook her head. "What's so different from before?"

Left helpless, she tried to smile through the awkwardness of finding the right words to explain how she felt.

"I- don't know what to say. You have always been the Sam I met when you first emerged from the cave." She hugged her and squeezed tightly. "And you will always be the Sam I know."

Sam hugged her back. Words echoing in her mind. "Thanks, I needed that." She took a deep breath and nodded.

A sense of determination brought her to a stand.

The sky was still dark when the boat shifted, stirring Cedar from her slumber.

"Wha-" She sat up, blinking hazily as she tried to get her bearings. Waves of unruly hair hogged her vision.

Rubbing her eyes and face, she became more alert. She turned her head to see the boys beginning to stir as Amph freed the boat from the mangrove trees and pushed them forward.

Cedar looked over to see Sam still sleeping easily. Her chest rising and falling with her breath.

Taking her own blanket, she covered the beams with it to give Sam a shelter from the sunlight that was streaming through the leaves and trunks of the mangroves.

Gingerly stepping over her, Cedar made her way to the tip of the boat, where her bag lay. She had started wearing makeup after seeing the beauty of the koimaids. The memory of asking her mother about it came back to her. Lin had sighed, saying she wasn't old enough.

But when Cedar had seen a shop full of fine clothes, jewelry, and *art for the skin*, curiosity got the better of her. The merchant woman had eagerly explained the basics, painting visions of elegance with every brushstroke. Cedar hadn't told Sam or Fin about the purchase—she didn't want Fin mocking her or Sam scolding her for spending money on something frivolous. Still, when she saw the makeup, she felt compelled to experiment.

Sitting now, she looked at her reflection in the water, brushing her hand over her cheek. She'd practiced applying it, but doubt still lingered.

Was it worth it?

"Here."

The voice startled her. She jolted upright, rocking the boat. Her heart hammered as she turned, meeting Bram's wide-eyed stare as he steadied himself.

"Sorry," she gasped, hand on her chest. "You scared me. I wasn't paying attention."

Bram laughed softly, sinking into a crouch to keep the boat balanced. "No, that's my bad. Should've announced myself." He held out an apple and a piece of cheese. "Brought you breakfast."

"Thank you." She took the food, her stomach grumbling its approval. Setting the apple on her bag, she bit into the cheese, savoring the taste with a small smile.

Bram's gaze drifted to the satchel beside her, where the paints and eyeliner lay half-hidden. "What were you doing over here, anyway?"

Her cheeks warmed as she quickly closed the bag. "Nothing."

He raised an eyebrow but said nothing. Cedar sighed, her resolve crumbling. "Fine. I bought some makeup in Vineke.

I've been practicing, but I didn't tell Sam or Fin. They'd just tease me or get mad."

Bram tilted his head. "Makeup? Is that the stuff you've been putting on your face?"

"Yes." She focused on the cheese in her hands. "It's supposed to cover spots or make you look prettier. Some women wear it when they get older, but I wanted to try."

Bram picked up the small eyeliner stick, turning it in his hands. "You don't have any spots that need covering. But..." He hesitated. "I guess it does make your eyes look kind of... like the golden trees in fall."

Her hand froze mid-motion. She stared at him, unsure if she'd heard correctly.

Bram blinked, realization dawning. "I—I didn't mean it like that. Or, I mean, I did, but not—" He groaned, rubbing the back of his neck. "Forget I said anything."

Cedar bit back a smile as his words tumbled over each other. The redness creeping up his neck mirrored her own. When he started to stand, she reached out and grabbed his arm.

"Wait, it's okay."

He hesitated, then sank back down. "Really?"

"Really." She tucked a stray strand of hair behind her ear, her cheeks still warm but her heart lighter. "Thank you. For saying that."

For a moment, neither spoke. The soft lapping of the water filled the silence. She picked up the apple, taking a bite as Bram leaned back, a small, sheepish smile tugging at his lips.

"So," he said, after a beat. "Are you going to teach me how to use that stuff, so I can be pretty, too?"

Cedar laughed, the sound echoing over the water. "You'd probably poke your eye out."

He grinned. "Probably. Maybe teach Fin, though. He kind of needs it."

She snorted.

Um... so, are you actually planning on leaving once we get to the mountains?" Cedar asked,.

"I don't know. There is just so much going on. My head feels jumbled with so many things I need to do and things I *want* to do." He rubbed his hand through his hair. His emotions weighed down by his thoughts. "Do you want me to leave?" he asked.

"No, we don't-.."

She paused.

"I... don't."

Cedar and Sam worked their way to the back of the boat around Ajax, who dozed in the sun, and around the items that had been lazily thrown about.

"Man, what a mess," she muttered.

Cedar agreed, adding, "We will need to pick up today, since it might be the last day here."

A heavy weight settled in her chest as thoughts of leaving Amph consumed her. She bit the inside of her lip.

"What are we going to do by ourselves in this floating city?"

A hand landed on her shoulder. "We'll figure something out. You don't need to worry. Also, did you do something with your hair? It looks like you finally washed it," Fin snarked.

She rotated on her heels. Her head slumped, and her eyes narrowed in response to her sarcastic friend.

"Ha Ha Ha, you're *soooo* funny." She replied flatly. Brushing his hand off and moving towards the back of the boat next to Amph and Bram.

"Well, *I* thought it was funny," he smirked at Cedar, who rolled her eyes at him.

"It does look good, though. I think Cedar needs to do mine next." He fluffed out his man bun and imitated having long hair.

Sam raised her eyebrow and snorted. "You're going to have to be treated for fleas first, dude."

Bram, Cedar, and Sam laughed in unison. Fin crossed his arms but couldn't help chuckle with them.

After a pause, he added, "but seriously, you know I don't have bugs right."

Bram slapped him on his back, smirking lightheartedly.

"I'm surprised we're so far from land now. I didn't think we would get this far already." Sam looked at Amph, changing the subject to why she came to the back.

"I started as the first sun peaked. We have been rowing for a while now. Soon we will have to switch completely to oars because the pole is barely reaching the bottom." To prove his point, he stuck the bamboo pole into the water. It came about a foot out. She raised her eyebrows in surprise.

"Ya, it sucks," Fin said, exhausted from rowing. He sprawled out from under the oars to rest.

"It hasn't been that bad," Bram snorted. "It has been nice arm work. He is just being dramatic."

"That's easy for you to say. Amph's also been rowing on your side!" Fin pointed to the extra oar. "I am doing twice as much work."

"Are you doing twice as much, or are they doing half the actual work?" Cedar jumped in, raising her eyebrow mischievously.

Fin's eyes widened, and he opened his mouth to respond. Instead he grabbed his head. He groaned and pressed his forehead on the soft wood.

Sam chuckled, "I'll help you Fin."

She reached back, stretched, and then sat down. Her eyes flickered towards him and Bram, a silent moment passing before she finally said something.

"Now, do you think you are only doing half the work or a quarter of the work?" she asked rhetorically and waited for Fin's reaction.

"Not you too." His head slumped backwards, and he groaned again. "Too much thinking."

"Is it really, though?" Bram asked, his eyes full of concern.

Fin made a face, mocking Bram. Sam cracked a smile at the two. The oar in her hands, she copied the way Amph held it.

Sam watched Cedar, who plopped down in front of them, next to Ajax in the middle of the boat.

"Mmmm, Cedar, are you not going to help row?" Sam asked, clicking her tongue.

"Mmmmmm, no." She clicked her tongue back in the same tone. "There are enough oars now and we don't want Fin to have an aneurysm," she said promptly, not leaving room for debate or discussion.

Sam rolled her eyes at Cedars' demeanor as the four of them started to row.

They continued for a couple of hours, switching out or taking breaks when someone tired.

"My arms are jelly," Sam complained, heaving herself away from the oar. Her arm muscles twitching slightly from the excessive use as she said it.

"How long until the city?" Fin asked, defeated.

"Now," Amph said, pointing a little left of the sun as it stood only a little ways above the horizon. There poked out the top of the floating city, hazy and contorted in the waves of the sea.

10

THE FLOATING ANCHOR

THE PROTECTORS OF THE REALMS REMAIN
SILENT, OBSERVANT.

THE TIRED GROUP APPROACHED the city. Its towering supports and expansive width left Sam in awe, wondering how a city built on water could support such massive structures.

The tall skeletal domes stood high above her as she rotated her head upward. A gigantic one, followed by two smaller ones positioned themselves closely behind. The domes were constructed with carefully shaped metal, gracefully curving and converging at the center. A few smaller pieces, similar in design, were welded together and connected horizontally.

Besides the three domes that loomed over their hexagonal bases, there were also smaller decks that connected to them, like a beehive. Sam could see that there were homes scattered on the outer banks of the massive domes. The bases not flat, but a gentle curve that encircled the edges. Despite their size, the homes were impressively crafted, walls made of mud and metal, roofs woven from dried kelp, and furniture intricately carved from logs or wood. The group noticed that the homes, while appearing simple, were made cozy with the use of ocean-colored paints and art on the walls.

"We should probably find somewhere to stay while we're here," Sam spoke up as they made their way past the first outer layer of floating homes and staring eyes.

"I know a place. It's been a while since I've come here, but there is a sort of inn you can stay at here in Anchor," Amph responded as they continued rowing.

"Anchor?" Fin asked.

"Yes, this Reef is called the Floatin' City of Anchor. It's the sixth of the Reefs and Lakes."

"Anchor... like an anchor?" Sam used her hands to visualize the heavy object dropping to the ground.

"Mhmm."

Sam made a face. "Why?"

"Well, half the city is the up top floatin' bit. Then the other half is way *dooowwnnn* at the bottom surrounding the anchor and its coral reefs." As he spoke, he motioned casually downward towards the sea.

"No way. You gotta be kidding." Bram leaned over the edge and stuck his body halfway over. "He's not joking. There's a massive chain leading to a coral reef at the bottom with a *huge* anchor."

Sam shook her head in disbelief but joined him and the others to look. Without even sticking her head into the water, she could already see a warm blue glow jumbled aimlessly at the bottom of the ocean.

As she peered down over the boat, she saw the silhouette of what Bram had described. A metal chain with links as big as the chief connected and raveled down to what Sam could only assume was the largest object she had seen in this new world so far. Around the base of the anchor was indeed a coral reef and homes carved into it.

"What?! How is that even possible? How does the chain not weigh down the entire island? How long has it been like that? It has to have been a while because of the reef growing around it," she continued to rattle off sporadic questions into the air.

He raised his hands in a calming alarm as she buzzed with excitement.

"Wooooaaahhhh, woah now. You're askin' all these questions to the wrong person, missy. You're goin' to wanna ask my buddy at Driftwood."

"Of course, there's an inn called Driftwood." Fin snorted. "Awesome."

Weaving through the floating homes, they made their way at last to the main docks, as Amph had called them. Driftwood was on one of the outer docks, on the opposite side.

"We will have to dock here and walk the rest of the way." Amph said as the boat knocked somewhat against the wooden planks. He jumped off. Cedar threw him the rope from the back and Bram tossed him the tie off from the front. They made sure to grab all of their items and bags, along with waking Ajax from his slumber. Once it was secured to the dock, they stepped out of the boat and onto the floating city.

Sam examined their new surroundings. Watching all the merfolk and sea faus go about their way. Some stopped to stare at the curious newcomers. As Sam double-checked Bram's mask, she absentmindedly brushed her cheek to confirm her own mask was in place too.

Only a sparse amount of mermaids and mermen were around.

"This must be how they get around," Sam noted.

She pointed to the almost hidden pathways in the water under the floating wooden docks.

"Why are there fewer merpeople here?" Fin asked, looking over at Amph and then back at his surroundings.

"I believe they enjoy it at the bottom of Anchor. It's probably more accessible for them to do things down there than up here," he responded. Fin nodded.

"Wait, so the Reef is down there and it's too far for us to hold our breath, but I thought Sam said that our sea walker is in a Reef." Bram stopped walking for a moment. "What's the plan, then? Find someone to look around for someone else that we also don't know..."

At that, Sam stopped. She hadn't thought about that.

So what were they going to do?...

"I don't know…" she responded. "Maybe we can figure something out. Like paying someone to look for her for a day."

"Well, I don't know how your s'possed to find this girl, but I know how you can deal with the breathin' underwater problem." Amph said.

The group started walking again and crossed a bridge to a different hexagonal dock, one that was sturdier and bigger than the one they arrived on.

"What do you mean?" Cedar asked as she readjusted her satchel, giving Ajax a scratch behind the ear.

"We can talk more about it with my buddy at Driftwood. They understand it better than I do," he said.

"Ok, well how about this then, the city of Anchor is made of wood. So it floats, but how does it not sink from all this weight? What if it gets lopsided or something?" Sam motioned around to the slow and steady life of the city.

"Mmm, I know some 'bout that." Amph scratched his chin as they turned a corner and continued down a smaller back road. "They put floating seaweed and other buoyant plants packed underneath. It keeps the city floating."

Thoughtfully, Sam blinked twice as she tried to rationalize his response.

"All right, I guess." She shrugged as they walked on.

Inside the city, it grew denser. And more packed with plant life than she would have assumed a floating city would have. The ground and buildings were carved in wood and smoothed to look seedless and beautiful. Moss and plants grew off the sides and roofs of the homes and shops. Metal bits were intertwined into the buildings as well; she could see that they were built into them to provide support, like the massive domes above them.

The metal beams towered above her. Painted in shades of blue and green, reminiscent of the ocean. Wrapped in a cloth of the same hues. Strips of the same cloth hung, gently blowing in the wind from where they were tied off.

They exited the center of the city and crossed over to another connecting hexagon. After walking for a couple more minutes, Amph strolled through a medium-sized entrance that was carved out of a large wooden wall garnished with flowers at the top. As the group passed it, she finally caught sight of their destination. Driftwood. Lavish and decorated with pillars of trimmed wood, trellises planted with lovely purple and blue hanging flowers. Patterns of blue mosaic tiles detailing the white painted walls.

"This is an inn?" Cedar asked, astonished as she took in the surroundings of the incredibly embellished building.

"No I just call it that. This is Driftwood. Home of Apollonia and Marcion Bermis. These are friends of mine and your father's. They have been waitin' for you."

Sam stopped. Both her and Cedar gave a confused look.

"Wait... what? You know Amos?"

"Of course I do. Why'd you think I was waitin' at the river?" He snorted and flashed a mischievous smile as he glanced her way.

Sam's mouth agape in protest at the unexpected news. She smirked, "Sounds like Amos."

Cedar blushed. "I can't believe you guys never told us." She put her hands to her cheeks in embarrassment.

"Well, he wanted you to go 'bout your business like when he was a kid. No need for extra dramatics." Amph chuckled as he knocked on the thick wooden door carved with sea creatures dancing in bubbles.

After a moment, it opened to a dark stout man with his hair pulled back into a bun. Feathers of red and green poked out on the sides. Large gills slit across his neck and shoulder's. He wore a no shirt but had on puffy red and blue patterned trousers that hugged at his ankles.

As the door opened, he saw Amph, and his arms went up in merriment. A wide grin spreading from ear to ear.

"Amph! Welcome, welcome! How long has it been, my friend?" The man spoke in loud excitement. "Apollonia, my love, they are here!" he called behind him and turned to fix his gaze on Sam and her friends.

His eyes shone an intense bright blue as he stared at each of them. "So, this must be the adventurers Amos wrote to me about," he leaned slightly to see Fin and Cedar in the back. "The red monkey boy must be Fin and the red fox girl is Cedar. Ah Cedar, so much like your mother," he pushed through to hug her tightly, lifting her into the air and setting her back down. Cedar laughed stiffly as she fixed a bit of fallen hair from her face.

"Y-yes, that's me..." she said shyly.

Marcion turned now to face the other two. "And these masked ones must be Sam and Bram." He said, smiling at both of them.

Hesitantly, Sam took off her mask and wiped the grime from her face. Bram did the same. Marcion nodded as if confirming a thought that he had.

"It is a sad time to have to hide your beautiful faces from the world," he said, shaking his head remorsefully.

Sam looked down awkwardly, not sure how to respond. Then his demeanor swiftly rotated back to merriment. "Nonetheless, you are safe to roam here at Driftwood! Isn't that right, my love?" He raised his hands in the sky again and looked past Sam and Bram to the archway.

They turned to find an extraordinarily tall woman standing there barefoot in a tropical dress designed the same to match Marcion. Her skin, a caramel colored. Long curly black hair flowed down past her back. Her eyes matched Marcion's in intensity, but their color was hazel. And her gills were hidden underneath a clump of pearls and shell necklaces.

"What a lively young group," she said cheerfully, "I am so glad you could make it. Marcion has been ecstatic for the company ever since Amos wrote to us." Her laugh sounded off like the soft jingling of bells.

"Well, come in, come in. Let's get you acquainted with the house." He motioned for them and hurried inside for everyone to follow. It was a one story home but sat large and long with similar style inside as the outside, decorated with mosaics here and there, and the walls painted in white with brown wood accents.

"This is Driftwood. We hope you find comfort here," Apollonia said as she motioned the symbol of the sea. Pulling her hand from her chest. "Our home is your home."

"Yes! How long will you be staying? I heard you are in search of a sea walker," Marcion said, he now motioned the land, sea, and sky symbol.

Sam's heart sank as she thought back to Lin, and her time in the Whispering Woods.

"We don't know how long, because we aren't sure where she is exactly. We know her name is Lyra. Do you know of anyone with that name?" Cedar asked, her tone full of hope as she took off her satchel and placed it on the wooden kitchen table.

The two looked at each other for a moment, but then disappointedly shook their heads.

"We know most who are of Anchor, but have never heard of a Lyra." Marcion frowned.

Fin crossed his arms. Bram shuffled. Sam and Cedar exchanged glances.

"But... I am sure there are some people who we have yet to meet. We don't go down to the reef that much anymore! Maybe they are there." Apollonia put her hands outward in a gesture of hope.

Sam nodded. "In my dreams there was a giant coral wall and when I touched it, it lit up with bioluminescent colors." She looked down at her hand, vaguely feeling the coarse touch of the coral under her fingertips.

"They need some aquabreath, Marcion, and someone to go down there with them. Unfortunately, I can't stay. I need to get back to Lorelei," Amph said from his spot on the couch he had found.

"Aquabreath?" Bram said thoughtfully.

"Wait, you're leaving so soon?" Cedar looked at him, surprised.

Amph met the concerned eyes that passed between the group. He sighed and stood after a moment.

"Kids, now I know you're nervous about bein' in a new place. But remember, you didn't even know who I was when we met. You didn't know anything about Vineke. You're s'pose to be adventurers, so now isn't the time to get spooked. Besides, these folks'll help you with what you need in Anchor, and then it'll be time to travel again."

"He's right, we got into this. We are going to have to keep going and move forward on our own," Fin spoke up from behind the group. Sam turned and stared at him. She rustled her hair before nodding in agreement.

"That was actually mature Fin," Cedar said, shocked again.

He quickly lost his composure. "Well, you don't have to sound so surprised." He rubbed the back of his neck.

"We can do this, guys. This is what we set out to do." Sam fixed herself and looked back at their new acquaintances. "Our best bet is to search the reefs and Amph said something about aquabreath? What is that?"

"Well, I don't know much about how it's made. I am not a fuananoid of science myself, but I do know it was invented by the sky folk to help those without gills breathe underwater."

"Something that helps you breathe underwater?..." she repeated slowly in confusion. "H-how is that possible?" She looked down at the table, focusing on the mosaic patterns and sea creatures carved into it, as she tried to visualize how what he said could be possible.

"Well- it's... a sort of mask." Marcion motioned to something that would go around his face. "And a gel-like packet holds a clear liquid that makes it possible for air breathers to breathe while underwater. So, it's basically a pouch of breathable liquid hanging from your nose and mouth." He nodded deliberately through his words as he worked through his own confusion of the description.

The group was silent for a moment as they digested what he had said.

"I have never heard of something like that before, that's-" Cedar didn't finish her statement.

"It is helpful for us, but mostly seen in the Reefs, not anywhere else. It's a relatively new product." Marcion weighed his hands back and forth.

"Ok- so the first thing we need to do is buy this aqua...breath. Then maybe tomorrow we will go down to the Reef. Is that ok with you, Apollonia and Marcion?" Sam looked at them for confirmation.

"We are ready to help in any way we can," Apollonia replied, "however, you must know that the Floating City has been on edge and wary of land and sky faus these past few years. So we need to be careful."

"They are tense with us? Why?" Fin asked, more alert now.

"Our Oracle, he is out for blood." Marcion sighed as a disappointed father would. "Over the years, he has grown more paranoid and turned against our ways of peace and humility. He is a man who was born to crave violence."

"It will be fine, though." Apollonia calmed the unnerved group. "We will do what we need to and not bring any extra attention to ourselves."

"That's interesting. I've not heard about this Oracle before. It is weird to hear of a hatred toward us when we don't even know him." Fin furrowed his brows, concerned.

"Thank you for letting us know. We will make sure not to draw any attention to ourselves." Sam eyed Fin and Bram to emphasize she meant them two.

Baffled, Fin crossed his arms. "Excuse you, I am not the one who *sat* in the middle of a salmon run." He pointed towards her.

"*Or* almost started a *fire* in the hills." He pointed towards Cedar.

"*Orr* almost *murdered* everyone I now know!" He exclaimed as he gestured towards Bram.

Cedar put her hands on her hips and glared at him.

"At least I'm not attracted to shiny things like a moth to a flame," Bram snarked back at him. Fin began to retort, but Sam got between the two.

"Ok, ok, point taken." She intervened with her hands up. "We'll *all* be on our best behavior, but seriously, no stealing, no burning things down, and definitely no murder." She glanced at each of them in turn and then uncomfortably at Bram, who did not make eye contact with any of them.

Fin gave a dramatic face but stayed quiet, giving his consent to what she had said.

She sighed and rubbed her eyebrows with her thumb and pointer finger.

"Other than that, I think we have a plan."

"We've been traveling for a while. Why don't we rest and then head back out when we say goodbye to Amph?" Bram suggested. Sam could see the tiredness on their faces, and she felt it sink into her as well.

"That might not be a bad idea. Ajax is already sleeping." She looked down to see him sprawled out on the floor.

"Yes, stay tonight. We'll eat and rest, then tomorrow we will deal with our troubles. Amph, please stay for the night. It's the least we can do," Apollonia said soothingly.

He rubbed the back of his neck with uncertainty as he tried to decide. "I guess it would be best to rest up and eat before I begin my journey back."

At that, the tension left Sam. It was good that Amph would stay for the night while the group became more acquainted with the Bermis family.

"That settles it then! Apollonia, please show our guests their rooms and I will begin preparations for our welcome feast!" Marcion clapped his hands and swiveled, walking out of the room.

"This way." She gestured toward the opposite way.

The group picked up their packs and made their way through the home. After the kitchen and dwelling space, the building took a sharp L and turned to the right. Rooms on the left had arched windows facing a central courtyard. To the right she could see outside where Marcion rummaged through the gardens for fresh fruits and vegetables. A smile played on her lips while she watched him dance for joy and pick at the green stems.

"This will be yours." She motioned for Cedar to enter a little room that was tidy enough for someone to have never set foot in.

"And you can stay here." Apollonia looked at Sam and opened the door for her and Ajax.

"Thank you so much." Sam said to her as she passed her and entered an identical room to Cedars.

"The boys will be in the hall on the other end and will have to share a room while Amph stays here."

Sam nodded, understanding. Bram and Fin grimaced and shot each other a glance.

"Hey." Sam poked her head out and stared the two of them down. "Be grateful you're not sleeping in the garden," she said firmly. They rolled their eyes but continued walking in silence.

Apollonia chuckled. "I will call for you when dinner is ready. Please make yourself at home and rest."

Sam smiled at her, thanking her for their hospitality again, and shut the door. She continued to go over the list of what needed to get done in her head as she put down her mask, leaned her staff against the bed, and placed her bag on the bench that sat underneath the window of the room.

With a sigh, she collapsed on the bed, sinking into the soft sheets and plush mattress. She stared at Ajax, who already found himself asleep near the foot of her bed.

He slept so much.

She watched him breathe until her eyes shut and she could no longer stay awake.

II

SCARS OF THE SWORD, WOUNDS OF THE HEART

KOI FOLK HAVE ONLY RARELY BEEN SPOTTED
IN THE REEFS.

The morning came as Sam rose and made her way out into the main room. She learned that Amph had left earlier that day. Marcion, Apollonia, and Cedar had seen him off, but no one else was awake to say goodbye.

"Ya, I guess that sounds like something he would do." Fin said, yawning.

"But I still wanted to say thank you," Sam replied, hurt by his sudden self dismissal.

"He knows you are grateful. He didn't do it for you to thank him. Amph did it because he wanted to." Apollonia said gently as she comforted Sam and the others.

"Besides, he isn't a man for emotional spats." Marcion spoke up. "Today is the day! Are you ready to buy the aquabreath and traverse into the deep?" He said in a spooky, fun tone.

Sam smiled, feeling better about the day, and Cedar chuckled.

"However, it's probably best that we split up. I will take two of you, and Apollonia will take the other two," he added.

"Wait, why do we need to split?" Bram said, concerned, as he sat up more alert from the fruit he was munching on.

"Because a big group can draw a crowd, and this time in Anchor is not the best for drawing attention," he responded in a more serious tone.

"Cedar and I will go together." Fin said with a sarcastic smile as he leaned in and side hugged Cedar.

As she was being moved back and forth by the hug, she made a face and flared her nostrils.

"Woah woah woah, why can't I go with Sam?" she protested, swatting him off.

"Because me and Bram don't *exactly* see eye to eye. And for some reason I feel like you don't like me, so we are going.... on a *friendship journey*," he said as he hugged her tighter and waved his other hand in the air with a sparkle in his eyes.

Cedar groaned in annoyance. They all knew how Bram and Fin would fight, so keeping them separate was the best way to stay on the low.

"That settles it then. I will take Sam and Bram." Marcion gestured to them, "And Apollonia, my sweet, you will take

Fin and Cedar. We will meet back here once all four have an aquabreath. Then plan to travel to the bottom."

With that, Cedar gave them each one scale to exchange for coins, and they separated.

As the morning wore on, Sam, Bram, and Marcion grew increasingly discouraged in their search for an aquabreath merchant. The crowded streets making it difficult to navigate.

"Try the vendors at the main dock. They sell the more *lucrative* items, if you catch my meaning," One vendor had said.

As they walked away, Sam asked, "Why haven't we already gone there? It seems to be a bigger shopping area."

"It is- but I was hoping to avoid that area altogether with you two." He laughed. "That's where a lot of our Oracles hooligans like to spend their time. But it might be where we have to go."

"Let's make this fast." Bram sighed. "I wonder if they're having better luck than we are."

Sam nodded as she thought about the other three. "Hopefully, they're staying safe."

The small group made their way to the center of the city, keeping their heads down and masks on. No one gave them a second glance as they walked through the busier streets of the central dock.

"Ahh, here we go," Marcion said after a while. He turned and stopped, waiting for a gap in the crowd, then shuffled up to a stall with what seemed to be aquabreaths laying on the counters.

They looked exactly how he had described them. Sam could see the sack made of a gel substance that held an invisible liquid inside. She walked up to the counter and poked the pouch, her finger sunk into it and she could see the clear liquid slide around underneath.

"Woah." She laughed quietly in disgust.

"You break it, you buy it." The vendor tsked and eyed her.

"S-sorry." Blushing under the mask, she quickly pulled her hands away and clasped them behind her back.

The vendor turned towards Marcion, "What can I do for you on this fine evening?"

"We would like to purchase two aquabreaths today," He said with a pleasant smile and placed a sac on the counter in front of the merchant. The coins inside clinked, settling into themselves.

"Ooooo, for these two?" He cooed, "Are they land lovers here to tour the city underneath?" He examined the two quiet ones. Sam looked down.

Marcion, however, laughed, "No, no, these are my grandchildren here to visit from the lakes." He leaned in closer to the vendor to speak in a hushed tone, "They have always wanted to see the reefs, but weren't old enough," he said, winking at him, and slapping Bram on the shoulder endearingly.

"Hmm." The vendor frowned, upset for them to not be what he wanted. He moved on.

"Well, then I am sure you know how these work. Remember, it will be completely out of air once it has turned a deep purple, *and* it can be quite stressful for first timers," he said, inspecting them.

Marcion laughed again. "Thank you my friend, I will make sure to come back and spend my money here again, such fine service." He smiled as they took the aquabreaths. With a gentle push, he set them in front of him, waving goodbye with a cheerful smile as they disappeared around the corner.

The group heaved a sigh and relaxed once they were out of sight from prying eyes. Sam and Bram both examined the devices they were given. Soft and light in her hands, she flipped it around.

"What did he mean, it turns purple?" she asked, looking at Marcion.

"When you breathe out, the liquid will turn purple, indicating that it is no longer good. Once the entire sack turns that color, then you better be close to the surface. We probably have about half a day's worth," he said. "Some nowadays even come with a plant in it that can clean the water. How neat is that?!" he exclaimed.

"And what did he mean by stressfu-"

A sharp pain erupted on her side. Bram elbowed her.

She grunted in irritation, then glared at him. He moved his eyes back out towards the street they were just on.

Standing in the street. Laughing a disgusting laugh and talking to two other faunanoid, was someone they were looking for.

"Toba." Her face darkened.

She turned towards Marcion and grumbled, "I'm sorry, we have to go. Please take these, and we will meet you back at Driftwood."

Hurriedly, they shoved the aquabreaths towards Marcion, but he quickly protested.

"What do you mean? What's going on?"

She grimaced at him with narrowed eyes through the mask.

"We have a score to settle with this one."

In a swift movement, she turned and released the latch on her staff, freeing it from its place behind her back. With it clenched tightly in her hand, Toba's laughter echoed in her ears, fueling her anger.

They emerged from the alley and found themselves amidst a bustling crowd, their eyes fixed on him until he finally glanced in their direction. Bram's clenched his fists, his face contorted with rage. Toba's eyes widened with realization.

He backed away, turning and forcing his way through the crowd. The two pursued him. The sound of agitated voices pierced their ears, echoing through the now chaotic crowd. With hearts pounding, their eyes never left their target as they maneuvered through the jostling bodies. Their stare fixed on him. The fau desperate to flee.

Sam ran faster in her anger. A fiery rage ignited within her, her grip tight on her staff as he tried to escape. The vivid flashback of that night in the lake city consumed her. She pushed herself to run faster, to catch him, to get back at him for what he'd done. Her rapid, shallow breaths struggled to escape the confines of her mask, suffocating her, while her hot breath stung her eyes. She stole a quick glance at Bram, whose effortless stride mirrored her own. Her determination heightened, Sam redirected her attention.

He knew Anchor. That was his biggest advantage. He rounded a corner, flipping some boxes and a vendor's table in their way. Bram hurdled it as Sam went around, they lost sight of him. Toba was gone.

Sam clenched her jaw as she looked for any sign of the attempted murderer. An angry merchant yelling and cursing at the event that just unfolded.

Her breathing was ragged. A lump formed in her throat. She tried swallowing back tears that were already streaking down her face. They smeared into her skin under the mask. Clutching her staff with shaking hands, she desperately tried to hide her annoyance.

"I can't believe we lost him," she said, defeated, as she crouched in the alley closest to them for a breath.

Bram came up to her, his breathing also ragged.

"He will show his face again. There's no doubt now that he knows we're here."

She looked at him for a moment without blinking, and then, attached her staff to her back belt.

"He won't get away next time."

Apollonia led the two of them straight to central dock where the massive beams overlooked all. Cedar glanced up at them as they judged all with their stoic unbiased stares. She could see the decorations more clearly now. In the places untouched by ribbons, there were intricate patterns of waves painted.

Looking around, she saw many interesting shops that were built like Driftwood, decorated the same. Many of the shops sold items not meant for survival but for hobbies instead; books, antiques, clothes, and trinkets for one's home.

"Here we are. The shop owner here has just about anything you could ask for." Apollonia pointed out a neat store front with white flowers planted out front and a sign that read *The Starfish, Anything and All.*

"Hmm, that's useful." Fin looked up to the sign and smiled.

Cedar rolled her eyes and walked past him, following Apollonia inside the shop.

"Wait here while I speak with the keeper." She turned back to them and pointed to a more secluded and well hidden spot of the shop. "We don't need him asking any unwanted questions." Apollonia gave them a wink, then vanished into the maze of items about the store.

Cedar glanced around the cluttered room, taking in the eclectic assortment of items. It was a treasure trove of oddities, everything from vintage toys to worn-out books, all nestled together in a comforting chaos.

Her fingers brushed against a small statue of a bird perched near a crumpled paper lantern, the light casting flickering shadows on the wall. She turned her attention to Fin, who was rummaging through a pile of vibrant fabrics draped over a nearby chair.

"So, you wanna tell me why you don't like me? Because honestly, I thought I was charming," he said, his voice teasing as he sifted through the fabrics.

Cedar blinked in surprise. "Wow, straight to the point, then," she muttered under her breath, then replied, "Look, I don't dislike you, but sometimes you're just so..." she scrunched her face in concentration, searching for the right word, "fake."

Fin scoffed, putting down the faux plants he'd been fiddling with to focus on her. "I am not *fake*," he emphasized, keeping his voice low to avoid attracting attention. "I'm a jokester." He crossed his arms defiantly and smirked.

"I doubt that," Cedar shot back, setting down the pen she had been absentmindedly twirling. She turned fully to face him. "Ever since we met, it's been nothing but corny jokes and jabs. It's obnoxious." She looked away for a moment, then returned her gaze, her resolve strengthening. "And another thing. I don't like that you act so phony because Sam trusts you. I want to trust you, too, but whatever this—" she gestured up and down at him—"facade is, I. Don't. Buy. It." She poked him in the chest with each word, then spun away, searching for a second of space space in the clustered shop.

Fin stood there, momentarily stunned. Cedar felt her heart race and heat rise to her cheeks. Regret washed over her as she forced herself to calm. Her eyes stapled to a pile of books as she forced an apology out. Before she could, Fin spoke up from behind a stack of the mismatched junk.

"I thought my jokes were funny. I didn't know they bothered you guys so much. I mean, I couldn't care less about what Bram thinks," he snorted, "but I don't want you... or, especially, Sam, to be annoyed with me. I'll try to stop." His gaze dropped to the floor, avoiding hers. A pang of guilt twisted in her stomach.

"I'm sorry," she admitted, stepping closer. "We want you to be yourself. It feels like you're hiding behind this act. You don't have to be like this with us." She reached out and touched his forearm gently.

"It's been... hard-" he cut short, his voice faltering as he cleared his throat.

In that moment, Cedar glimpsed the vulnerable child hiding behind Fin's bravado. He had wrapped himself in humor and smiles, shielding his pain from the world. Even if it meant tricking himself.

"Fin," she frowned. Without thinking, she wrapped her arms around him in a comforting hug. "I didn't think. But now I'm starting to understand. It's been tough for me to make light of everything we've faced, but having you here helps."

He let out a deep sigh as she released him. "Thanks, Cedar," he said, a small laugh escaping his lips. "It feels good to get it off my chest." He looked at her with gratitude, and she could sense a fragile bond began to form.

A loud, prominent voice cut through the store, bringing the two of them back to their surroundings.

"Apollonia, you must visit more. You know I love seeing you, darling. I hope the aquabreaths suit your needs."

"Thank you dear, you always come through for me, until next time." Apollonia turned to wave delicately to the unknown man and as she turned back, she eyed them for a moment, motioned with her eyes for them to follow.

The door shut. The two put the items they rummaged through back down and left without looking at the man. They caught up to Apollonia and began their stroll back towards Driftwood.

After walking a distance away, yells of distress and cursing rang through the square. Cedar searched for the source. A man ran through the middle of the street their direction. Wildly shoving and pushing past bystanders.

She halted. Her eyes grew wild.

"Toba." She snarled at him as he passed them.

Their eyes met. Shocked, he paled further. Fire erupted, engulfing her arm. Furiously, she launched herself at him. Her surroundings fading into oblivion.

Without warning, a forceful arm wrapped tightly around her, stopping her movement.

Fury filled her, Cedar's eyes blazed, the fire now engulfing her upper body. The screams of those around her grew louder. She twisted to confront the person who held a tight grip on her.

Instantly, she quelled the flames.

"Fin! Fin! I'm sorry I burnt you." Cedar blurted, flustered by her abrupt rage. Her hands hovered over his singed clothing.

"Now's not the time Cedar." His eyes never leaving Toba. "Stay with Apollonia. I'm going to follow him. I'll meet you back at their place."

With his clothing still smoking, he merged into the crowd seamlessly, darting past them and vanishing into the faus.

"No! Fin!" she called out. It was too late. He was already gone. "I *cannot* believe that we saw him," she groaned.

"Sweetness, I am not sure what is going on, but we *must* go. Eyes watch you now." Apollonia drew near her, holding the aquabreaths. She used her other free arm to wrap Cedar and escort her away from the circle of onlookers.

"Fin will be fine. I'm sure he can handle himself," Apollonia whispered to comfort the distressed girl.

"You're right, he can."

"What... happened?!" Marcion exclaimed to the exhausted group as they collapsed on the couch.

He and Apollonia set the four newly acquired aquabreaths onto the kitchen table and stood in front of the three of them, both concerned.

"Where is the other boy?!" He asked equally shocked.

"Fin ran off after a man named Toba." Cedar slumped further into the couch and looked over at Sam and Bram. "O ya, we saw Toba running for his life, by the way."

Sam was hunched over, her head buried in her hands, as she fiercely rubbed her tired eyes.

"That was us."

"We chased him until he vanished. He must have seen you guys soon after. Hopefully, Fin doesn't screw this up," Bram said as he took an orange from the fruit bowl and peeled it.

"So then, you all obviously knew that man." Marcion slumped his shoulders. "That is no good. He looked like one of the Oracle's men."

At that, Sam sat up straighter, "Wait *seriously*?"

Apollonia nodded solemnly.

"Who is this Oracle? I thought the leaders of each city had to be for its faunanoid. Why is he so *terrible*?" Cedar emphasized in her still slumped position.

"Well, he started out as a helper to the Oracle before him. He seemed to grow more envious of the position as time went on, then when the position opened, he grabbed at the power and-didn't let go," Marcion said.

"He always seemed violent if you caught him off guard. But now that he is Oracle, he has no need for secrecy." Apollonia put her palm on her cheek and stared out the window at her garden. She continued, "Then when the people wanted him gone, he hired thugs to *keep the peace*." She sighed. "It has been getting worse since."

Marcion walked to Apollonia, embracing her and comforting the somber woman. "Oracle Barclay is a twisted, selfish soul."

"Barclay." Cedar mumbled in distaste.

"Why does the city let it happen?" Sam interjected.

Marcion smiled with sad eyes.

"Those who are strong fight for him and those who are weak fight for survival. Change will not be made until those who are weak grow angry enough."

"Oracle!"

"Oracle!"

Toba ran through the door of his Oracles home, bursting through the rooms of the elaborately lavish abode.

"Oracle Barclay, I have news!" Rapidly, he pushed the two doors to the main hall open .

As he did, a small polished Damascus steel throwing knife whizzed past his head and lodged itself into the dark brown pillar carved with a coral reef.

He jolted and nervously cast a sideways glance at the menacing blade. Beads of sweat rolled down his cheek, he swallowed.

"Be careful what you call me," a deep voice started, "or you might lose an eye."

"S-sorry- Sir..." He kneeled where he was, his mouth dry, and his body shaking with adrenaline.

"Proceed," the malicious voice sounded from the center of the room.

He stood up and cautiously made his way forward, to the fau who was seated in the expansive pool of water at the center. Adorned with deep blue and white mosaic tiles, the pool was the perfect depth for both faus and merfolk to use. Toba waded through the pool, feeling the cool water against his skin, stopping only a yard in front of him.

"Sorry to bother you. I have news," Toba repeated, rubbing his damp hands down his pants.

"Spit it out then, or leave," Barclay snarled as he threw another knife into the pillar. It dug itself into the wood close to the first.

Toba glanced back, anxiously nodding as he stammered. "I-It's the land faus I told you about. They are here, in Anchor."

Barclay looked at Toba now, involved. He sat up straight. A crooked smile forming on his lips.

"You mean the plain one?" He leaned forward, a strip of pitch black hair fell over his pale face.

Toba nodded rapidly. Another bead of sweat rolled down his face.

Barclay sat back in his chair and chuckled to himself.

"Now, this- will be interesting."

He threw his third and last knife, piercing the heart of the carved Lady in the Water.

12

A CITY ABOVE, A REEF BELOW

THE DEEPEST REEF IS ONLY REACHABLE TO THOSE WHO KNOW NO FEAR OF THE DARK.

"WHERE'S FIN?" SAM PACED the entrance corridor and she bit her nails. "It's almost noon. We *need* to get to the reef soon. There isn't any time to waste now," she groaned.

"Ya," Bram snorted. "Now that this *Oracle Barclay* knows we're here," he said mockingly.

"I feel that we have waited for him long enough. It is time to head to the reef, yes?" Marcion asked cautiously.

The group exchanged looks. Hesitant to make a decision, they stayed silent. Sam stared at the arabesque tiling of the floor.

After a brief pause, she took the responsibility of making the decision for them.

"Let's go guys, we've got work to do."

She grabbed her aquabreath carefully off the table, and patted Ajax's side for a goodbye as the others roused to get ready for departure.

"I'm sure he will be here when we get back, but maybe we leave him a note?" Cedar asked.

"I think that's smart," Sam nodded, and then flashed an embarrassed, lopsided grin. "I don't know how to write that well, though." Her cheeks bloomed the color of rose and she scratched her chin as she tried not to laugh at herself.

In a small voice, almost louder than a whisper, Bram added, "I can't read or write."

The girls stopped and stared at Bram. Sam's jaw dropped, raising her eyebrows. She couldn't help but quirk a smile.

Bram looked up through his brows and gave a goofy grin as he stifled a laugh. At that, Sam cracked up while she and Bram laughed together. Marcion and Apollonia chuckled from the couch.

Cedar groaned as she tried to hold in a smile.

"Can we borrow a paper and quill?" she asked while shaking her head.

He nodded, still laughing as he got up and came back into the room a few moments later with what she had asked for.

She slapped it down on the counter, looking at Sam and Bram in goofy annoyance.

"Bunch of illiterates," she said through a small chuckle as she sprawled out some letters on the paper.

"There. I wrote, *'You took too long, we are going to the reef. Stay here.'* How does that sound?"

Sam nodded as she cleared her throat and wiped the tears from her eyes.

"Perfect."

Cedar snatched up her aquabreath, still eyeing Bram and Sam. Then, just as fast, she added in a stern tone.

"*You're* going to learn how to read and write!" She pointed accusingly at Bram, then pointing to Sam. "And *you're* going to work on your writing! I am putting my foot down on this! I will not be the youngest *and* the only literate fau in this group!"

Finally, her eyes darted back and forth between the two as she squished her mouth shut with an affirmed look. She turned and marched out the door. The rest followed in quiet snickering as they marched out of Driftwood and through the entryway of the front courtyard.

Apollonia swept to her side, and wrapping her in her arm, she pecked the top of Cedar's head. "This way, my child, you are too kind to be so hard on yourself." Apollonia turned and winked at the two of them as they quieted down to a soft chuckle and continued on their way.

"So, where are we going exactly?" Sam asked after she relaxed. "Isn't it right below us? Can't we just jump in the water and swim down?"

"Hmmm, yes, that is quite a good question, curious one," Marcion said. He pointed forward. "This way is the gateway to the reef. It is the safest and fastest. The merfolk who live here can enter wherever but for you three... it would be better to enter at the gate."

"Why?" Bram asked.

"There is a pulley system that is connected to the chain of Anchor. It will take us to the bottom quickly. It would be much harder to swim straight down."

Sam nodded as she tried to imagine a pulley system in her mind.

The merchant said that it was a stressful experience for first timers. Sam pondered what he said.

She twisted a strand of her hair that fell over her shoulder as her mind wandered to the many things he was trying to say.

"It's just up ahead now." Apollonia alerted them.

When Sam looked up, she was surprised to find a crowd of sea faunanoids all around her. She strained her eyes to catch a glimpse beyond the crowd, but the constant movement of people made it nearly impossible.

They cut through, walking straight to the fountain of the marketplace. The giant circular fountain base, made of stone, featured a metal centerpiece adorned with a variety of sea creatures swimming in currents of metal water. In the middle, a woman dressed in a flowing chiton, looked forward, extending one hand outward. In the evening sunlight, she shimmered. With a serene expression on her face, she held out her hand, and from it flowed a soft, tranquil stream of water.

Enamored by the masterpiece before her, she leaned over the fountain's edge and her eyes danced across each of the different animals she saw that surrounded the woman. As her gaze lowered, she looked into the water and froze.

"Sam, what's wrong?" Marcion asked, concerned.

"There's no bottom… to the fountain." She pointed.

Cedar and Brams' eyes widened and they bent over the edge. Cedar gasped. Bram muttered under his breath.

"That's… *deep,*" he added.

"Calm, girls, this," Marcion gestured to the fountain, "*is* the gateway to the reef below."

"You're joking?" Sam looked at him.

He shook his head. Sam glanced back to the newly appointed gateway.

Once more, leaning over, she braced herself against the railing, completely captivated by the breathtaking sight of the reef stretching out far beneath them. She glanced back up to the woman, and squinting, noticed that in her other hand, there was a type of stringed instrument.

"Apollonia," Sam called. "What is that?" she asked, pointing up at it.

"The Lady in the Water loved this instrument dearly. A skilled artisan, she played it so masterfully that her music could entrance all who listened. This instrument is called the Lyra."

Sam turned to her. Her mind raced, but her voice could not start. She stared at the fountain with the creatures dancing around the Lady of the Water as she held her Lyra.

"That's the name of who we are looking for." Cedar bounded up to Sam excitedly. "Maybe that means she's here!" She grabbed her arm and shook her from her thoughts.

"Ya, that's... kinda crazy, isn't it?" Sam breathed.

"Let's hope we find who you are looking for, but it's time to show you how to use the aquabreaths." Marcion motioned to the masks that were in their grasp as he and Apollonia exchanged nervous glances.

Sam's heart skipped a beat as she shifted it in her hand. Her uneasiness grew as she observed their reactions.

She shifted where she stood. "Why is everyone nervous about this thing other than us? What do we not know?"

Apollonia sympathized with her, making a sorrowful face when she responded, "I don't know if it will be better for you to experience it or if we should tell you beforehand..."

"I would rather know what's going to happen," Bram said.

"Ok- well," she looked at each of them. "Just so you know, you are not in any danger, the liquid is quite safe for your lungs and even healthy for them, it acts as a cleaning agent and many people use it to help them breathe, but-" she cut short as she smoothed out her dress.

"You're freaking me out," Cedar said.

"It's going to feel like you're drowning," Marcion spoke plainly, him and Apollonia were quiet as they watched the wave of reactions from the group.

Sam looked at Bram and Cedar for confirmation to what they heard. She could feel her heartbeat in her fingertips. Her body jittered nervously and she looked down at the device, trembling as she imagined what was about to happen next.

"Ok, ok," she said shakingly, "but are we actually?" She held her hands close to her chest to stop herself from trembling.

"No, no, you will feel like it because your body is not used to breathing in liquid, but after a couple of minutes, it will feel completely normal. That being said," Apollonia tapped on the mask that Sam held, "it would be wise to not take it off until you are completely finished with it, otherwise you will cough up the liquid and have to repeat the unpleasant process of putting it back on."

"Liquid to air, then air to liquid isn't the best repeating process. It's best to do one or the other for long periods of time," Marcion added while weighing his hands.

Sam nodded, dread building in her chest as the time passed.

Did she have to do this? What would happen if they didn't? Could they find Lyra without her?

Her thoughts raced like a whirlwind, a sense of urgency gripping her as she desperately tried to come up with any alternative to finding Lyra without resorting to, to this. With her eyes tightly shut, she pressed her trembling hand against her temple, feeling the cold sweat trickling down her face as she struggled to steady her breath.

No. No she needed to do this. Lyra is out there, somewhere.

As she opened her eyes, she turned to her friends. Cedar's eyes widened, her body trembling, mirroring the same terror that consumed her. Sam observed Bram, who appeared to conceal his fear better than both of them. But she could see the unease in his eyes as well.

"I am going to do it." She walked closer to the two of them and grabbed Cedars' hands for comfort. "You don't have to if you don't want to. This is *a lot* for me to ask," she added. "You can go back with Apollonia. Me and Marcion can go look for Lyra."

"I'll do it," Cedar said abruptly, "I- I want to do it."

Bram nodded in agreement, and Sam let out a relieved sigh.

"Remember, you can back out at any time," Sam said reassuringly to them and to a small part of herself.

She turned to Marcion, "I guess we're ready..."

"Then we will do it one at a time so that we can be there to comfort the one who is adjusting. Who is going first?" Apollonia asked, her eyes never leaving Sams.

Sam understood what she meant and stepped forward. "Let's do this."

"Find somewhere where you can be comfortable."

Sam sat on the edge, flipping around. Her feet splashed into the water. A decent sized lip lay between her and the vast empty beneath, for people to stand on before diving in. She looked up towards the woman and the sea creatures, who stared back.

Comforted by the statue. Sam lowered her gaze to her feet and towards the reef below that waited for them. She took a deep breath as she tried to steady herself. While closing her eyes, she nodded once more.

Cedar and Bram sat on either side of her. Marcion stood behind her, and Apollonia kneeled in front on the stone slab that sat under the water's surface and offered the mask up to her.

Her hand trembled as she grabbed the aquabreath. While her other hand took off the fox mask and placed it in her lap. It stared up at her as she fixed the new mask around her neck, and one palm slipped the aquabreath around her nose and mouth.

It felt warm on her face. Her fingertips felt the edges where the mask met her cheeks. She could feel the gel on her fingers, but her nose and mouth felt nothing. She held her breath as she opened her eyes and blinked a couple of times. Curiously, she questioned the reason behind the others' concern about what was going to happen.

Naturally, she went to take a breath, but her body stopped. The watery substance rushed into her nose and she stood in a panic as she tried to take the mask off to take a breath. Her body convulsed as she choked and desperately expelled the liquid, her eyes wide with terror. Sam's mind went blank as the warnings faded away. Consumed by the rush of adrenaline surging through her veins, leaving her shaking and gasping for breath. Her fingers desperately clawed at the mask, but hands abruptly clamped around her arms, freezing her in terror. Tears welled up in her eyes as she struggled.

Someone was speaking to her, but she couldn't make out the words as her body fought breathing in the water. Sam squinted her eyes shut and collapsed into the fountain's water. Apollonia held her gently. Cedar was at her side, and Bram stood in front of her so she didn't fall into the sea. She pleaded with them as she battled the urge to take a simple breath in. Her lungs burning in the absence of what they needed most.

Sam put her hand up to the mask, shaking her head. Her body shook as it begged for air. Tears slid down her cheeks, falling into the water.

"Sam, breathe, you will be ok, don't think. Just breathe." Apollonia whispered in her ear as her hand caressed her back.

She could hear them now, telling her to breathe. Sam stopped moving and focused on making her lungs inhale. Her brain splintering into a headache as she lost her sight. Carefully steadying herself, she counted down from three and inhaled.

Water filled her lungs and she backed up against the fountain's wall as she sat in the water. She could feel her body calming down as she breathed in the mask. She had fought so hard to deny it, but as she took more deep breaths, it grew more unnoticeable.

With her head laid back against the wall, she looked up at the statue. Cedar peeked into her gaze.

"Hey." Sam leaned her head to look at her.

Cedar smiled, relieved. "We thought you were dying!"

"*I thought* I was dying." She smeared the drying tears and stood wobbly through her receding headache. Her fingers traced the foreign object stuck to her nose and mouth as she tried to grow accustomed to it.

"Wait." She touched it more. "How am I talking?"

Apollonia chuckled, "You sound a bit muffled, but we can still understand."

Surprised Sam plopped down on the fountain's edge again as she continued to examine the strange object on her face.

"Ok, now who's next?" Marcion clapped his hands and turned to Bram and Cedar, who avoided his gaze.

Bram touched his face like Sam had done earlier.

"See, after a moment, it's not that bad." Cedar smiled as she mimicked him and poked at the gel that covered her nose and mouth.

"That was- rough though. Fin's gonna have a *blast*." Bram rolled his eyes.

"Now there is no time to waste, we must not delay. There is a finite amount of breathable liquid in your masks, so let's get going." Marcion pointed to Sam's aquabreath, and as she narrowed her eyes to peer down at it, she could see a strain of purple appearing.

Apollonia put her hand up for them to pause. In her other hand, she revealed three goggles with attachments on them.

"For obvious reasons, these are needed, too." She attached it to a clip that had gone unnoticed on Sam's mask. Then did the same for Bram and Cedar.

"Hold it in place. They will suction to your face once you're under the water," she added once they were all secured.

Marcion jumped into the water and disappeared under the surface. Apollonia gestured for them to follow, Bram dived in while Cedar and Sam sat on the edge, dropping in gently.

Once they were in, it took Sam a minute to train her brain to breathe in the mask, but she felt eager at the possibility of being able to stay underwater for a prolonged amount of time.

As she swam forward, she couldn't help but steal a glance at the edges of her and Bram's animal masks peeking out of Cedar's satchel. She wondered if it would be safe to leave them behind and not wear them in this underwater city. As she was lost in her thoughts, her attention quickly diverted to something moving in front of her.

Her eyes adjusted to the goggles. She noticed it was a rope where one end moved downward and the other end moved upward. Apollonia came up to her, her hair dancing in the water as she looked at Sam with a twinkle in her eye.

"This is the pulley that will take us to the bottom faster."

Sam nodded in acknowledgement and looked back at it, examining its parts with curiosity.

First, Marcion grabbed a hook and sunk with it to the floor. Then Cedar cautiously copied as it passed her, Sam got the next one. Then Bram. Last, Apollonia.

As they descended, Sam's gaze swept over the reef city unfurling below. Miles of coral spread out in intricate patterns—some towering and grand, others delicate and modest. The descent ended sooner than she'd expected; the city lay closer to the surface than she had imagined, bringing a surprising sense of relief.

The reef was a kaleidoscope of beauty. Sunlight filtered through the water, casting golden rays that danced across the coral, while bioluminescent plants, underwater mushrooms, and glowing coral added an ethereal brilliance. The subtle interplay of shifting colors caught her attention, and as she looked closer, she realized it wasn't random. It was a mesmerizing collaboration, orchestrated by the merfolk and the sea creatures living in harmony.

Yet, even amidst the vibrant life of the reef, a vast emptiness lingered in her periphery. The endless expanse of the ocean stretched before her, filling her with a strange mixture of awe and insignificance. Her rational mind dismissed it as just an endless sheet of blue, but something deeper felt the weight of the water pressing around her, its presence immense and inescapable.

Beyond the reef's edge, past the steep drop-off, she spotted movement—a massive creature gliding silently into the abyss. Its form melted into the shadows, leaving an eerie stillness in its wake. The black void beyond seemed alive with untold secrets, and as it loomed near, a chill crept through her veins.

With a kick up of sand they landed on the seafloor near the massive anchor. Sam turned and stared up at it in admiration of the anchor's enormous size and watched the nook she had previously held onto turn and travel back to the surface.

Was this anchor a remnant from her time, or a time after?

"What's the plan?" Bram asked as he finished landing next to her.

"We should probably divide and conquer," Sam stated as she saw the road forked both to the left and to the right.

"Well, the reef does somewhat go in a circle. Both ways lead back here, so that can work," Marcion spoke up as he walked over to the downward floating Apollonia and caught her.

"Yes, I will take Cedar and Bram, if you wish, and you can take Sam," Apollonia said as she chuckled in his arms.

"Very well, my love." Marcion pecked her cheek and set her on the sand.

Sam looked at the other two, "Remember her name is Lyra, we don't have that much to go on," she lifted her head to the rippling water of the surface, gathering courage, then looking back at them she added, "But we have got to try. Stay safe, and we will meet you back here in a couple of hours."

"Agreed." Bram nodded and Cedar hugged her as they made it to a rocky path and swam the opposite way.

Once they turned out of sight, she looked to Marcion. "I guess it's time to get started."

They searched for hours, asking the merfolk who swam past them and working their way gradually through the reef. Sam met the merfolk, many were combinations of fish or creatures that lived in a reef. There was a clownfish merman, an eel mermaid, and many other vibrant and exotic looking colors and patterns of fish that she recognized but couldn't name.

Marcion had warned her to be careful of the anemone as they swam past it.

"Only those prepared and used to it can enter. It will harm the rest," he had said as she gave it a wide berth.

He had also warned her not to scrape against the coral once she got too close to a beautifully salmon colored one.

"It is alive like you and me. And it can grow on anything, *even* on skin."

Sam made a face and decided it would be best not to let her curiosity win her over.

The homes of the merfolk were engraved into the coral and rock. The few who lived in the anemone seemed to live sparsely with few items, but she could see the seagrass beds and mats where they would live. Much of the wood she saw was made of bamboo and other types of lumber that adhered better to the ocean. There were also shops that she peeked in and could see how they looked similar to the homes.

Every once in a while, there would be a manta ray or whale that swam over the reef. Sam and Marcion would stop to watch it swim nimbly, undisturbed by the civilization around it.

During their time, she also saw a sight that took her breath away. The gigantic creature that vanished in the void reappeared. The massive whale shark mermaid glided over them peacefully with an entourage of mermaids and fish gathered around her.

"They're so beautiful." Sam said to herself as another large manta ray with white on its belly swam overhead. A group of silver fish clustering its presence.

"I never imagined I would be on this side of it." She smiled softly.

"Well, there are many wondrous things in this world indeed." Marcion stopped to watch as well. "You know, I have gotten so used to them. It took fresh eyes to make me see how special it truly is."

"It feels like time moves slower here," she replied.

They watched together as it vanished into the dense ocean cover.

"I am sorry to say, Sam, but I think we might be at a loss for finding your sea walker here. I wonder if the others have had any luck," he said after they started swimming again.

"I know." Sam frowned. She ran her fingers through her floating hair, which had become a new fascination for her, and her stomach growled. "There's no way to eat with this thing on, is there?"

Marcion chuckled, which gave her the answer she needed.

"Alright, well, let's head back to the anchor and wait for them, I suppose, and then we can eat and get Fin caught up on everything that has happened."

When they arrived, they spotted the others were already there and waiting for them. Sam could tell they had no luck either, with the frown settled on Cedars' face.

"Sorry Sam," she said, shifting her bag.

"We can try later. Let's go eat and see Fin. Besides, your aquabreath has way more purple now." Sam pointed to her mask and the larger strains of velvet that seeped through.

Cedar touched her face and replied, "So has yours... I guess we need to search faster next time."

Sam swam over to the pulley and waited for one to pass her as she latched on and swam up with it. When she looked down, she saw the others joining her and the reef shrinking in size as they continued their ascent. A group of fish entertained them on their journey up to the surface.

Finally, she split through the surface and swam towards the sitting spot once she let go of the rope. Shortly after, everyone was sitting, and Marcion explained how to take the masks off.

"It would be good for you to stay in the water here. You will cough up the aquabreath liquid for a moment as you switch to air. It's going to be *awful,* but just work through it." He gave them an honest and hopeful smile as Sam pulled off her mask and the liquid projected itself out of her painfully. She coughed harshly. Each time, liquid poured out of her nose and mouth. Sam couldn't get a breath as she continued to heave. Her lungs consumed by fire.

Eventually, all the liquid was purged, and she gulped down air again. Exhausted, she collapsed against the stone, her head resting heavily as she struggled to regulate her body. She noticed the stunned expressions on Bram and Cedar's faces, realizing they had endured the same ordeal as she had. Her energy drained, she closed her eyes to rest.

"Finally," Cedar said, relieved as the entryway of Driftwood caught her eyesight. She slumped as she walked through the front door. To be polite, she laid on the floor instead of the furniture as she continued to drip and air dry her clothes. Bram and Sam had joined her, and there they lay, heaving from the intense experience. Marcion and Apollonia went to find them a change of clothes.

"Fin!" Sam tried to yell out for him from the floor, but fell short. "Fin, come here!"

They listened for any sound of him, but all they heard was Ajax bleat sleepily and emerge with tired eyes from Sam's room. He came over to them and licked their salted faces.

"Please don't," Bram groaned and weakly waved him away from his face.

Ajax made his way over to Cedar, who giggled, then to Sam, who patted him on his side.

"Alright that's enough of that."

He bleated, more alert, and laid down next to them.

"Where is Fin?" Sam sat up concerned, she looked around. "Did he come back?" She looked at Ajax and he ruffled his growing mane in a confused look.

She got up, stretching and walked over to the letter and aquabreath that still sat on the counter.

When she got closer, she noticed another slip of paper on top.

"Guys!" Sam yelled in hurried dread. She launched over to the counter and snatched up the paper, crumpling it in the process.

The piece of paper bore a harsh red symbol in the circular shape of a shark.

13

RIPPLES OF THE BLUE

"CRACKS HAVE FORMED BETWEEN THE REALMS AND THEY ONLY SEEM TO BE GETTING BIGGER." -IKE, A QUEEN FROM THE 5TH GENERATION

Curiously, Cedar leaned over Sam's shoulder to sneak a peek at the crumpled paper she held. She noticed the circular emblem of a shark, colored in vibrant crimson red. Droplets of ink trickled from the sign. Cedar stared at it, unable to think.

"I- I can't believe he is gone..." she said, finally breaking the air of silence.

"He isn't gone! We have to help him. He's our *friend*," Sam barked.

"Ya, I know- that's not what I meant. I meant... This is kind of crazy. What are we going to do?" Cedar wrapped her fingers around Sam's arm gently. She could feel the tense muscles jammed together.

"I don't know." Sam replied.

Bram snorted from where he lay on the floor. "What a dope. Of course, he would be the one to get caught."

Mockingly in Fin's voice, he added. "I got this guy. *I'm* the sneak."

Cedar grunted in agreement and rested her forehead in her palm as she leaned against her knee.

What was he thinking?!

Her mind flashed back to the last time she saw him earlier that morning. Regret filled her chest as she thought back to when he stopped her from going.

Footsteps drew her attention to the hallway entrance.

"Well, first things first. Let's get you changed out of those damp clothes and then we will come up with a plan on how to get him back. I mean, for all we know he could be fine and this is a calling card for you to go see Oracle Barclay." Marcion added doubtfully as they entered the room with neatly folded clothes draped over their forearms.

"Here you go, girls." Apollonia walked over to them and laid them down, picking up the piece of cloth colored in deep coral green with wavy patterns and rustling it out of its fold. It was a type of loose jumpsuit.

Apollonia held it up in front of Sam and checked to see if it would fit her correctly. Sam looked wearily at her from the outfit. But shortly after, she gave a curt nod and laid it in Sam's lap, approving of the size.

"Here is the bralette that goes underneath it." Apollonia picked up a small piece of tan knitted clothing and handed it to her.

Cedar continued to watch Sam mindlessly examine the pieces. Apollonia turned to her and placed a dress out in front of her with the same design as Apollonias outfit.

"This will do. Go change girls. Dry yourselves and freshen up. We have much to discuss." She corralled them out of their seats and down the hallway.

Cedar hesitated at her door. Her hand hovering above the doorknob. A sense of unease gripping her. Before Sam could enter her own room, she caught her attention.

"Sam, it's going to be ok, I promise." Cedar gave her an encouraging smile.

Sam looked up with exhaustion in her eyes. "I know, thanks Cedar. I'm just- tired from the reef."

With a click of the latch, she turned and went into her room, leaving Cedar to anxiously watch after her. Her damp clothes clung to her body. Peeling them off hastily, she was left with feeling refreshed. Then she rustled the new outfit into a comfortable position. The sensation of being free from the cold, damp clothes brought her a sense of comfort, but her thoughts remained fixated on the dilemma of what to do about Fin. She sat on her bed, straining her ears for the click of Sam's door, but only silence filled the air.

As she wiped her hands down on her new attire, the soft fabric against her skin, giving her a sense of contentment as she opened the door. Cedar approached Sam's room with hushed footsteps. Her hand gently resting on the polished wooden frame as she cautiously turned the knob. When she leaned in, she could see Sam in bed. Her eyes shut and a sense of tranquility filling the room.

A relieved sigh escaped her lips. Quietly entering, she retrieved her soaked clothes strewn across the floor and brought them along. With one last look at Sam, she left her in her afternoon slumber.

After she took their clothes and leaned them over the window's edge that looked out to the inner courtyard and garden, she joined the others back in the main room.

"Sam's exhausted. I caught her asleep. She needs rest for now," she said, sitting on the couch and leaning her head back as she stared at the white ceiling.

"She can sleep while we figure out what to do." Bram sat up cross-legged from laying on the floor.

Cedar looked at him for a moment. "She puts too much on her own shoulders. I wish she understood that we aren't *completely* useless."

Marcion plopped down next to her with a grunt. "I am most certain she does not think that. I think that she needs to protect her friends at all costs, which means that she needs to take everything headfirst."

Apollonia walked in and handed out a cup of warm tea to everyone. "Hmm, yes, we know someone who was like that once," she said, eyeing Cedar.

"I believe it was your father," she added as she sat and sipped her drink.

Cedar choked a bit on the tea.

My dad, Amos the Otso?...." she asked, looking for reassurance in what she heard.

Marcion nodded. "He was a headstrong fau when we were all younger."

"He still is." She flashed back to how long it took for him to be convinced she could leave the Whispering Woods.

"Well, you're here, so that says something," he chuckled.

"Ya, I guess." She sipped on her tea as homesickness seeped into her heart.

"Not to change the subject, but what do you think we should do about Fin?" Bram said as he scooted over to the lower table.

"Well, the only thing we *can* do is go get him. We are going to have to be careful, though. This guy sounds dangerous." She scrunched her nose.

The Oracles Court was on the edge of one of the outer docks. Sam hadn't seen it before now. It was symmetrical, with four wooden pillars, two on each side, supported by carved stone. The roof and foundation were constructed from wood. While the exterior walls were built with stacked stone, standing slightly taller than the surrounding structures, not as grand as she had imagined a significant person's building to be.

Double doors with metal knockers of seahorses in the middle of each. Her eyes trailed the rounded stairs that led up to the center and sighed.

"Let's get this over with."

"Sam, are you sure this is the best way?" Bram asked, looking at her with concern for the first time.

"We don't know that much about him. Maybe it will be ok, and we have backup in case it goes sideways." Sam gestured to Marcion, "A Summoner, and a fighter, too." She turned to him. "We have to do something."

"Then hold on to this. I'll take your fox and dog masks." She rustled through her satchel and brought out their used aquabreaths.

Sam gave her a curious look, but took it.

"It's just in case they try something sneaky."

Sam took off her mask and handed it to her, revealing a tired yet determined expression on her face. Bram did as well, and Cedar put both of their animal masks in her bag. Sam stretched the mask over her face, adjusting it to sit comfortably on her neck, ensuring that she had it on without using the liquid inside.

"Ok, then let's go rescue doofus," Bram cracked a smile as he turned back to the large doors.

Marcion stayed outside. If they were not back in time, then he would go find others to help in their cause.

With one last glance towards him, Sam turned and made her way up the stairs. She took hold of the ring that the seahorse held in its mouth and banged it against the door three times.

CLANG

    CLANG

        CLANG

They listened to it echo and fade before the door was opened by an older faunanoid. He watched them enter and pointed down the hallway to another set of doors.

"Watch the water," he muttered before turning to shut the doors and walk away.

The three of them exchanged glances and Sam unhooked her staff. Cedar lit her right arm aflame and held it up to the dim lighting of the room.

Sam scanned at her surroundings. The court itself was beautiful, just stained in the chaotic light of its master. She saw the intricate carvings and furnishings that held the history of the sea and its faus. Walking to one side, she ran her fingers over a table made of smooth marble.

"Fit for a king," she grimaced.

Bram already made his way to the door, with Cedar behind him lighting the area and Sam catching up. He pushed open the door. The hinges creaking steadily. Shivers ran down Sam's spine, and the hair on her neck stood when she glimpsed what was about to come.

Toba.

He stood in the center of a shallow pool with a toothy grin stuck to his face and a sword glinting against the light of lanterns. His shadow danced hectically from the glow of Cedar's flames.

"You got a lot of nerve standing there with that smile on your face, *coward,*" Sam spit out the last word. Her face convulsed at the sight of him while her hands twisted on the engravings of her staff.

"He has been waiting for you," Toba started, pointing his sword directly at Sam.

"We have been waiting to see *him,* too," Cedar fumed, her flames reacting to her emotions, growing more intense with each word.

"Not you," he snapped, "he doesn't want to see you either, you can stay here..." He smiled at Bram, "with us." As if on cue, two more men came out of the shadows, one dragging his sword, creating sparks as it screeched across the stone.

"What are you talking about?" Sam asked, curling her lip up in disgust.

"He said he will let you all go, if you go talk to him. *They* can wait here. And I almost forgot, your other friend is there with him, too." He set his sword on his shoulder and smirked again. "Don't worry, they'll be safe with me."

Sweat rolled down her face, making her aware that her heart was racing and her mind reeling with anxious adrenaline. She looked at the others for a sign of what to do. Cedar shook her head while Bram looked at her calmly.

She turned to glare back at Toba. He pointed his sword slowly to the shadows and into the darkness.

There.

Sam could barely see the semblance of a door. She took a step.

"Sam, no." Cedar grabbed her hand, pleading with her.

Sam put her hand on Cedar's. Her gaze fixed as she studied her. Finally, she spoke, "Fin's there. I *have* to help him." They stared at each other for a while in a quiet argument. "Trust me," Sam whispered. Cedar gave in and nodded.

Her hand slipped out of Cedar's grasp. She headed into the dark towards the door, eyeing Toba and the other two. Scowling at them as she passed, daring them to try something. Once she reached the wall, she felt for the door and searched to find a knob. The smooth metal jutted out and she turned it. The door opened easily and she slipped into the next room, taking one last look at her friends as she shut the door behind her.

The noise of rushing water hit her. Sam's eyes adjusted to the dim lighting in the room. Her heart pounded as she noticed a torrent of water gushing through a thick opening in the floor, its relentless force threatening to engulf everything in its path. The room she entered was reminiscent of the one before, with shallow water covering most of the floor.

The old man's voice rang through her mind.

Watch the water.

Carefully eyeing it, she took a cautious step forward. She could feel the presence of chaos somewhere, but the room lay still beside the flickering of the lit flames. The water grew deeper towards the center. Once she got past a tall chair that sat blocking her gaze to a part of the room, she could see a something laying on the stone.

"Fin!" Sam gasped at the sight of his crumpled body half out of the water on the floor. She stumbled towards him. Her steps hesitant as she waded through the water and eyes wide with horror. With tears streaming down her face, she dropped her staff to the ground and embraced him, the weight of grief heavy. Her words stuck in her throat as a helpless cry made its way out.

His face was a gruesome sight, bruised and bloodied, with one eye swollen shut, leaving her terrified of what had caused such mutilation. Fin's arms wrapping, curling into himself. The horrific evidence of slashes carving through both of them. Too many to count, slicing through his flesh.

"S-" He tried to speak, but could only manage a broken whisper. "-am."

"No- no," her voice cracked, "don't say anything... save your energy." She held him, shivering as she tried to hold herself together. Her head rested on his arms, shielding him, trying to protect him from what had already happened.

"I'm so sorry Fin." She whimpered despairingly.

His fingers lifted, catching a piece of her hair gently.

"Just lovely." A voice came from behind.

Her heart jolted. Distracted by Fin, Sam had completely forgotten about the other person who was supposed to be in the room. Her eyes widened at the malice that hung in the air.

Fin groaned in response to the voice, shrinking into himself. Her eyes drew over him, begging for forgiveness.

"It's going to be ok," she said, whispering again as she tried to hold herself together. A tear rolled down her cheek that created an easy pathway for more to follow.

Fin shook his head faintly. Harshly gripping a string of her hair in protest at what she was about to do.

"No-" Fin struggled to get up but collapsed, yelling out in pain.

A trembling smile made its way to her face. More tears streaked down. Her courage to do what was right had dissipated. All other emotions faded, leaving behind an unwavering need to keep her friend safe. Tenderly grabbing the hair, she pulled it out of his fingers, took her staff and stood to face the fau the voice belonged to.

She saw him in the light. He stood, standing with his white and gray tail. Two dorsal fins stuck out the back. His upper body toned with lean muscle, and his arms covered in sharp tattoos.

The shark symbol flashed through her mind.

Her fear continued to rise, her eyesight blurring.

"You're not what I expected," he smirked.

Sam glanced at his pointed teeth.

"Neither are you…" she caught herself, "but I have to ask… were you born with pointed teeth or did you do that to yourself?" She made a pained face as she ran her tongue over her own teeth.

"I heard there was a plain one in the realms, but they were whispers. So, when Toba confirmed it," he stopped talking and smiled. His face was carved handsomely, but his eyes held a sinister darkness to them that unnerved Sam.

"Plain one?" she asked.

Waves of hostility ebbed off of him in his stance. She put her staff defensively between herself and her enemy.

"Yes," he sighed impatiently, waving his hand in circles to drone on with his words, "Plain one, ancient one."

Sam stepped back, her heart racing at the mention of her true self.

How did he know?

She swallowed. "Oracle Barclay, I-"

A knife whizzed past her face. She turned, wide eyed. It dug itself deep into the soft wood.

"*No!* Not Oracle! *Never Oracle!*" His body shook violently. Then almost instantaneously calmed down. She forced herself to swallow the lump in her throat.

He looked at her. "Oracles are spineless lumps who work for a king who uses the sea to his advantage." He shifted and threw another knife into a wooden table.

"You… call me Barclay."

"Barclay, I have come for my frie-."

Before she could finish, he was in front of her. His massive hand engulfed half of her face, her staff slipped from her grasp, clattering to the floor.

Despite her effort, she lacked the strength to overcome him. Desperate, she clawed at his arm, but he remained unaffected as he effortlessly lifted her from the ground.

Her feet kicked frantically in the air, and her hands clawed at the powerful grip around her throat. A ragged gasp escaped her lips, eyes wide as her body jerked and twisted, trying desperately to break free. The fingers around her neck tightened, cutting off her breath, and her vision blurred as the world began to spin.

"Stop!" Fin said from below, grabbing at Barclay's tail fin.

Barclay looked down in disgust.

"Don't touch me, tree rat," he fumed, spitting on Fin before turning and smacking him in the face with his tail.

Sam cried out, her face twisting in agony as Fin lay unconscious on the ground. She struggled in his hand as he dragged her through the water, closer to the opposite end of the room.

"You're brave, *Samihanee*. Brave to face me." His voice was a blade, slicing through the space between them. "But that doesn't make you strong... or smart."

The moment he released her, she stumbled back onto the jagged stone that met the rushing current. The roar of water filled her ears.

Barclay loomed over her, his shadow swallowing the dim light. His voice dropped lower, more insidious. "And you don't belong in this world. *My* world. Not anymore"

Sam clenched her jaw and turned away, refusing to meet his gaze. His nails closed around her jaw, forcing her back. His grip was iron, pressing into her skin. He leaned in, his breath warm, suffocating.

"Your eyes tell me everything." His own burned with something dark, something cruel. "This... gray claims no sky, no sea, no land. *Empty.* You are nothing, Samihanee. You have no fin. No claws. No feathers." He released her with a small shove, crossing his arms as if he had already dismissed her.

Sam staggered, her breath catching in her throat. She bent forward, hands on her knees, forcing air into her lungs. *Inhale. Exhale.* Each breath scraped against her ribs.

Barclay watched her struggle with amusement. "There is no room in these realms for something like you. I was chosen by the sea, *Sam.* " He moved closer, his voice a whisper that curled into her ear. "It is time for you to drift into the void."

A chill crawled down her spine. Her muscles locked, every instinct screaming at her to run. She lifted her head to meet his gaze, and the weight of it pressed into her, crushing, suffocating.

"You don't belong here." He flicked his hand in distaste. "The time of our ancestors is *over.* The era of the Seaborne is beginning."

Heat rose in her chest, her pulse pounding in her ears. Her fists curled, nails biting into her palms. Then, she straightened. Standing taller. The fear, the doubt, the trembling hesitation—it *burned* away.

"You don't know what you're talking about." Her voice was steady now, cutting.

His expression twitched, just fast enough for her to almost miss it. Sam took a step forward, her finger jabbing toward him. "These faunanoid aren't your playthings. You weren't chosen, Barclay. You're just using power to hide behind because without it, you're *nothing*."

Silence. Barclay frowned, his face twisting in thought. But his fingers twitched at his sides. The river roared behind them, hungry and waiting.

The door that Sam had come through opened. Cedar and Bram rushed through. Sam could see behind them lay a crisped and smoking body.

"I think it's time for us to be taking our friend and leaving," she said cautiously, glancing between Fin, Cedar, and Bram.

He growled again. Then yanked her arm into an awkward angle as he lifted her into the air and held her over the water that flowed to nowhere. A cry escaped her lips and her face twisted in agony.

"Stay back." Sam whimpered in pain, holding out her other hand. "He's too strong." Her fingers raked over his hand in a feeble attempt to escape. The ends of her sandals scraping against the edge.

"Sam!" Cedar yelled as she drew closer to them. Bram stopped her.

Barclay snickered. "You might be brave, but are you brave enough to sacrifice yourself for them?"

Sam's breathing caught. A wave of nausea passed through her. The water below grew louder.

"Please, don't," she cried softly, shaking her head and grabbing at his arm, holding onto the only life raft she had.

"Sam!" Cedar yelled again, fighting against Bram. Tears streamed down Sam's face.

"If you want, I can slaughter them all in front of you, then you will know that you are truly alone," he chuckled in her ear. Cruelty seeped from his voice as she felt his breath go down her neck.

"But if you sacrifice yourself, I'll let them live."

Uncontrollably she shook her head, her gaze fixed on her friends. Emotions forced themselves up, rising like the tide. She cried out.

"Pick one. Your life or theirs," he growled, growing impatient and held her further out over the water.

She blinked rapidly, her eyelids fluttering, but the tears still clung, refusing to fall. Her chest tightened, each breath shaky as she fought to hold them back. Cedar collapsed in Bram's arms and Fin lay almost dead in the water.

Her eyes closed. The hand that held his arm went limp. In hopes for a glimpse of mercy she studied his unyielding eyes.

"What a waste." He frowned, releasing his grip.

Sam cried out. Her fingers grasped for the stone that slipped away.

Her body hit the water.

Everything went dark.

14

HYMNS OF THE SEA

"CONNECTION WITH THE WATER BRINGS CREATION." -TENZIN OF THE MOUNTAIN CITY

"CEDAR, PAY ATTENTION TO what's in front of you." Bram hissed.

She looked past Toba. Her eyes stapled to the last sights of Sam as she shut the door behind her.

"Right, sorry." She shook her head to gain focus, furrowing her brow as she stared at the three fau blocking their path.

"Do you honestly think you will get past us?" Toba sneered as he walked to the side.

"I think we won that last fight. I seem to recall the fear on your face," Bram snapped back calmly.

Anger flared on Toba's face. "That won't happen again."

The other two men followed as he held his sword in position by his side.

Bram looked to Cedar. She balanced herself and held her right palm out with the flames engulfing it as it lit the room in a shadowy dance. Excitement surged through him as he clenched and unclenched his hands. His mind buzzing with apprehension of the battle that awaited.

Bram closed his eyes, hoping that this was the best decision to make. He opened them and focused on the first faunanoid in front of him. To the right of Toba.

"Cedar," he whispered, "create a fog. Keep your distance. I'll deal with them."

Cedar tried to argue, but, hesitated when she saw the unyielding determination etched on his face. Her body involuntarily took a step back, hands balling into fists. After a moment, she summoned a ball of condensed fire that burned yellow, and aiming it at the pool, she tossed it.

The water screamed. A steam clouded the room in a hot cover. Bram waited until she backed away more until he began his prowl. The faint scent of sweat and fear hung in the air. Stealthily circling around, his heart pounded in his chest as he closed in on his unsuspecting target, his breath shallow and his senses heightened. He lurched forward, clinging to the man's back and face as they both struggled for victory. Bram could feel his body urging to fight. To rip his throat open. He recalled the familiarity of what it was like when he was a shifter.

Control it. Hold it in. The dark green fau fell to the floor with a splash.

"Where are you?!" Toba yelled, but Bram had already made his way to his next victim.

The steam began to settle as Bram launched himself onto the second henchman. The man struggled against him, wrapping his hand around his neck.

Bram froze.

Toba discovered Cedar and pressed his sword against her neck. Fury and helplessness flared in her eyes.

"This looks familiar, doesn't it?" He grabbed her forearm, holding her hostage in front of him.

"Let him go, or she dies!" Toba yelled across the room.

Bram reluctantly released the man. His slender opponent fell into the pool, desperately gasping for air.

"Looks like we are in the same situation as last time," Toba snarled, pushing his sword deeper into Cedar's throat. She sucked in a breath. A trail of blood lining the blade.

"No. We aren't." Cedar clutched Toba's arms with her hands. Bram could see her fox nails dig into his skin as she torched him. He howled, dropping his sword and falling to the floor.

"Do you want to know why?" Cedar leaned towards him as he writhed in the water, he clutched his now steaming and singed arm.

"Because I don't have to worry about destroying someone I love... I can *finally*.. Let. It. All. Out."

She focused her attention on Bram. Her eyes became embers that sat at the bottom of the flames.

"You're going to want to go for a swim."

He haltered a bit, but she turned and grew brighter. Her body a glowing source of illuminated building. The screams of Toba were shrouded as Bram dove into the water at the last second. As soon as he fully submerged himself, a flash of light and heat that pulsed through the room. Bram instinctively shielded his face. Forcefully, pushed back by the explosion.

He broke the surface a minute later. The room steamed from the heat. Scorch marks blackened the walls and ceiling. Most of the water evaporated from the pool. Bram looked for the second man and saw he had collapsed with burns covering his body, his scales sizzling.

Cedar stood hovering over the charred body of Toba. Still gripping his arms. Then, leaned upwards, blowing smoke from her mouth, she collapsed. The body of Toba melted away into a pile of nothing more than a mixture of ash and water.

Bram stood, examining his surroundings in terrified awe. As he approached Cedar, he lifted her head, and she blinked back at him weakly.

"So that's what that looks like on the other side of it," he said with a soft chuckle.

Weakly, she smiled back at him. "I told you I can handle myself."

She stood, her legs shaking. The remains of Toba dusted her hands, face, and clothes. When she wiped at the ash, it only further smeared into her skin. Bram hesitated, watching, waiting for her reaction. Her hands trembled under their gaze as she took in what she had done. Cedar held a breath as she dipped her hands into the water.

"Why won't it come off?" she asked, scrubbing her skin and using her nails to scrape the dark stain out of her fur. Bram's heart sunk. He haltered, unsure.

"Cedar-"

"Let's go get Sam and Fin." Quickly, she stood. Sizzling came from her skin, her body heated and the small droplets that stuck to her began to evaporate.

They made it to the wooden door and pushed it open. Bram haltered, his eyes widened in terror. A shadowed figure lurked in the flickering lantern light, clutching Sam tightly. Dread dropped in Bram's stomach. Her eyes showed defeat. His dismay gave way to more anger. He stepped forward.

"Stay back," she cried out to them. Bram stopped, surprised. "He's too strong."

He could see the tears staining her cheeks.

"Sam!" Cedar lurched forward. Instinctively, Bram grabbed her before she moved any closer. With a heavy heart, he clasped her arm. Tears welled in his eyes, as he witnessed the man he now knew to be Barclay and Sam's transaction unfold.

"What are you doing? Bram? Let go!" She shot him a look of pained confusion as she unsuccessfully tried to push his arms off. He gripped tighter.

"I'm sorry." He said, low enough for only Cedar to hear.

Her eyes widened in realization.

"Samm!" She fought harder, crying in frustration.

Barclay leaned in closer to whisper something in Sam's ears. She turned to look at them, blinking furiously. Bram could see it on her face. She shook her head no. Agony ripped through his heart.

"Please," Bram mouthed to her, distraught. Sam turned back to the shark fau and let her body go limp.

Bram and Cedar watched as the Oracle of Anchor tossed their friend into the rippling current.

And all at once, she was gone.

Emptiness consumed her. Sam couldn't tell if she was staring at the endless bottom of the ocean. Or if she faced upwards to where the horizon met the sea. Every so often, she would twitch her fingers faintly to remind herself she was in the ocean and not floating through the void of space. Her emotions had tired themselves, and she drifted, blinking in and out of existence. It would be easy to sleep. So easy. Her breathing slowed in the aquabreath. It told her she was running out of time.

Sam closed her eyes. The laughter and conversations with her friends echoed in her thoughts. She hoped their faces would bring her comfort. She hoped that Barclay would keep his word. Maybe they could return to their lives from before her.

I'm sorry, Lyra. I wasn't able to help you after all.

It doesn't matter. None of it really mattered.

Barclay was right. I don't belong in this new world. Maybe, maybe this is for the best.

Her world was gone, the past was just that, the past. Why did she have any right to be here when the rest of humanity was gone? Dead. Buried with the history.

She smiled lightly to herself ironically as she thought about how she came into this world, alone without answers, and now she would leave the same way.

Her hair brushed against her cheek, tickling her.

Slowly moving her hand towards her face, she couldn't help but picture her fox mask. Then her mind shifted to the staff she had found. Both a part of her. Both left behind for her friends to safeguard with her memory.

At that, her mind reminisced, flowing from scene to scene. She could see them clearly, as if she were there again.

The Chief, Amos, Lin, and Atlas looked at her from the forest of the Whispering Woods.

Nakoia camouflaged in the branches of the deep jungle, watching her from under the stars.

The Centaur tribes as they stampeded over the Hills of Yoid.

Vineke with its koimaids who humbled themselves among the manatee and fireflies.

Her mind became a canvas as a flood of more vivid scenes crossed her view.

The woods where she spent her time on the moss that grew plush in a dense green, and the tree of life sitting in the hidden valley with its maroon and shimmering gold leaves. Its guardian standing next to it, touching its trunk as she watched Sam.

Muninn.

I don't want to die.

Someone... anyone please...

She covered her face as if afraid someone would see her cry. Her nose scrunched itself, and her throat closed. Her tears merged into the water of the ocean as they vanished. Overwhelmed by fear, she curled into a ball, squeezing her eyes shut as she continued to cry. Her breaths shallow.

Something silky bumped her arm.

It wasn't real, it was her imagination. There was *nothing* where she was.

A soft object brushed across her leg this time.

Drearily, her eyes opened to a blurry pink blob floating next to her. Sam tried to focus her faded sight on the object. After a moment of confusion, she could see what it was.

A... jellyfish?

The plump creature, the size of her arm, meandered next to her for a moment before spreading out its body and pushing itself up and away. As it moved, her gaze followed it. A multitude of blurred pinks flowed around her now.

She uncurled herself. Stretched out. Laying to watch them swim. Many more appeared around her from the depths and continued past her, lighting the sea and creating a beautiful endless landscape of glowing pinks and purples mixed with the ocean blue.

The surrounding mass grew more dense until barely any water was visible. She watched the tentacles float. With the light now illuminating the darkness, she caught a glimpse of the aquabreath. A complete shade of velvet purple.

Embracing the sight of the jellyfish, she felt weightless, floating effortlessly among them in the tranquil water.

A call from a large animal cut through the water, breaking the silence.

The noise was deep and sad. Her heart filled with longing as it sang to her. The creature sang out a deep pulsing call, then clicking combined with high and low whistles. She closed her eyes to listen.

The jellyfish faded above her now. But below, the new creature emerged. Their singing grew louder as they neared. Then stopped completely. She could feel them. Their presence reached for her, soothing her.

She opened her eyes and forced her head to turn. To her right, she saw the eye of a whale.

Sam smiled.

Hello.

As she reached out, her fingers brushed against its leathery side. Feeling the gentle pulse beneath her touch. It was not one, but a pod of them. A little calf came up to Sam and nudged her. Chuckling weakly, she put her hand on its back, brushing its flipper as it chirped at her delightfully. Five or six of them swam gracefully around her. Her eyesight blurred. She blinked a couple times, confused. Tired.

A series of pulses rang out, and she felt the baby whale swim. It pulled on her arm. Sam ascended. Releasing its fin and rotating in the water, she caught a fleeting glimpse of the expansive sea below. She frowned, unsure if they were playing tricks on her.

Down, into the abyss, she caught glimpses of structures and pieces of metal that jutted out as if trying to reach for her. It was only a short glance however as one of the bigger whales moved and placed her on its back as they started upward.

She could see a pink light approaching her now. Soon, the pod of whales easily passed and left the swarm of jellyfish behind.

Light approached them. She saw the waves of water on the surface of the sea as it crashed down from above.

The whale slowed, allowing Sam to witness the gentle breach and be bathed in the ethereal glow of the starlight.

How long had it been since she was carried away?

She reached for her mask. Her body was weak, but still fought to take it off. There was not much clean liquid left. With her face in her hand, she desperately reached for the gel, only to have it slip through her fingers. Sam took in a labored breath as she tried to refocus. The mask was her only obstacle for air now.

The second time, she came from below, prying it off with what little energy she had left. After another moment of struggle, she pushed it up enough and forced it off the rest of the way.

A deep purple liquid purged itself from her lungs as she relentlessly battled for air. Her now useless aquabreath fell limply out of her hand and she watched it slide off the whale's back and sink into the deep, towards the curious structures that lay beneath.

She coughed up more purple as she wheezed in the cool air. "Thank you."

She fell onto her stomach and lay there. Sapped of energy and unable to move. Their sounds of melancholy and joy pierced the night as she listened to the way they called out to her. They ruptured through the star patterned water, splitting it open and flying into the air before descending again.

The whale underneath her hummed softly. The sound reverberating through her body, calming her more. Her eyes drifted open to close and open again until they could no longer watch the celebration of the magnificent creatures before her.

"Is she dead?" A voice whispered close to her.

"No, she isn't. You can see her breathing," another voice snipped back, irritated at the first.

The first smacked his teeth to the second's response. "Well… she *looks* dead. So, I don't know why you would be surprised by my question."

Sam groaned. Life stirred around her. Still the whale hummed gently under her. In the blurriness of her vision, a dark silhouette floated near. Three figures were on the whale's back with her, each a darkened silhouette against the reflective water.

She struggled to concentrate and lifted her head in an attempt to clear her mind.

"It's a good thing she told us you were here girly, otherwise you'd be dead by now. Ain't that right Lahs?" the third said as he leaned down and patted the back of the whale. The whale pulsed in acknowledgement of the man.

Her head, too heavy to bear, collapsed back down. Unable to keep her attention on anything.

"She looks completely out of it. Let's get'er onboard," he sighed, concerned.

"Oi, set a course for Nim, we found the girl!" He called up to the ship and a merriment of responses rang out.

Sam faded more out of consciousness as he picked her up. She opened her eyes to the whales dipping under the water and quickly she was lost to the void of sleep once more.

Sam awoke to the clambering of footsteps above her and felt the rocking of a boat as she groaned and cradled her head. With a deep breath, she endured the discomfort until it subsided, and then cautiously opened her eyes. Turning over, she felt a mattress under her and a thick blanket covering her. Around was a small room decorated in trinkets from the sea, clothing, and other items a ship would need.

Sam slowly got up and made her way over to a desk that sat in the middle of the room. She wracked her brain, trying to piece together the events that led her to her current location. Groggily, she picked up a telescope and weighed it in her hands as she looked around the room for further information. Flashes of purple and whales singing flashed through her memory.

The sound of the door handle clicking startled her, causing her to swiftly abandon the telescope and retreat behind the desk for protection.

"I see you're awake now." He smiled at her warmly.

Sam recognized it as one of the voices from when she had woken before. She haltered at the sight of him.

"You're- You're human."

Without hesitation, she took two long steps around the desk towards him as she examined his face. He was tanned from being in the sun for too long, and shaggy dirty blonde hair was being tormented under a dark blue beanie that corresponded with his blue eyes. He wore a long, slick coat above a sweater and pants that were tucked into tall rubber boots.

"I… I don't understand. How is this *possible*? I was told there weren't any humans." She staggered in building excitement as she swallowed down the nausea, and pushed through another headache.

He made a pained face at her. "Sorry, don't mean to disappoint." He gave her a crooked smile and held out his hand. Wiggling his webbed fingers, she looked down and little sparks of lightning zapped.

She stepped back as her heart sank. "You're- a Summoner." She sat back down on the bed and rubbed her hands on the soft material. "I'm sorry. I wasn't thinking straight." She shook her head, looking down at the planked flooring.

"I didn't mean to make you upset. I wanted to come in and check on you. You've been out for a while." He chuckled softly and came in to put some stuff from his pockets into a drawer in the dresser.

"This is your room?" she asked curiously.

"Yes, you're aboard my ship. I am the Captain of this humble fishing vessel." He took a sarcastic bow and threw a smile at her.

"Thanks for saving me then, but what happened to the whales?" She peeked out the window to the opened sea, hoping to catch a peak of one of their blue backs.

"They went ahead to the Isle of Nim. She sent all of us to get you. I was wondering what was so special about one person. But now it makes sense. There hasn't been a human in a *long* time." He stared out the window as well, looking back to a time that no longer existed.

Sam's head drummed in pain again. She winced and waited for the pain to subside.

"What's wrong?"

"My head, it's been hurting since I woke up." She grimaced and squinted through the aching.

"You're probably dehydrated. Let's get some water."

Sam nodded, then stopped. "Wait, you haven't told me your name."

"I guess I haven't. It's Sideon. And I don't believe I know your name either."

"Samihanee, but people call me Sam."

"Well Sam, welcome to my ship, the Agalon." He opened the door and gestured for her to follow.

She walked after him and braced herself against the morning sunlight as she tried to gather her surroundings. The ship was the classic ship that she knew from the time before. Built with sturdy wood and massive sails that hung on rope and wind. The crew, at least the ones she saw, consisted mostly of arctic creatures. She saw men faus of white foxes, seals, penguins, and one specifically large man who was a bulk of white fur with a polar bear's head.

Sideon noticed her staring.

"That's Brogie, don't worry 'bout him. He is tough on the outside, but a warm cuddle bug on the inside. Isn't that right?" he said in a sugary voice at him.

Brogie let out a deep breath, shaking his head disappointedly at Sideon, and rolling his eyes. He gave Sam a curt nod and then continued his work at the helm.

"See! There's nothing to be afraid of." He smiled mischievously as they continued walking.

"He looks like he could eat you if he *really* wanted to," Sam said, glancing back at the polar bear helmsman.

"Nah, he's fun." He waved off Sam's concerns. "Here's the kitchen. We keep the barrels of fresh water down here." The Captain led the way and walked down a set of short stairs.

Sam found the barrel. Her tongue dried as she spotted it. Gulping down the fresh water, her mind cleared, the fog lifted. Embarrassed, she made eye contact with Sideon. His gaze fixed on her.

"Why are you staring? You know that's considered rude?" She wiped her mouth and fixed her hair.

He shrugged. "No reason. I just like to watch people." At that, he jumped up and turned to the entrance, heading up the stairs. He added. "We should be there by now. She isn't far."

Sam followed him out of the kitchen and to the front of the ship. The smell of fish clung to the air with the feel of a static charge.

"Is the static electricity from you?" She felt her hair beginning to friz as she patted it down. Sam glanced around and saw the crew worked through it as if they didn't notice it. And she held back a chortle at Brogie's puffed up fur.

"Sorry, that happens sometimes." He stopped, rubbing his hands together momentarily, then clapped, causing a miniature thunder clap to be heard throughout the area. After that, the frizz and static in the air had dissipated.

"How's that?" Sideon smiled at her, happy to show off his skills.

"Hmm, neat." Sam touched her hair again and felt the small hairs on her arms return to normal.

"Look, we're here." Sideon herded her to the tip of the boat and pointed out. Sam could see an island approaching them. It was a simple piece of land. Only big enough for one house.

"This is the Isle of Nim?" Sam squinted as she leaned forward.

"You know about this place?" He looked at her, impressed, as he handed her the telescope that had been on his desk earlier.

She opened it up and put it against her eye. "Only from when I heard you talking about it last night. On the back of Lahs, the whale. And I'm guessing you were the one that picked me up and carried me on board." She said, then glancing down, she added in a quiet voice. "I thought I was going to die, so- thank you."

"I thought you were out of it. I tried talking to you, but it didn't seem like you were all there." He laughed and gripped the railing. "But really, it was Nim who saved you. We got a message from her to bring her the one lost at sea with Lahs and the rest of the pod. If there is anybody you should thank, it's her." He leaned against the railing and they watched as the island grew closer to them. "We should be there shortly."

Sam leaned against the railing with him, and looking into the water, she could see three manta rays swimming along with the ship. They danced in the water gracefully as the Agalon tugged along.

"Her name is Nim?" Sam scrunched her nose.

Sideon cracked a smile. "She gave herself that name for the people to call her, but she is otherwise known as the Lady in the Water."

15

LADY IN THE WATER

LIGHT SUMMONERS FROM THE GUARDIAN
MOUNTAINS HAVE BEEN KNOWN TO SPREAD
THEIR ILLUSIONS AS FAR AS THE LAKE OF
TIDECREST

THE SMALL ROWBOAT BUMPED against the sand and slowed to a stop on the island's beach. Sideon jumped over the side and grabbed the boat, heaving it ashore and onto the burning sand. Sam stood and stared at the island for a moment.

"It's smaller than I thought it was going to be." She could see the entire island in her view with its few trees, beautiful flowers bowing back and forth in the soft breeze, and the cottage that sat on it.

Sideon rested his hands on his hips and looked around with her, shrugging, he said, "She seems to like it."

He gestured for her to come ashore with him. In a wobbly effort, she made her way to the front. Sideon held out his hand. She grabbed, climbing out of the boat that was lodged securely.

Once they were both out, Sam made her way to the house but stopped when she noticed Sideon was not with her. She looked back to see him bent over and wrestling with his shoes, taking them off one by one and placing them in the boat with his socks hiding inside them. She looked at him and raised her eyebrow.

"She has a no shoes policy," he said.

Of course she did.

Sam pursed her lips, then nodding in defeat. She trudged through the sand and back to the boat to take off the sandals that were given to her by Apollonia. As she paused, she closed her eyes and savored the feeling of the sand slowly engulfing her feet. She could feel each of the tiny grains warming in the morning sun. The sensation of the sand rubbing between her toes made her smile to herself. Relishing in the tiny, prickly pains it brought.

"Well, come on then," Sideon hollered back at her. He was halfway to the grassy hill when she looked up.

She laughed to herself as she struggled through the sand. With each step she took, her back foot dug deeper into it, making it hard to walk. So she galloped her way to Sideon.

"I'm glad you're enjoying yourself," he said with a small smile. "I don't think I have seen you happy since we picked you up."

She stopped, out of breath. "Well, I haven't been in the sand since I woke up. But I can remember the feeling of it. It makes me feel like I'm recalling something."

He stopped too and looked back to their footsteps, the small rowboat and to his fishing vessal in the distance.

"For obvious reasons, water has always been in my family. We've lived in a watery port town all my life, so when I discovered Nim and her island, it made me see the ocean in a different light."

"A port town? They call them Lakes or Reefs, I thought? There aren't any port towns in the realms." Sam looked at him.

His eyes connected with hers, and for a moment she saw surprise behind them. With a sly smile and a wink, he looked on ahead.

"Come on."

Hesitating, Sam stared after him as he continued to the cottage. Thoughts filled her mind as she followed, trying to understand what he meant. She shook her head, distracted by his words, and decided to ask him about it later.

As she arrived at the start of the short lampposts, she felt the smoothness of the stoned pathway beneath her feet and breathed in the sweet scent of clover. Sam walked down the path as the plants underneath tickled the bottom of her feet. Upon closer inspection, she could see intricate carvings in the base and head of the lamps. Her fingers reached to trace over the designs. As they got closer, Sam could see a garden of vegetables and flowers to her left, protected by a stone fence that went up to her waist.

The cottage itself was small, but unique looking. A massive bay window stood at the center of the home and sculpted itself into the walls circularly. The walls were made of wood and stone and the soft pointed roof consisted mostly of wood paneling. Sideon made his way past the welcome gate and into the garden. Sam continued with him. Hidden on the other side of the bay window was a door that was long and arched at the top with the stones turned into a keystone fashion.

Sam peeked inside the large window and could see an unlit kitchen and living room inside. Sideon opened the door without knocking and went in. Baffled, Sam followed him uneasily.

"Are you sure we can walk into her home like this?" Sam crossed her arms in front of herself and searched for any sign of life.

Sideon chuckled, "she knows we're here."

Sam let out a relieved breath and let her arms down to wander as well.

"You can take a look around if you want. She'll be back in a little bit." He sat down on the couch as if it was his own and took out the book that was in his coat.

She looked at him a moment longer before deciding what to do. It wasn't long before curiosity overtook her and she made her way through the small home.

It didn't look like the other homes she'd seen in the realms. It had items she hadn't seen in a long time. The kitchen had two circular conclaves in its stone walls, the larger one in the corner was a clay fireplace with a chimney going out the top, the other was a sink built into the wall with mosaic tiles decorating the inside that depicted a meadow of golden wheat with a colorful sky. There were pans hanging above the oven. Plants and herbs hung or sat in every corner, surrounded by the usual kitchen trinkets scattered throughout the room.

She continued on to the living room, where Sideon enjoyed his book in silence on a light blue couch. Paintings of beautiful landscapes hung all over the walls. Sam ran her hand along the surface of a smooth bookshelf containing jars of dried leaves, books, and other nicknacks. Gently, she released a book from its secure spot. She opened it and felt the delicate pages slip through her fingers, capturing the scent of time within them. Then, stopping suddenly, Sam noticed the words, recognizing them.

"This book... is in English," she said awestruck as she looked at Sideon, her mouth opened in shock.

"They are all... in English," he mimicked her as he held up the book he was reading and she could see that it was also written in the language she hadn't seen since she had woken up.

With a couple of blinks, she turned the pages, the sound of rustling paper filling the air. She held it tightly against her chest, feeling its presence, before carefully setting it on the armrest of the couch. If there was a dull moment, she wanted to spend it with the little remnant of her past.

Moving on, she reached a locked door, so she continued past it. From the living room, a larger two-door exit opened to a view of trees and flowers, leading out to the endless ocean. The doorframe spotted with colored tiles in its glass, the wood between danced unevenly on the door creating gaps for the glass in unsymmetrical segments.

She turned the handle of the right one and walked outside, leaving the door open behind her as she stared out to the cloudless sky and the calm, open ocean. She could see another stoned trail leading to the beach. There were a couple of cushions on the short patio with exotic plants in large, painted vases. She walked over to the nearest plant and felt its flower and leaves in her fingers, then looking out to the water, she noticed something odd. Curiously, she leaned forward, squinting her eyes in an attempt to see more clearly.

"Hey... Sideon, the water's being weird!" She called back into the cottage.

On the beach, she saw a small stream of water make its way upward from the ocean, more water from the island rolled downward to meet it. The streams joined. Swirling around each other and gaining speed, until they formed a pillar that defied gravity.

Sam saw more pieces of water floating towards it from the ocean and joining into the pillar. It stopped growing in height and slowed. As it did, it gained color. It morphed from the water's clear blue into a white tunic and long, wavy hair.

Sam stepped back in shock, bumping into Sideon. She stared at him, not knowing what to say. Her mouth hung open again as she looked back and forth between the two.

"Welcome back Nim!" He yelled down to the woman on the beach.

"You have one minute to leave." Barclay said flatly. "Or I'm killing you all." With a twisted smile on his face, he gave them one last look and turned, leaving through a door close behind him.

Bram released Cedar from his grip and she collapsed to the ground.

"Sam-" she said, barely letting her friend's name leave her lips. Covering her face, she hunched over, her body crumpling into the water.

What's happening?

I don't understand.

This wasn't supposed to happen.

She yelled out, wailing louder than the rushing water that had destroyed her life. She screamed louder, letting it go on until she couldn't breathe anymore, and her head pulsed with her heartbeat.

Gasping for air, she stayed there unmoving until she felt Bram touching her back. Dazed, she sat up and looked at him. In his arms lay the unconscious and bloodied Fin.

"Fin... no." She shut her eyes and rested her forehead on his arm while she held his limp hand. "I'm so sorry." A couple of tears fell as she listened to his breathing and stood. Aware of the gravity of the situation, she nodded to Bram, and they departed from the Oracles Court.

"Children!" Marcion ran up to meet them as they walked down the stairs. His face twisted as his eyes scoured over Fin's beaten body.

"Is he-" Marcion haltered, and looked at Cedar before he finished what he was saying.

"No," she croaked, her voice still wavering, "but we need to get him to Driftwood, where I can help him."

"Where's Sam?" His concern rising.

Bram shook his head. "Now's not the time."

Cedar's eyes welled, and she put her hand over her mouth to stop from crying out again.

Marcion looked back and forth for a moment. Then nodded furiously and gestured for them to follow.

They had made it halfway back to Driftwood and were passing the fountain of the Lady in the Water, when Cedar could feel the intensity of someone's gaze from the fountain. A woman standing immersed in the water, fixated her gaze on them. A sense of unease settled in her. She looked away but remained aware of the mysterious woman.

"Hello, Cedar the Flame Summoner."

The hairs on the back of Cedar's neck stood. She stopped and turned back to her, lighting her fingers on fire. The group stopped as well. Marcion shuffled Fin in his grasp.

"Who are you?" Cedar spoke as she tried to hide the sorrow.

The woman stepped out of the water, over the edge, and onto the stone. They backed up. Guarded and broken from their recent encounters.

"You don't have to be afraid. I am here to help." Her voice flowed like honey and beckoned them to come closer.

"Who are you?" Cedar repeated, forceful this time.

"I have been called by many names over the years. As of now, I go by Nim." She held out her hand and water dripped from it. The water continued to fall and streamed itself through the cracks of the stones towards Cedar. Once it reached her, the water went around her, then back on track to its true target.

The water flowed up Brams' leg to Fin. It reached him and snaked over his body to his face. As it touched the gashes that were scattered over his arms, the flesh folded together, and the dried blood washed away.

"Bring the boy here, put him in the water," she said calmly.

Bram looked at Cedar for a moment, and then together they walked up to the woman who called herself Nim.

Her skin was olive, and she had wavy chestnut brown hair that went down to her thighs. A white tunic covered her body that adorned a clasped at the shoulder with a golden wave circling itself. Partnered with her deep green eyes, Nim had the look of a comforting mother as she stooped to hold Fin in the water.

The water rippled around him and hummed as it danced in repetition. Little streams flowed upward to his face again.

"It will take time to heal properly, and he will have scars on his arms from the deep wounds but he will live." Nim said.

She brushed his hair back, and he groaned, blinking his eyes open.

"Did I die?" he whispered.

She chuckled, "No, you're still alive."

"I don't understand." He sat up by himself, examining the scars where his skin fused itself together and touched his face.

"Water has healing properties if used correctly. It is life, after all," Nim responded.

He stood. Cedar watched him continue to examine his arms. The scars were deep, and many. The thought of Barclay cutting him, slicing through his body with those daggers made her stomach churn. Hatred built in her throat as she swallowed down the tears. No longer able to look, she plastered her gaze to the cobblestone.

"Where's Sam?" Fin asked. Bram's face dropped.

Cedar covered her eyes as tears fell freely.

"She's gone, Fin," Brams' tone was soft. Barely a whisper.

"What do you mean, gone? She was there, I- I saw her," Fin faltered, his hands limp at his side.

"He let go of her over a current. She disappeared into the sea." Bram slumped onto the fountain's edge. "She's gone," He repeated himself.

Cedar fell in the water and cried, her body was heated with the anger of her uselessness as the seeping coldness of dread paralyzed her.

"No, no, that's not true." Fin looked to Marcion. He turned away, unable to meet his gaze.

"She can't be... *gone.*" Fin covered his eyes as his face scrunched together in pain.

"Peace, children, she's alive." Nim spoke to the group.

Cedar sniffled.

"What?" she asked.

"Samihanee is with me. I can feel her. I have sent my whales to fetch her and bring her to my home." She pointed out to the sea.

"How?" Bram stood defensively.

He clenched his fists and felt the pent-up anger bubbling within him. Ready to explode.

"Sam is in the middle of the ocean being carried away by a current."

"I am the ocean. I am the current. I feel her now." Nim lifted her hand in the air, copying the statue of her above and water droplets formed, swirling, "I surround her, I protect her, she is not floating aimlessly, there is a reason for everything." Then, in an instant, the droplets fell back into the water to create a rippling pattern in the sea.

"Yes, because she is the Lady in the Water." Marcion stepped forward and completed the symbol of touching his chest and pulling it away.

She nodded. "It is time for you three to leave Anchor and meet your friend at my home."

"Sam's alive?" Cedar said out loud to herself, baffled as the thought came to her. She gawked at Bram and Fin with shock lingering in her eyes.

"Sam's alive!" She jumped up and hugged them again. "I can't believe it. We're going to see her!" She buried her head into her friends and they laughed together in merriment. Relief once again washed over them as they celebrated together in the fountain's waters.

Sam and Sideon watched her walk up to the path and towards her home. Sam's heart ached at the sight of her. She had so many questions that raced through her mind but held back from bombarding the woman with questions. As she got closer, a strange intuition tugged at her, signaling that there was something peculiar about the Lady in the Water.

As if Nim could read her thoughts, she spoke up, "Sam, I can see on your face that you have noticed I am not of the realms. I am from before, long ago, like you."

Sam stumbled on herself, "I-" She struggled to find the words to say.

Nim held her hand up. "I am wary, let's sit and then we can talk."

Sam nodded and let her pass. Nim walked into the living room and into the kitchen. She sat at the thick wooden table and waited for Sam to join her.

"I know you have many questions. Let's make some tea first."

With a flick of his fingers, Sideon conjured two small bolts that ignited the oven, filling the air with the scent of burning wood. Simultaneously, he effortlessly retrieved the cups from the cabinet, their cool porcelain surface contrasting with the warmth of the room. Meanwhile, water materialized from a nearby vase, and gracefully floated through the air and poured itself into the kettle that sat atop the crackling flames. Sideon then placed dried herbs, flowers, and fruits on the table for them to choose from.

Sam watched in wonderment as the two worked together so naturally to complete the task. She also noticed that the water around her moved without Nim telling it to, as if it had a mind of its own.

"How are you doing that?" Sam asked curiously.

"I am different from Sideon. He was born in this time and can *control* lighting. I was one of the original Elementals and *am* the water."

"So, Cedar, Muninn, and Sideon can only create or control their element. They aren't made of it," Sam thought out loud to herself.

"She catches on quick, doesn't she? You told me we were rescuing a smart one," he said with a chuckle and plucked an orange peel up. With a playful smile, he placed it in his cup.

"Yes," Nim said as the boiling water lifted itself from the kettle and made its way towards them. "Careful now."

Sam moved aside and watched it split into three as it dropped, filling their cups perfectly.

She let out a breath.

"That's amazing."

"Thank you, but I know you have more important things you want to ask me now." Nim picked up three rose petals and dropped them into her cup. The water stirred itself gingerly for a moment.

Sam burst at the seams with questions. Her mind had been racing since she saw Nim arrive on the island, but there was only one question that was truly important to her at that moment.

"Are my friends ok?" Sam rattled the question out faster than she could think of it.

Nim chuckled, "I was surprised you waited so long to ask. Yes, they are fine. They are on the way here now."

Her heart flipped. She sat up straighter in her seat. "Fin?"

"He's fine. I was there waiting for them to pass by. I healed him to the extent of my powers."

She let out a breath and gripped her steaming cup handle tighter. "Thank you." She looked down at her cup, her lip quivered. "I don't understand. Why are you helping us?" She swiped at her watery eyes.

"There are many reasons, reasons that you *need* to know, and reasons that you *cannot* know. Right now, the main reason is that you and your friends have a quest ahead of you."

Sam picked up mint and raspberries from a bowl and put them in her cup, then dripped honey into the steaming water. The spoon tinked against the sides as the honey dissolved and the water turned to the light pink color of berries.

Nim continued, "You are looking for Lyra. Your sea walker."

Sam's eyes shot up. "How-" She stopped herself. "You already knew that."

Nim's eyes twinkle with laughter. "Yes, I did. Do you know what her name means?"

Sam shook her head.

"It means Song of the Sea. Lyra is my descendant."

Sam's eyes widened.

"She is in danger, and you have been destined to help save her. That is why Muninn has been sending you into the dreamscape to speak with her. Lyra has been forced into a deep sleep."

"Why?"

"Her name was given to her because that is what she is. She *is* the Song of the Sea," Nim sighed. "When she was born, I could feel it ripple through the ocean. She isn't a Summoner like Sideon, but she has an interesting power that is new to the world. She can see the dance of water. It sings to her. She sees the currents flow in different colors. And it has made her a target."

Sam thought back to the forest and the soft voices that echoed through on the quietest days. She shifted in her seat.

"You seem powerful, though. Why can't you help?" She asked.

She was silent.

"I was told not to intervene, and that *someone* would show up at the time to help. Not long after, I felt your presence in Vineke," Nim responded.

"Who told you not to help your granddaughter?" she asked, baffled.

Nim looked at her again, then took a sip of her tea and said, "That is something you cannot know for now."

"Ok-" Sam started, upset by her answer. She pushed herself past it with another question. "What is the danger that me and my friends are going to have to face when we find Lyra?"

Sideon set down his cup to answer this time, "It is a beast of the sea, protective and monstrous. The Sotrolden."

Sam made a face. Nim's teacup clinked as she set it down on its plate also.

"It resembles the Kraken from our time," she added, releasing the air of confusion.

Sam didn't speak for a moment. "You mean-" She made a tentacle motion with her hand. "*The* Kraken? I thought it was a myth?"

"The original Elementals tried to keep out of the affairs of the four realms, but as you have seen so far, things from across old mythological cultures have slipped through." She sighed.

"Sam, I hope you are taking this seriously. If you can navigate the castle without being caught you will be fine. But this beast is dangerous, and I am not allowed to intervene. Sideon will come with you to help. However, I worry for Lyra." Nim's face grew even more concerned as she spoke.

Sam placed her hand over Nims. "I'm sure it'll be ok, especially if we added a lightning man to the group." She shot him a smile.

Sideon laughed, "Well, I will only join you for this short part, unfortunately I cannot go deeper into your realms."

"*My* realms?"

"Sideon is from the outer lands. He is not from the valley," Nim interjected. "The world is much bigger than just the protected realms."

"I guess I knew that."

"Are there any more questions you have? It is about time that you rest before your friends arrive."

Sam finished the last bit of her tea and felt the tart on her tongue. "When the pod of whales rescued me, I saw something big and metal in the water. What was that?"

Nim paused.

"That... was the fossilized remnants of our civilization."

16

PATHWAYS THROUGH THE DARK

"FROM THE ROOTS, TO THE WATER, AND
THE STARS, WE FIND REASONS TO BE
CONNECTED. SO WHY DO WE DEFY NATURE
AND PUSH OURSELVES APART?" -JORMUND,
6TH CENTURY

FIN TWITCHED NERVOUSLY. HIS tail flicked as his mind raced through the events of what happened the other night. Over and over again. Sam's distraught face stained his sight each time he closed his eyes.

Breathless and determined, he had been running after Toba for what felt like ages. Fin grimaced to himself at the thought of the thug. He followed him to the Oracles Court. After Toba went inside, he looked for a way in.

Fin closed his eyes.

That's when they found him. Then beat him mercilessly and took him to Barclay.

His hair stood on end, thinking about what Barclay had said. Fin scrunched his face together. The mere thought of Barclay's words to Sam filled him with repulsion, a mix of unsettling emotions that he desperately wanted to purge.

Going there was a mistake.

Agitated, Fin scratched at his leg, trying to resist the urge to touch or even look at the new scars covering his body. He looked down at the rest of the ship. Nim healed him, then she said they were to get their things and leave to her island as soon as possible. So that's what they did. Sam was there, waiting. At the thought, Fin's stomach dropped.

"Why are you being so weird?" Bram grunted as he climbed up the rope and sat next to him on the sails beam.

"Why would you care?" Fin retorted in the same tone.

Fin could feel Brams stare, and turned to meet it. He didn't need to answer his question out loud. Fin could see he was trying to find a common ground.

A sigh escaped his lips.

"Sorry, I'm not used to people actually *caring*." His mind jumped to his younger brothers and father back in the deep jungle.

"I don't know what Sam is going to say when she sees me. Is she going to be mad? I got us into this mess. Do you think she will kick me from the group?" Fin asked, turning to look at the sea and straining to see an island that had yet come into view.

"That's stupid."

Fin flashed him a look.

"Fin, I tried to *murder* you guys and I'm still here. It was a good thing I didn't, of course, but still, I think the bar to be kicked out would have to be pretty high."

"I guess-" Fin fidgeted again, unconvinced.

"We both know Sam. Do you *really* think that she would just drop you like that?" He asked, trying to emphasize his point.

"No, she wouldn't."

"Then why are you so worried?"

"I wanted to do something right. The whole group thinks I'm some goofball who can't handle anything." Fin took out one of his black pins, twisting it in his fingers.

"So, I felt like I needed to prove myself. Catching him would have made her see me differently. Then *I* got caught and-" He gripped his pin, wincing as he felt the pain arise. His healing wounds caught his eyesight again.

So many scars.

"Then *he* hurt her." He turned away, grimacing through his rigidness. "I'm- I'm just a burden."

"That's not true," Cedar's voice rang out sternly.

He kept his eyes shut, but could feel her settling on the beam to the other side of him. He looked down again, trying to avoid eye contact with either of them.

"No privacy at all." He cracked a trembling smile as he tried to persuade them and himself that he was alright.

"Sam loves you. She loves all of us. Do you know how my village treated her when she first arrived?" Cedar asked. "I was one of the first ones to see her climb out of the Forbidden Cave. Do you know how *I* treated her?" Cedar's voice cracked.

"I treated her like a monster. We *all* did." Her tone, full of shame.

"She came out. Only muddied skin and bones, barely able to stand, begging for someone to help her." Cedar gripped her jumper tightly. Her claws dug into her palm.

"And we ran away terrified of the monster that had shown itself. Then, when I was being attacked by a hog, she *still* helped me. She was weak and unable to stand properly, but she found a way to rescue me. I will never forget that day that she came into my life. She taught me to be stronger."

Cedar sighed as she tried to calm herself down, and in a much more leveled tone, she added. "Sam is not the type of person to dismiss others because of their mistakes."

Fin looked down at the crew below. Wandering about their business as they completed their jobs.

"Ya."

After another moment, Cedar spoke up. "I'm gonna go back down. Ajax looks like he is getting anxious down there by himself. And being up here *terrifies* me." She laughed as she climbed back down the twinned rope ladder.

"Im gonna go too," Bram said. He patted Fin's shoulder and left him to his thoughts.

On the cusp of the horizon, a small dot appeared.

Through narrowed eyes, he spotted the island they had been sailing towards. The thought of seeing Sam sent a wave of nausea through his stomach.

His tail flicked again. In frustration, he wrapped it securely around his waist and began his descent down to let the others know they were drawing near.

"I saw it," he said as he jumped the last two feet down from the ladder.

"Saw what?" Cedar asked as she pet Ajax and he rubbed up against her.

"The island we have been heading to this whole time, *duh*."

Cedar shot him a look. "Back to it already, huh?"

Fin smirked. "I'm done moping around and looking for a pity party. It's time to get some work done."

Bram and Cedar's eyes met, and they smiled. "It's good to see you feeling better," Bram added.

A thump sounded on the boat, and they rocked at a pace that didn't match the ocean waves. All three looked at each other for a moment as they tried to figure out what had happened. A bigger thump sounded, and they huddled to the side of the boat to find the source of the strange occurrence.

"There!" One of the fishermen called as he pointed into the waves.

The group peered over to see a large sea turtle bumping into the side of their boat. Pale green with a square pattern covering its shell. It thumped against the boat again.

"Hey!" Fin yelled down, "You're gonna hurt yourself, stop."

The turtle looked up at him, and when it did, they saw that there was a bottle with a note strapped to its neck.

"Drop anchor! We'll stop here!" the Captain hollered to his crew.

The ship slowed and came to a stop as it continued to rock back and forth in the waves. The Captain used a pole to grab the bottle and broke it over the sea. Once he pulled the note out, he looked at it for a moment and then handed it to Fin as he began blasting orders to his crew.

Fin took the note and they read it. Huddling over it and fighting for space to inspect it.

"It says that the turtle will take us the rest of the way." He looked up and handed it to Bram.

Bram denied the paper. "I believe you."

Cedar rolled her eyes and snatched up the parchment. "Ya, because you can't read." Then she read it.

Fin's eyes widened, a smile caked across his entire face as he stared at Bram. "I'm sorry... what did she just say?" He barely managed through his laugh.

"Cedar," Bram huffed as he turned, "you didn't have to tell him."

"It does say the turtle will take us the rest of the way. I guess we need to get our stuff and Ajax and load up."

"When were you going to tell me you couldn't read?" Fin leaned in, trying to pester him.

"Never! You were never going to know that." Bram threw his hands into the air and walked off towards the bunker below. "And just so you know-" He shot back around and paused as Fin guffawed at him. "Sam also can barely write. So-there… do with that what you will."

Fin turned to Cedar for acknowledgement. She looked at him blankly for a moment and then pursed her lips, nodding slightly. At that, Fin burst into roaring tears.

"How can not one, but *two* of our group not know how to read and write?" He wiped the tears from his eyes.

"Don't be rude or I'm going to make you teach them." Cedar furrowed her brow.

"This is *too* much." He breathed through his laughter.

"Get your stuff dummy, we are leaving in five." Cedar huffed and turned towards the stairs and followed where Bram had disappeared below.

Playfully, Ajax trotted up next to him and swatted at him with his growing antlers.

"Not you too!" Fin said in amusement. "How can I be the only one to find this *hilarious?*" he said as Ajax ushered him to the stairs and into the room where they all stayed.

Soon they were packed and being lowered down to the turtle in a rowboat. As they hit the water, they rocked harshly. Fin grabbed the sides and waited for the boat to steady before he picked up the oar laying next to his feet and began rowing.

"I guess this turtle is going to be our guide the rest of the way," Cedar stated as she pet it.

"I guess so." Fin joined her and could feel the furry algae growing on its tough exterior.

"Let's get there so we can see Sam." Bram picked up the other oar, and they turned the tip of the boat to follow the turtle.

Every once in a while, it would turn to check on them, but continue on its way. Fin saw the small speck of the island from the top of the boat, but there, amongst the waves, he saw nothing but water and sky.

They swapped turns on rowing between the three of them a couple of times before Fin could see the island. After spending a couple more hours and with the sun gradually sinking in the sky, they reached their destination and obediently followed the turtle onto the warm sands of the small island.

"I can't believe we made it," Fin said, exhausted as the three of them dragged the rowboat through the sand.

"It's going to be night soon." Bram looked back out the way they came.

Ajax bleated, stumbling awkwardly out of the boat. When he caught his footing, he jumped through the sand. Carefully navigating his steps, he maneuvered towards the softness of the grass.

Fin finally saw what Ajax was struggling to get to. He sucked in a breath.

"Sam."

"They are here." Nim said.

Sam looked up from her tea, and Nim gestured to the back door. With the scraping of the legs on the tiled flooring, she scrambled out of her chair. She scurried to the large back door with the glass carved into it and peeked out of one of the top glass pieces. Ajax ran towards the house with Fin, Cedar, and Bram struggling to drag the boat aboard. She snorted and cracked a smile at the common shenanigans of the group. As she did, she noticed a large sea turtle scuttling up the beach with them.

"Who's that Nim? Another one of your helpers?" she asked, glancing back at her.

She joined her by the window. "That is Jilla. She is in training, so I asked her to go find the boat that was bringing them and escort them the rest of the way. She is beautiful, isn't she?" Nim smiled happily.

"I didn't know turtles got that big. She looks longer than Ajax," Sam said in awe.

"She is just a baby right now, but I'm wondering why you're wasting time talking about sea turtles when we both know you want to see your friends." Nim looked at her with a mischievous twinkle in her eye.

Sam glanced at the doorknob, then back to Nim. Understanding the unspoken question, Nim nodded and Sam turned the knob. With a burst of energy, she bounded onto the patio and began leaping from stepping stone to stepping stone. Her heart pounding with the thrill of the imaginary lava beneath her. Once she made it to the sand, she ran faster, making her way to her friends.

"Hey! You guysss!" She waved her hand in the air. Fin had already seen her, but Cedar and Bram stopped. A smile formed across each of their faces, and Cedar ran to meet her.

Her hand brushed against Ajax as she passed him. He happily bleated and leaped as he returned from the grass to join them back on the sand.

"Ajax, I missed you so much buddy!" Sam grabbed him with her body, hugging him ferociously.

"Sam!" Cedar had caught up to the two of them and hooked on to her at full speed.

Sam grunted as they fell backwards, laughing in the sand together.

"I can't believe you're alive!"

"You're one of the *luckiest* people I've ever met." Bram came up and helped them stand. As they stood, Fin walked over, joining them.

"Sam." He swallowed.

She paused and observed him, noticing that he not only seemed better but appeared healed.

"You look.. different.. since the last time I saw you." Her smile faltered. His body. She ran her hand slowly over the raised scars that now decorated his arms.

She choked back her pain. "Fin- I-"

"I feel better now... that we finally got back to you," he chuckled, putting his hand reassuringly over hers and squeezing it lightly.

Sam forced the tears down. Blinking past her regrets.

"Me too." She wiped the tear from her cheek.

"I am so glad you were finally able to make it to my home," Nim started from behind Sam.

Sam turned to look at her, and Nim added. "I think you deserve a rest while we catch up on the next step of the plan."

They walked up the steps and through the door to the back of the cottage. Sam could see Sideon waiting for them in the living room.

"It's good to finally meet the friends of Sam that I have heard so much about." Sideon gestured to the couch and the other cushions around the room. "Please sit. I will get you some tea."

As they walked in, Cedar whispered to Sam, "Who's that?"

"That's Sideon. He is the one who rescued me... well, Lahs the whale rescued me, but Sideon picked me up." Sam said.

Bewildered, Cedar looked at her with a puzzled expression. Sam waved off the comment.

"I'll tell you later," she whispered back.

Cedar nodded, and Sam glanced at Bram and Fin to see how they were faring. Bram seemed to try to get comfortable on a thick cushion that sat on the floor while Fin leaned against the wall, taking in his surroundings.

Sideon brought them cups, and just like before. Nim let boiling water float through the air into them. After letting them steep for a couple minutes, they were ready to be sipped on.

"So... Sam, would you like to catch up with them and after go over the plan to save Lyra?" Nim asked.

Sam nodded and told them everything that had happened from the time that she had been shot into the ocean to the moment she saw them beached with Jilla, the sea turtle. Night had fallen on the island and several cups of tea had been steeped by the time the group was caught up with her.

"Wait," Fin interjected, "you know Sam's past, but you're not allowed to tell her." He made a face at Sam, then looked back to Nim for an answer.

"Fin, don't be rude," Sam said in embarrassment, her cheeks flushing.

Nim held up her hand, "No, he's right Sam. I'm sorry that I can't help you with any of it. But I have been told that I cannot interject or indulge in the past because it could divert from the plan."

"Basically, it is out of her hands," Sideon added, shrugging.

"That being said," he stood and stretched, "it is going to be time to leave soon."

"Pearls Gate." Sam repeated the name as she imagined what the Reef would look like.

"Sideon and I must go over the plans here before you all leave, so if you'd like, you can roam the island or the cottage until it is time to go." Nim gestured to the starry night outside.

Sam stood, "Do y'all want to go to the beach for our last peaceful night?" She started for the doors and the others joined her.

"We'll be down at the beach if you need us." Sam smiled at Sideon and Nim as she shut the door behind her and they made their way back down to the ocean.

The group settled into the sand and Sam wiggled her feet into where she could only see her ankles and she felt each grain between her toes. They stared out at the lapping water as the soft noise of the waves lulled them into a calm demeanor.

"I missed you guys," she sighed and leaned back to lie in the sand and look up at the bright stars. Fin on one side, Cedar and Bram on the other.

"We missed you too, Sammi." Cedar grabbed her hand and squeezed it.

Sam approached the limitless wall. "Lyra!" she yelled at it excitedly.

"Sam?" Her voice sounded unsure at first.

"You're back! You've been gone for such a long time!" she cried out in dismay, "I thought I'd never hear from you again."

Sam sat cross-legged and faced the wall. The one piece of coral still lit up from the time before.

"Well... There was a close call, but it turned out alright." Sam stopped for a moment, hesitating. "Your- grandmother, Nim, saved me from drowning at sea."

"What?! You almost died? What happened?" Her voice sounded shocked.

Sam caught her up on everything that happened in Anchor with Barclay. Once she told her about Sideon, the island, and her ancestor Nim, Sam stopped and waited for Lyra to respond.

"I'm glad that she was able to help you, then. I don't see her much, so I'm a little surprised that she knew I was in trouble at all," Lyra said quietly, her voice softening behind the wall.

"Lyra- she called you the Song of the Sea. Do you know anything about that?" Sam leaned forward, waiting.

"Yes, I can see the currents and movements of the ocean. When I was a child, I thought everyone could see the different colors moving around like streams of rivers in the water, but then Nim came to me and told me what it truly was," she paused for a moment, then added, "it doesn't do much. I can blur it in and out so the colors aren't extreme, but other than that, I don't have that much use for it."

Sam nodded, thinking about what she said. It was quiet.

Lyra was quiet.

"Lyra?" Sam called out.

"Sam, I don't think you should come."

Sam blinked, baffled. "What?" She breathed out. "That's nonsense."

"The Sotrolden is a terrible monster of the sea. I can't have someone getting hurt on my accord. Especially a group of people that I have grown fond of." Lyra's voice cracked. "You have told me so much about your band of misfits. I imagine myself going on adventures with you, when there is nothing but my own imagination to keep me company.... Now that you are actually on the way, I couldn't bear it if something happened to any of you."

Sam could hear the quiet tears in her voice. She restrained herself as she tried to decide what she was going to say.

"I'm sorry that you've been trapped here." Sam stood, walking to the coral wall. She placed her hand on a piece and a light blue color lit up.

"We're coming for you Lyra. Nothing is going to stop us" Another coral lit up purple towards the top of the wall. As she stared at it, wondering how one so high up and away could light up without being touched, a thought occurred to her.

"The Sotrolden is monstrous. But we have a Fire Summoner and now a lightning one too." Her mind flashed to Cedar and Sideon, and a smile formed on her face. More coral lit themselves.

"An obnoxious thief and a fighter that matches no one." The wall became dotted with the colorful coral as she imagined Bram and Fin.

"Then me and my trusted partner, who won't stop fighting until our friends are safe." Her mind went to Ajax and she could see that the wall was almost completely covered in glowing coral now.

"And to top it off, we have someone who can see things no one else can. They see pathways through the dark. All they need... is someone to believe in them."

The wall glowed brighter. It was complete. Cracks formed, starting from tiny bits and growing larger as Sam faded backwards into the void.

"Lyra! I think you're waking up! We will find you! Stay in Pearls Gate." Sam called as loud as she could. Hoping her voice reached her friend.

"Sammm!" She could hear her calling from a distance. "Thank you!" Lyra's voice stretched into the nothingness as she watched the impenetrable wall crumble into dust because of the resilient mind of their sea walker.

17

TO SAVE A SONG

WHERE DID THE ELEMENTALS GO?

LYRA WOKE, BLINKING INTO the lights. Gingerly, she sat, her consciousness grabbing at the long awaited reality of her bedroom before her. She scanned her surroundings, feeling the soft silk bed sheets beneath her fingertips. She saw her mirror and desk with the many pens and papers she used to write letters with. Her coral armor hung on her blue room divider and noticed that it had been recently filed down.

They had been taking care of her armor while she slept.

Her Damascus tipped spear, leaned delicately against it, left there, awaiting her return. Groggily, she turned towards the far wall where her bay window sat, the window was left open for the air to cycle in the room. A stack of books piled high. And, as always, one less book from toppling over.

She swallowed, her mouth dry from the unknown amount of time she spent asleep and her head beginning to spike from the dehydration. Her long legs dropped to the rug that shielded her from the cold marble. Lyra reached for the glass cup of water that sat on her table side and she sipped at it eagerly until the glass was emptied. By accident, she carelessly returned it to the table, only to watch it teeter and then plummet to the marbled flooring, where it shattered into countless glimmering shards.

She winced as voices arose from outside her door and she stumbled to stand. Weakly gripping the side of the bed, she mustered the strength to push herself up. Soon after, her bedroom door opened and two guards dressed in similar coral armor came in. As they saw Lyra awake, one hurried to her side, assisting her, as the other yelled out the door.

"She's awake! Song Lyra's awake! Message for the Dowager and call the Medic!" he yelled out.

"No," she croaked, her voice stale from under-use.

She coughed for a moment, then repeated herself in a stern voice. "No, belay that order."

The guard at the door hesitated for a moment, then called out. "Cancel that order. We were mistaken."

"Song Lyra, what do you mean? You have been asleep for months. Why should we not call for the doctor?" The guard asked shocked as she sat back on the bed.

She looked at them both individually before stating, "There is something wrong in Pearls Gate. I did not *fall* asleep. I was *put* to sleep by someone here."

The guards looked at each other.

Then she added, "I need food, please, and I need help to get into my armor, but *no one* must know I am awake. Do you understand?"

She locked eyes with them briefly before they both nodded in unison.

Lyra breathed a sigh of relief. "Thank you. What are your names?"

"This is Ermas," the guard next to her pointed to the other guard. "I'm Tark."

She nodded. "Ermas, can you get me some food and water, please? Tark, grab my armor."

Ermas headed out to the hallway. She could hear him yelling for fruits and bread as Tark gathered her armor and brought it to her. He handed her the chest piece first and put the other pieces on the bed as they waited for Ermas and the food.

Lyra ran her hand over her armor. She could tell that it had been filled and smoothed, kept in the correct condition that a soldier should keep it in.

"Who has been keeping it clean?" she asked, looking up at him.

"The guards on weekly duty have been assigned to keep it filed and polished. Is it adequate?"

"Yes, it's perfect, thank you."

Ermas came into the room. In one hand, he held a plate of bread, fruits, and cheeses, then in the other, a vase of water. He placed it on the table and stood back with Tark.

"Thank you both," she said tiredly. "Could you guard the door while I eat and change?"

"Ma'am." They stood alert before turning, then left, closing the heavy door behind them.

After patiently waiting for the door to be completely shut, she seized the pear on the porcelain plate and took a massive bite. As the juice from the pear dripped down her chin, she hurriedly poured herself another glass of water and gulped it down. Her body craved the food in front of her as she tried to restrain herself from eating too fast and getting sick.

After she had wiped the plate clean of all food and the vase was half empty, she stood and stretched her body. All of her muscles ached and called out to her in strained agony. She stood and took the black skin suit off the bed and swapped it for her sleeping tunic. Next, she slipped into her brown pants and once she had the base of her armor on, she grabbed her chest piece and slipped it over her head while pulling out her long hair from under the piece. Then she grabbed the shoulder and side pieces and clasped them to her chest.

Lyra shuffled around in her old suit, trying to regain normality. She glimpsed herself in the mirror and stood appalled at the mass of salmon colored hair that surrounded her and dropped to her thighs.

She looked like she had slept for longer than a couple of months.

With a sigh, she settled into her chair and reached for her brush, feeling the bristles against her scalp as she carefully pulled her hair back into a neat ponytail. After it was up, she braided her dangling hair into different braided strands. She stood, admiring it, now shorter and less disastrous. Lyra took in her reflection. She was taller and leaner than most, with her skin a coral blue and her hair colored in salmon. She stuck out like a sore thumb. As she nervously chewed on the inside of her lip, her fingers absentmindedly played with the freshly braided strands of hair.

How was she supposed to move around unnoticed?

Her eyes traveled downward to a book that lay on her dresser with a bow wrapped around it. She brushed off the ribbon. It read, '*Stories of the First and his comrades, History of the First King*'.

The front was edged in silver outlines of a landscape in the background and in the foreground were the outlines of the First King, King Arthur, and his comrades. Lyra ran her fingers over the engraved images, tracing the outlines. She opened the book and found a note written to her on the first page.

Lyra,

We wait for the day you awaken, but in this time that you sleep, here are the stories you have loved since you were a child.

Sincerely,

Akros, Adviser to the Dowager Queen

She sighed again, uncertain now of anyone she could trust. Her eyes lingered on the First King, depicted in the book with his battle armor, the intricate details etched into the leather catching her attention. At that, a thought came to her.

Carefully using a book holster to attach it snugly to one of her belt loops, she walked over to her bay window and opened a hidden compartment underneath. Hesitantly, she reached into the silver and gold adorned chest and pulled out an overgrown coral helmet, the remnants of a forgotten era.

Dad.

Lyra examined it and saw that the metal lining was still intact. No coral had penetrated the inside. It was safe to wear. She also pulled out a large folded white cloak that engulfed the majority of her body when she put it on.

After collecting herself, she positioned the helmet on her head and stared at her own reflection in the mirror. Lyra's two most obvious outliers were hidden by the cape and the helmet.

No one would know she woke up. Lyra would be just another soldier walking the halls.

The sun was rising on the ocean, glistening sparkles dashed off the waves that rocked Sideon's fishing vessel gently from side to side. He had woken them up not too long ago, letting them know that they had arrived. As they left their temporary quarters, they were met with Pearls Gate.

Sam could see portions of the castle sticking out of the water. It was made of smoothed white marble with coral accents dotting the exterior of the shimmering palace. From the edge, Sam's gaze fell upon the castle below, its imposing presence accentuated by the vast reef garden that embellished its lower walls and stretched out into the distance. She also saw a marbled dock with a large arched entryway. Many boats were docked and guards monitored those who entered and exited through their post.

"That's- Pearls Gate?" Sam asked in astonishment as she took in the vision of magnificence before her.

"Yep. A true beauty," Sideon said, standing next to her.

"It's a castle," Cedar said.

"That's half submerged in the ocean?" Bram added.

"Yep," Sideon repeated himself. He rocked back on his heels and went into the captain's quarters, then returned with five aquabreaths.

"So, we will be needing these for our search." He handed one to each of them.

"Not again," she groaned as Sideon dropped it into her hands mercilessly.

Cedar whined as well while Bram remained quiet in his fate.

"What's so bad about the aquabreaths?" Fin asked as he shifted it in his hands.

"Ya, I forgot, you weren't there when we searched the reef of Anchor." Cedar flashed a sly smile at Sam. "It will be his first time experiencing *it*."

Fin scowled, "*it*? What's *it*?"

"All you need to know is we will be right there if you need us." Sam said, giving him a pity smile.

"Remember guys, we are here to find Lyra. Sam told us that she is awake now. We are not here to fight the Sotrolden unless we have to." Through his brow, he glanced back and forth between the four of them.

Bram put his hands up innocently. "We don't randomly pick fights with people... at least not anymore." He scratched his chin while laughing at what he had said.

Sideon shook his head, "Ok, well, the plan is to go to Pearls Gate, search the top half and if no luck then we use the aquabreaths and search the bottom."

"We can just walk in? That doesn't seem right..." Cedar looked at him, concerned.

"You can, if you have this." Sideon flashed a crooked smile while taking out a metal token as big as his palm with a circular wave symbol on it.

"And that is?..." Fin asked, waving his hand for an explanation.

"This is the semblance of Nim. It shows that we are here for her and are welcomed," he said.

"But still, it would be good not to draw attention to ourselves." Sam added as she strapped on the fresh aquabreath and adjusted it comfortably around her neck.

The others nodded in agreement. Cedar dug through her bag for a moment.

"Here." She pulled out both Sam's fox mask and Bram's dog mask. They took them. Sam stared at hers for a moment as she imagined the last time she wore it before running into Barclay.

As she took a deep breath, she could feel the cool breeze against her, refreshing her senses. With the mask on and her staff clipped to her back, she felt strangely whole again in that moment. Her knuckles rapped on her chest piece, and she felt more confident in their plight against the odds of finding Lyra and having to handle the Sotrolden.

"We can do this, one step at a time," Sam said as the ship bumped against the dock of the upper castle.

She stood on the bridge as she gathered the courage to take the first step. Ajax bleated from behind her. She turned to see him staring up at her expectantly.

"No, Ajax, I'm sorry, this mission isn't for you. You're gonna have to stay with the ship for now, alright?" She kneeled down in front of him and rustled his head. He stared at her, disappointed, but then laid down next to the helmsman.

Bram made it down the stairs with Fin and Sideon.

"Ready?" Cedar asked her.

Sam nodded, and they headed down together. They walked through the boat dock, passing the crates, barrels, and busy faus.

"Reason for visit?" The guards barked, blocking the group's path with both of their spears.

"We are here as messengers of Nim." Sideon bowed his head slightly and flashed the symbol of the sea quickly.

The guards snorted and looked at each other. "Ya. Sure... Messengers. What's your message?"

"We are here to leave a letter and gifts for Song Lyra from her ancestor Nim, the Lady in the Water." Sideon kept his head down. The guards looked past his shoulder to the four of them that had stayed quiet.

Sam turned her head, avoiding eye contact with the guards. Cedar shifted uncomfortably.

"Hmph, where's your pass?" he asked, annoyed by the prolonged conversation.

Sideon brought out a letter and gave them the token he had shown them earlier. The guard inspected it with a scowl. Time passed. Sam glanced up to see him thoroughly examining the letter. It grew hotter by the second under the mask as beads of sweat formed on her temple and forehead.

"You may enter," he said flatly as he moved his spear aside. The other did the same.

They walked through. Sam sighed in relief once they had cleared their first obstacle.

"We're in, now what?" Fin hissed to Sideon.

"We head to her room," he shrugged. "it's in the upper castle, up the side stairwell to the left and down the hallway. Most of the more important people live either high up or on the seabed." He motioned the pathway to her room that Nim had mapped out.

"If she is not there, then what?" Sam asked.

"We search around, making our way down into the lower castle to the Master Advisor's room. Lyra is his apprentice, so if she isn't in her room, then she's there."

Sam nodded.

"This way," he said as he started down the long hallway that was designed similar to the exterior of the castle. Sam noticed, however, that there were slight engravings in the walls that depicted sea creatures swimming.

"The animals on the wall swim that way, though," Sam remarked.

"That way is the throne room for the royal who occupies the castle. That is *most definitely* not the way we need to go," he added sarcastically.

"Royals, who occupy the castle?" Bram repeated Sideon's wording and made a face at Cedar.

Sideon groaned, "Yes, when someone from the Realm of Sea marries a High King or High Queen of the four realms then this is their home along with their family members. The Dowager Queen lives here by herself right now. She is the protector of the sea and councils with the High King." He stopped and turned to face them. "The Sotrolden is also the protector of the sea, but once Song Lyra fell into her slumber, Nim and I learned of a plot to manipulate them both for power." He swiveled and continued his way down the hallway.

Eeriness took Sam, the hair on the back of her neck raised. Every few minutes, she would glance over her shoulder, her eyes darting around as if she sensed a presence.

They reached the stairs when heavy footsteps rushed down them. Sideon ushered them to the side, hiding against the curved walls as a tall soldier clad in a white cloak and coral armor rushed passed. As the guard continued on without noticing them, they hurried silently up the stairs.

"That's a nice spear they had." Fin's eyes sparkled mischievously as he grinned at Sam.

She groaned, rolling her eyes and slapped him with the motherly look of disappointment. "Please don't."

"She isn't anywhere in the upper castle, but we haven't checked the throne room yet." Sam looked expectantly towards Sideon.

He grimaced, understanding that it meant to at least risk a peek inside to see if they could spot her.

"Alright, but only one of us and just... *sooo* quickly please," he responded urgently.

Before the others could have time to volunteer, Sam raised her hand and waved it back and forth in silent excitement. She grinned at him as he tried to convince himself that this was a good idea.

"Fine- fine, hurry," he said, exasperated.

Sam took that as a personal victory and scuttled to the large arched doors that mimicked the entryway to the dock. The sun pierced through a veil of spotted clouds and shone on the doors. Hesitantly, she looked at the others for confirmation. In perfect synchronization, the rest of the group nodded urgently and waved her off. Sam delicately turned the knob and opened the right door, which emitted a faint creak. Once the gap was big enough for her to poke her head through, she peeked in.

The throne room was a massive circular room with marbled walls and pillars supporting the roof above. In the center was also a gigantic circular pool that lapped around its shallow edges as the fountain did in Anchor.

That must lead to the lower parts of the castle.

Cautiously eyeing it for a moment, she followed her gaze to the two thrones that sat on the opposite end of the room. One taller, one shorter, both carved marble with coral engraved into them. They were similar to the pillars and the circular room was engraved with sea creatures of their actual life size as they swam around the entire wall. In the group of engraved sea animals, she noticed first the whales, dolphins, sharks, manta rays, whale sharks, and orcas. The smaller creatures, clustered together, in a multitude of numbers. Tiny seahorses near her, fish of the reef, jellyfish, an octopus here and there. She spotted a few mermaids etched in with the circling animals, and even a pair of otters danced in the water.

The room of majesty shrouded Sam's thoughts as she continued to marvel at the circular engravings and its plentiful creatures. A tap rapped on her shoulder, drawing her back to what she was supposed to do. She drew her head out of the door and saw Cedar was next to her.

"What's going on? Is there anyone there?" she asked softly.

Sam shook her head as she straightened up. "No. I got distracted by the carvings on the walls, and the room." She blushed a little.

Bram rolled his eyes.

"Goodness me, we have an enthusiast for pretty walls," Fin snorted.

"And roofs, and floors, don't forget the roofs and floors." Sam shot him a look, then cracked a smile.

"Well, if no one is in there, I want to take a look. Might as well, right?" Cedar said as she pushed through Sam. Fin and Bram silently agreed as they followed her in.

"Wait- but..." Sideon pleaded to an empty audience.

Sam gave him an understanding look of pity, "they never listen, do they?" she said as she turned and followed them in.

Sideon closed the door behind them, and the group wandered into the room in awe of its features.

"Wow, Sammi, you were right, this room is gorgeous." Cedar cooed as her eyes sparkled with delight.

They walked towards the center where the water called to them.

"There are even thrones in here for them, look." Fin pointed to the thrones across from them and the pool of water.

"Fin, it's a *throne*... room, there's going to be thrones in a throne room," Bram emphasized.

Fin made a mimicking face at Bram, but stayed silent. Cedar's soft laugh echoed in the massive chamber.

"Let's head out to the stairs for the lower levels. This room might be empty, but I know that the throne room below is not." Sideon pointed to the gaping hole in the center.

As Sam stared at the water, her imagination painted a vivid picture of a throne room below, complete with its guardian lurking in the shadows. A shiver ran up her spine and she grabbed Cedar by her elbow.

"I think it's time we moved on," Sam said, jabbing her thumb towards the doors behind them.

"Fine, fine. Someone's scared," Fin teased as they started that way.

As Sideon reached for the door, a gong sounded in the distance, high above them. He turned, panic growing across his face. He looked at each of them and locked eyes with Sam last.

"That's not good."

18

WHAT LIES BENEATH

AN ELEMENTAL AND A SUMMONER ARE TWO
DIFFERENT ABILITIES.

SHE TOOK A HESITANT step back.

"How did they find us?"

"I don't know. We had the token. I thought we were set. Someone must have seen us come in here." He shot a look at Sam as he backed up next to her.

All eyes stayed plastered to the door. The gong rang five times, each echoing over itself until it died out. They waited for guards to bust through the throne room doors.

A bead of sweat dripped down Sam's face. She could feel the palpable tension in the air as everyone hovered above their weapons. The rowdy steps of soldiers grew louder by the second. In an effort to calm down, Sam focused on releasing the tension in her muscles.

As the footsteps grew to their loudest, Sideon put himself into a fighting stance. The others, seeing this, readied themselves as well. She sucked in a short breath, then held it. Focused on the clanging of metal boots colliding with the marbled floors.

Then, as they grew, they faded, becoming more and more distant. Sam imagined the soldiers that paired with the noises of scraping metal disappearing down the hallway and then it was quiet.

"Wha-" Cedar started.

Sideon raised his hand, signifying silence. He turned his head to the side to get a glance of the four of them behind him. "It could be a trap," he said in a steady and low tone.

They waited. Minutes passed.

Sam's heartbeat drummed in her ears.

Nothing.

She relaxed, releasing herself from the protective stance. "I think we're good."

Out of nowhere, Sideon and Cedar collided with the floor, causing a loud thud that reverberated through the marbled room. Sam jumped back in surprise. When she turned sideways, she saw what made them fall.

As fast as they had hit the ground, Cedar and Sideon were dragged backwards and flung high into the air above the two thrones and above the entrance to the lower room. A massive tentacle wrapped around both their feet and dangled them far above.

A plethora of thick, slimy tentacles the color of purple mud and seaweed snuck their way out of the pool, and slithered across the floor towards the other three. The Sotrolden found them, its massive mud brown and dark purple balloon head stuck out but Sam couldn't see its face under the rippling water. Her instinct told her that the eyes were stapled to them though, the enemy.

Cedar and Sideon's battle had already begun, while Cedar threw fire at it in aimless panic. Sideon grabbed for any parts he could electrocute.

Fin grunted, stepping to the side and slicing through a tentacle that was heading towards him.

"Why did it have to grab *both* of the Summoners?" Bram groaned agitatedly.

"Because that's *our* type of luck," Sam grunted as a larger tentacle lifted itself and fell on her. Her staff held it off. Twisting the golden rod around the tentacle, she threw it to the ground. Unsheathing her lotus dagger from the small of her back, she sliced outward, cutting it. Without hesitation, she mercilessly thrust the blade into yet another appendage that came towards her. Purple blood splattered everywhere. The tentacle retracted into itself, writhing in pain, and retreated into the water below. Only for another one to take its place.

The three of them fought their ground as the two hanging high above the water tried to escape.

"Sammm! I could use some help here!" Cedar yelled, her voice wavering as she was thrown back and forth by the largest tentacle. Sam examined her surroundings. Her body itching to race towards her. Cedar clutched onto the wet rubbery skin and burned a hole through it.

In response, each of the tentacles became more sporadic and frenzied. The room shook for a moment and a deep howl rang out from underneath them. Dread filled Sam as the tentacles started retracting in multitudes.

Cedar yelled, but she was cut short as the tentacles that had her and Sideon dropped almost weightlessly into the water, taking them with it. In only a couple of moments, it had arrived and then completely disappeared, leaving only a few bits of sliced tentacles and blood as evidence of its existence.

"Cedar, Sideon!" Sam yelled breathlessly. The group ran closer to the pool but stopped short.

She stood, catching her breath as she knew what they had to do. She fumbled for the aquabreath around her neck and paused momentarily. Sam saw Bram and Fin doing the same and stopped them.

"Fin- you haven't done the aquabreath yet. Maybe you should stay here." Sam put her hand on his mask to keep him from putting it on.

"What?" He looked at them, confused.

"It was overwhelming when we put it on for the first time and you haven't experienced it yet," her words stumbled out in a haste.

"No way, I'm helping!"

Sam saw desperation in his eyes. "I am not going to be completely useless on this journey, first Barclay, and now you're telling me to... to what? Sit here and watch my friends get killed by *that*?!" His face scrunched in torment.

"That's not what I meant..." She lowered her gaze to the floor.

He grumbled, "I'm sorry, but we need to help Cedar. Don't worry about me." He gave her a crooked smile.

Gradually, her hand slipped off his mask, and she nodded. "Ok."

"I don't want to rush this, but they are still under," Bram prompted.

Fin looked at him. He felt the mask's gelatinous texture as he carefully wrapped it around his face, shutting his eyes tight.

Sam looked at Bram and gestured to the water. "You go, I'll help him."

"Good luck." Bram said sarcastically as he glanced towards Fin, then back at her.

He jogged over to the pool and looked back towards them before diving and disappearing into the throne room beneath.

Fin collapsed to the floor, trembling. Sam kneeled over him, trying to reassure him.

"It'll be over in a second. Just breathe, Fin, breathe." She wrapped her arm around his back and glanced worriedly towards the watery entrance. He grabbed her forearm and Sam brought her attention back to his struggle, in doing so, she didn't notice the other tentacle sneak its way out.

Before she could think or react, it had wrapped itself around her leg. Briskly yanking her away from Fin. As she hit the ground, her elbow took the brunt of the fall. She cried out in agony. Pain coursing through her arm.

"Fin!" Sam yelled, straining for his hand. With one hand trying to rip off his mask and the other reaching for her, Fin grasped her fingertips as she felt the water soaking her lower body.

She choked out a sob in desperation and fear as she disappeared into the room below. Water filled her mouth. The final image that burned into her mind was the massive marbled doors swinging open.

"Akros!" Lyra called from the doorway. It creaked open the rest of the way to reveal an empty and darkened *Office of the Royals Advisor*. She shut the door, plunging herself into darkness, and she stumbled forward, the weight of her armor clanking loudly with each movement. It was not stealthy at all.

She grumbled to herself.

The room was medium-sized. Designed to the liking of Akros with stars and constellations painted on the walls while the collection of books, and other worldly items he found of interest decorated the area. There was a door in the right corner that led to a short set of winding stairs and his chambers. Then to the left was a cluster of windows looking out to the reef gardens. The sunlight streamed in and danced through the waves onto the walls and into the room.

She made her way past the deep blue velvet chairs studded with round metal pieces on the edges. An off placed letter caught her eye, but what truly made her interest peak was the name it was addressed from.

It read.

To: Akros, Master Advisor of the Dowager Queen
From: Barclay

Barclay? The Oracle turned rogue? Sam mentioned him.

Lyra picked up the letter, feeling the soft paper under her fingers. She popped open an odd wax crest seal of a shark circling itself and noticed it had already been opened. Unfurled and flattened in her fingers, she read the letter.

Her eyes widened. She swallowed, feeling a lump in her throat, and took a shallow breath to steady herself.

He betrayed them. He betrayed her.

Akros had written back and forth with Barclay to conspire for Pearls Gate.

He wants to take the threshold farthest from to the King's Realm.

"How could he do this to us?" her voice trembled as she spoke out loud.

"This- This can't be possible," she shook her head.

How was he supposed to overcome the Dowager Queen? He would still have to find a reason as to why he would become king.

"It's very much possible Song Lyra," a voice called from behind her.

She hadn't heard the door open.

"I see you've awakened."

She swiveled, panicked.

He was standing in the doorway between her and the way out.

"Akros," her voice cracked. She gripped the paper in one hand, while her other fell to her side. "How *could* you do this to us?" Her voice pleaded for a reason behind the betrayal.

"Do what?" He challenged her to speak the unspoken.

She flashed the letter before folding it and stuffing it in her armor.

"I wouldn't do that if I were you." His eyes darkened as he stepped into the room.

An uneasy feeling settled in the pit of her stomach. She added, "What was your plan? After you murdered her, how were you going to explain what happened to the High King and the Royals from the other realms?" she asked sternly, placing her spear between the two of them.

"Well," he started, closing the door behind him and walking calmly through the room to a table by the windows. Akros opened a chest that sat small and unnoticed. Delicately he took out a vial that held a shimmering black liquid swirling in it.

"I have been experimenting on the special effects and uses of the Sotroldens' ink and venom and have found many *fascinating* things about it." He smiled and held it up. "It can be a powerful hallucinogenic. It can also be a lethal poison to end a life. But do you know the most *interesting* benefit that I have found?" He looked at her. Her stomach churned and her eyes watered. "Mixed with specific plants, it can put someone permanently to sleep, well... a *normal* fau, that is," he said flatly.

She shook her head in defiance. "How could you do this?" Tears brimmed her eyes as they forced an escape.

"Barclay and I have decided we no longer want the lives we have been settled with. It's time for a change in leadership," he hissed. In his hand, he held two small throwing knives, their blades dripping with a sleek, black glaze.

"And we can't have the Lady in the Water or her descendant interfering with our plans." He shot one dagger at her. She jerked to the side. It collided with her shoulder. Dazed by the dagger's clanging echo, Lyra reached up to the gash. Her fingers brushed against jagged coral embedded in her skin, and she winced. The black ink smeared across her hand and glistened in the dim light.

Backing away, she stumbled into a chair and crashed to the floor. Akros was on her in an instant, closing the distance with deadly intent, his dagger raised to strike again.

Adrenaline surged through her veins. She swung her spear wildly, forcing him to falter, his steps hesitating just enough for her to scramble back. Her free hand searched frantically, desperate for anything, fingers finding the chair she'd fallen over. Fueled by rage and survival, she hurled it with all her strength.

The impact knocked Akros to the ground with a grunt.

Lyra staggered to her feet, her chest heaving. She spared one last, fleeting look at the man she once called a friend.

Then she ran.

Halfway down the hall, she heard his voice echoing through the corridor.

"Guards! Guards! Song Lyra is awake and is to be arrested for treason against the High King and Dowager Queen! Guards!" His orders sounded through the vast empty hallway with the sound of her feet. Akros rang the bell that hung on his wall.. The clambering of soldiers started their way.

No.

She paused, trying to find a way through the maze of questions, answers, and paths that ran through her head, blocking her train of thought.

They rounded the corner.

"Attack on sight! She is armed and dangerous!" Akros bellowed out, pointing towards her.

No!

She stepped towards them, hoping for them to see reason, but the two in the front had already begun setting for a spear throw.

They hurled them at her. Panic once again found its way into her thoughts, controlling her movements. As the spears clanked around her, digging into the marbled walls and pillars, she cowered.

"Stay there! You are under arrest for conspiracy of treason!" The guard in front barked at her as he ran her way.

Panic gripped her chest like a vice. Lyra stood frozen, torn between two impossible choices—fight the guards who had sworn to protect her home or run and live to fight another day. Her mind scrambled for clarity, but only one thought broke through the chaos.

Sam. She had to find Sam.

The thought hit her like a spark in dry grass, igniting her legs into motion. At first, she wasn't sure if she'd decided to run or if her body had simply acted on its own. Either way, she was moving. Away from Akros. Away from the guards shouting after her. Toward the docks. Toward her friends.

The gong thundered behind her, the sound chasing her like a hunter's horn.

Traitor. Traitor. Traitor.

The word echoed in her head, growing heavier with each step.

She kept running, lungs burning with every breath. The armor weighed her down, threatening to collapse her with every stride. Still, she pushed forward, her eyes scanning the dim corridors for the faintest glimmer of hope.

When she emerged into the open air of the lower levels, a single thought fueled her: the docks. Her sanctuary.

Then a scream split the air.

Lyra skidded to a halt, heart hammering. Her head whipped toward the sound, toward the massive throne room doors. Behind them, the muffled sounds of a struggle reached her ears.

The sweet aroma spread around Sam. Comforting her into a peace she'd never felt before. Her body floated weightlessly, unobscured by its surroundings. In front of her showed the deep forest with its spotted sunshine falling through the trees.

Behind her, in the sounds of the life of the forest, she heard something odd. Something out of place was calling to her.

No. Not something. Someone.

She pushed through the bird calls, the creek babbling, and the leaves rustling together in their own harmony to see if she could make out what they were saying.

Sam, Sam, we miss you. Come here Sam. Come home.

Two shadowed silhouettes came into view. They cooed and beckoned towards themselves. Her arm weightless. Immovable, as she struggled to reach her hand out to them longingly.

"Sam, samm please!" Cedar cried out.

Sam, Sammm come to us!

Sam pushed herself further towards them. Every fiber in her being aching to reach them. To be close to them. To be with them.

"No, Sam." Cedar searched frantically for a solution. Bram was the closest to her, but he had to battle his own way through the Soltroldens' grip.

"Sideon, help her! I can't lose her again!" Cedar pleaded with him as they both clawed at the tentacles encasing their legs.

"I can't! It might hit her or Bram. Lightning is less controllable under water." He barked furiously as he stabbed a small dagger into the dark purple tentacle that held him.

Cedar and Sideon had been dragged into the water, forcing them to hastily adorne their aquabreaths. However, Sam was dragged, maskless, through the cloud of ink the Soltrolden tried to use on them. Cedar could see her reaching further towards the beast now.

"The ink must be making her see things. Sam!" she called again desperately. Her voice muffled by the aquabreath.

Cedar writhed sporadically under its grasp. The tentacles tightened. She looked at her hands, focusing on a tiny flame or even a spark to assist her friend.

She covered her eyes with her palms. Weakness gathering in her as she lost hope. The water enveloped her. Offering solace as her friend disappeared further into the darkness. Her mind drifted to her family; Fern and her gardening, the laughing face of Atlas, her dad's embracing hug, and her mother caressing her face.

Bringing her thoughts to her soft spoken mother. Cedar was reminded of something that Lin told her when she was a child.

"Cedar," Lin brushed her long, thin fingers through her daughter's hair, "fire is the symbol of rebirth. It will give life, but can will also take it. Understand the flame and respect it before you wield it. If you don't, you can burn yourself, or worse, the others around you. I know now that you struggle to summon it forth, but with practice and patience, you will realize that even in the coldest reaches, there is life. And where there is life, there is heat. All you have to do is feel for it."

She calmed her mind and breathed through the aquabreath. Cedar focused on the water. Her eyes closed, letting go of the moment, she looked for signs of heat around her.

There. A small whisper. She could feel it.

It called for her, from far away. She could sense the geysers and warmth under the castle, in the ground under them. As she reached further, she could feel the gentle warmth of the water's current caressing her skin. In the bodies of Sideon, Bram, Sam, and even in the Sotrolden was the warmth of life. She had found the simmer.

Cedar opened her eyes. Holding her hands open in front of her. She focused on the energy rising in her and water cycled over her hands from the heat.

She surged with energy. Her body jittered. Cedar had never felt an immense power like this flow through her before, or for so long. She could feel her control breaking under the pure force. Her will cracked with fear.

Cedar focused the growing cyclone of boiling water towards her opponent as it grew to its greatest. With her hands, she twisted her fingers in a circle commanding the cyclone to narrow out its current into a flow that was as ruthless as it was merciless.

As if it was a sword in her hands, she sliced downward slowly, breaking through the marbled ceiling and cutting through the pillars as she laid it down on the monstrous Sotrolden before her. No blood oozed from its wounds. The cut was precise, and the heat cauterized them immediately.

The beast's screech echoed through the room deafeningly as it retracted its body together tightly. It let go of all the prisoners it held. They floated towards the floor as they watched it recall itself to a dark corner of the lower throne room. The energy rushed out of Cedar with the cyclone, leaving her almost an empty husk. She landed on the floor, trying to muster any strength she could find.

Severed tentacles floated upwards, and Cedar could see that there were still two small tentacles stuck to Sam as she drifted down.

Her heart raced as Sideon swam towards the limp body of her friend and adjusted the aquabreath to her face.

"Come on." Cedar struggled to get up. Bram swam up to her, and she put her arm around his shoulder.

"Thanks," she breathed.

"You have surprised me yet again, flame summoner." Bram flashed a laughing smile towards her. She returned it weakly, then looked back to Sam and Sideon, who had now fallen to the floor.

A low bellowing sounded in the room and dismay fell on Cedar as her stomach flipped to the sound. Tentacles seethed from the darkness again as the Sotrolden started to click and bellow in angry defiance.

"No." Cedar closed her eyes in defeat and sunk back to the floor under Brams arms. Drained of energy with no other cards left to play.

Bram set her down. Cedar watched him and Sideon stand and walk towards the beast for the next round.

As the full body of the Soltrolden seeped from the shadows, Cedar could feel the malice exude from it. It stared at her. Acknowledging the one who had mutilated its body. Then turned its attention towards the other two waiting in front of it. Sideon handed Bram his dagger, and they both braced themselves for the fight.

The beast lunged. Its whole body hurled towards the two of them. A split second before their mighty collision, a spear zoomed past Cedar, sinking into its body. It let out a piercing screech of agony.

Before anyone could react. Another spear, much larger than the first, whizzed past Cedar's head with enough force to push her to the floor. It struck the Sotrolden with precision and strength. The monster flew backwards with it and hung stapled to the wall from its enormous head. Its purple blood trailed the decorated Damascus and down its shaft before congealing into the seawater and slowly sinking downward in dense bubbles.

Cedar turned to see where it had come from. She smiled, relieved to see Fin had joined the battle, but quickly became wary when she noticed the tall soldier from before with the long white cape stood behind him watching the scene unfold.

With one last look towards the strange guard and Fin, she swam to Sam and huddled over her as she tried to wake her.

"Sam," Cedar shook her shoulders back and forth softly, "Sam."

Her aquabreath had a mix of black and purple in it that Cedar felt was unnatural to be leaving Sam's lungs. She bit her lip in concern as she brushed Sam's floating hair from her face. The others joined her while the masked figure stood by the door, watching.

Sam's eyes fluttered, and she grumbled before struggling to sit up.

"What happened?"

"You missed the battle. I saved the day again. No need to thank me," Fin chimed in.

She winced, but tried to smile at them. "I see you worked out the mask situation, huh?"

His face flushed and didn't respond.

"I don't think he did it alone," Bram spoke up, turning to the spears hanging out of the Sotrolden's limp body. Cedar and the others followed his gaze. They saw the soldier pulling their spear from the body. As it was removed, the lifeless monster slid limply to the floor. With a blood-covered spear in one hand, the soldier used the other to unclasp their cloak, letting it fall to the floor. They removed their helmet.

It was a woman, a couple of years older than Sam.

Cedar had noticed the woman's height immediately, but now she could see the sharpness in her expression as well. Yet it was her hair that truly caught Cedar's attention. A striking salmon pink, pulled back into a ponytail, with a few loose strands framing her face. The end of the ponytail was intricately braided into multiple pieces that cascaded down her back.

Her skin was a pale blue, and as Cedar looked closer, she noticed faint patterns etched across it—so subtle they almost blended with her complexion. In the shadows, however, the patterns revealed themselves, glowing softly with an otherworldly light.

It disappeared quickly, however, as the woman stepped forward fully into the light of the room and walked towards the group.

She hesitated for a moment, but then looked at them. And, in a hopeful tone, she spoke up.

"Sam?"

19

THE WAY THE WATER MOVES

"SAMMI." CEDAR SHOOK HER softly.

As she lifted herself, Sam's head throbbed. A foggy sensation clouded her thoughts.

"Wait- what happened?" She grimaced as Cedar helped her stand. "The last thing I remember was Fin putting on his mask."

Her brain kicked a wave of adrenaline through her body. "The Kraken!" She jolted around, looking for the battle that had already ceased.

Her eyes fell to the beast's body crumpled in a mess of its own tentacles and its blood smeared in a downward trail on the white marbled wall. The group was quiet. Something was happening she had not caught on to yet. As her surroundings became clearer, she noticed Fin, Bram, and Cedar huddled around her, their faces etched with worry. Fin had his aquabreath on.

"I see you were able to finally join the battle, hmm?" She gave him a smirk.

"Ya but not without some help..." he said, his cheeks growing red in embarrassment. Then his eyes went from Sam's to someone behind her.

Sam rotated. A tall woman in coral armor stood before them. Her grip tight on a bloodied spear. She blinked, connecting the dots.

A grin spread across their faces. They eagerly embraced each other with excitement.

"I can't believe I found all of you here, in the throne room, no doubt." Lyra beamed as they released from their hug.

Sam laughed. "I'm guessing you're the one we have to thank for the Sotrolden?" she said, gazing from the blood covered spear to the dead heap.

"No! No, Fin helped! He threw the other spear. I found him up there and he seemed to be new to the aquabreath so I helped him, and when he was adjusted, he pulled me down here" She smiled at Fin.

"Yep! You heard it from her folks, I- Finnigan, killed the mighty Sotrolden with only a spear." He bowed.

"I think it died when she stapled its brains to the wall." Bram said flatly.

Fin retorted, "Well, at least *I* was being productive. What were you doing again? *Biting* the tentacles?"

Bram glared at him in silence.

"Alright, that's enough of that." Cedar broke in.

Suddenly, the gong rang again. Sam sucked in a breath when she heard footsteps trampling down the hallway.

"How did they find us?" Bram asked.

"I don't know, but get ready for another fight." Sideon said, squaring himself to the doors.

"They aren't looking for you." Lyra spoke up.

Sam turned to her.

"What do you mean? Who would they be looking for then?" Sam glanced at the doors to the sounds of armored footsteps that grew louder, then back to Lyra, concerned.

"They're looking for me."

"What?" Sam asked in disbelief.

They all faced Lyra now with the same attentiveness. Cedar shuffled back and forth nervously.

"What do you mean Lyra? Why would they be searching for you?" Sideon stepped towards her.

Lyra's face distorted in agony, twisting itself as she brought her free palm to her eyes, trying to block the tears from forming.

"I don't think I can join you on your journey. I'm now wanted for treason, and attempted murder of Akros and the Queen Dowager." Her voice trembled as she spoke.

Sam shook her head in disbelief, blinking away the confusion as she tried to understand what she had heard.

"I- I am being set up by the advisor," Lyra added quickly, "it was him." Her tone sharp through the tears. "He was the reason I was put to sleep. He drugged me with a mixture of the monster's venom. Then I found a letter from Barclay to him talking about killing the Queen Dowager and that's when he found me and turned the whole of Pearls Gate against me." She fell to her knees, her spear and helmet clanking to the floor. Holding her head in her hands, she hid her face as Sideon comforted her quietly.

Sam's alertness rose at the mention of Barclay. His face of vice flashed in her mind, and the rushing current of the sea swept her back to the recent memory of almost being lost to the void.

She cursed him under her breath and faced her friends to see their reactions. The burning hatred behind each of their eyes, made the decision without even a spoken word between the four of them. Sam picked up Lyra's helmet, feeling the overgrown coral scrap her fingertips, then reached down to pick her sea walker off the floor.

"I think you'll be needing this on our journey. Do you have everything you might need?" Sam's mouth curved up at the ends, forming a gentle smile.

"But the whole realm will believe I'm a traitor once the word gets out."

"Well, good thing we are going to the Realm of Sky, then," Bram said.

Doubt covered her face. She reached into her armor and pulled out a thin piece of paper with a stamp weighing down one end. "I need to get this to the Queen. This will clear my name. It shows that Akros and Barclay are conspiring for the crown, not me."

"Why can't you just show the guards this?" Sideon took the letter and read it over.

"Akros is smart. He knows how to handle a crowd of people. He will say it's fake or a trick. But I know if I can get this to the Queen, she'll believe me." Her eyes glinted. Hope reluctantly appearing behind them.

Sam nodded. "Then we have our plan. We will give this to her when we get to the King's Realm."

"But what are we going to do *right now?*" Sideon snuck a glance at the doors again.

"I think it's time to go." Bram handed Lyra her spear.

Lyra fastened the cloak on and sunk the helmet over her head before looking up to the hole in the ceiling.

"That way will be faster. It's almost a straight shot to the docks from the upper throne room," she pointed.

A soldier's voice rang out from the hall. "I hear something here!"

"That's our cue," Sideon called out and pushed off the floor.

Lyra squatted down, using the force in her thighs to propel herself upwards as she used her spear to slice through the water faster. The others followed her example and heard the large doors opening as they made it to the top.

Sam grabbed the edge and wiggled her body as she tried to flop out of the water. Sideon and Lyra were already standing when she fell to the floor, soaking. Cedar joined right after. Once they were all out, the floor dripped in seawater and blood. Sam bent over, holding her knees for support. She used one hand to pry the mask off.

"Come on, come onnn!" Fin waved for them to hurry. "You have to take the mask off right now?!"

Sam shot him a mean look. "Yes. I'm not keeping this thing on any longer than I need to."

Fin groaned but didn't respond.

She gasped for breath, then straightened out and hurriedly made her way to Cedar, offering comfort as she battled through a fit of coughing as well.

They covered half the distance to the doors when a sudden groaning noise caught their attention - the doors were opening.

Sam's stomach knotted as she skidded to a stop. Sideon was ahead of her, Cedar standing by her side, and Lyra, Bram, and Fin halted behind her.

Two guards ran in.

"Song Lyra and others, you are under arrest for treason and conspiracy of murder," the one on the left barked. They held their spears out in front of them as Sam prepared for the worst.

"Put your hands up!" the other one yelled.

Sideon took a step forward.

"Hold it! Don't move!" The one on the left shuffled and jutted his spear.

"Wait, wait." Lyra pushed past Sam and stood next to Sideon. She put her arm out between him and the guards.

"Ermas? Tark?"

They shuffled again, and she took her helmet off. She held it against her hip, her left hand slowly rising in a gesture of surrender.

"Please, you know I would never do anything to betray Pearls Gate. This is my home. You *have* to see I'm being set up," she pleaded with them.

The air was silent. None moved. Sam's heart fought its way up her throat as she held her breath.

More footsteps grew in the hallway.

"Soldiers!" someone yelled down the hall. "Is the throne room clear?" the guards called out loudly for an answer.

"Please." She looked at them.

The decision rested with the two who blocked their path.

"Respond!" he roared louder.

Their gazes met. Sam's hand trembled above her dagger, the tension rapidly becoming unbearable. A moment later, the person standing on the right side spoke out.

"All clear, Sir!"

Sam could hear Cedar breathe a sigh of relief.

They had made it to the ship, getting past Ermas and Tark was the only real obstacle that they faced. In the rush of panic placed amongst the people, the group found it easier than they thought to make their way to the ship and set off with the new found member of their group.

Pearls Gate stood behind them now as they set out for the next stop in their journey. Lyra watched her home dwindle in the distance. The sun that set high in the sky now baked her in her helmet. She released her hair from its prison and combed her bangs off her sweaty forehead.

"It's a beautiful place to live." Cedar leaned on the railing and watched the castle fade away with her.

She saw Sam and the others join her as well.

"Yes, it is. It's been my home for as long as I can remember."

"So, are you supposed to be a princess or something? Do we have to call you 'her majesty'?" Fin said with a smirk, and Bram punched the back of his shoulder.

"Ow," Fin laughed lightheartedly, "it was a joke," he remarked as he rubbed the wounded spot.

"No." Lyra smiled softly. She sat on the deck, her back against the railing. "I became the apprentice advisor to the

Queen when I turned ten. Then when I was old enough, maybe a year or two later, Nim informed me to join the guards and learn to defend myself."

"Why did that guard call you Song Lyra, then? Is that your name?" Cedar asked.

"Song's like a title. It was never a secret that I had abilities, thus the nickname Song of the Sea, and then the title Song Lyra." She paused for a moment, then scratching at a spot on the wooden deck, she added softly, "Now I see that it probably would have been better to be discreet about it."

Lyra covered her face.

"I feel so stupid. I can't believe I *trusted* him," she added scornfully.

"Lyra, it isn't your fault. Did you ever have any reason to believe this advisor guy would do something like this?" Sam asked.

"I mean- no, but I was around him more than anyone else was. I should have... I should've seen it. Now, because of my arrogance, I'm a traitor to my queen."

"It's going to be ok, I promise. We have a plan in place. All we need is to keep that letter safe in the meantime." Sam comforted her.

"Not to change the subject, but... what exactly can you do?" Fin asked, his voice curious. Lyra noticed that all of them leaned in slightly as the question hung in the air.

"Didn't Nim tell you about it?" she asked, glancing at the others.

"Oh, she did," Fin said, his tone brightening. "But we thought it'd be better to... see it for ourselves."

He sat down cross-legged, his eagerness palpable.

Lyra hesitated for a moment, then closed her eyes, centering herself. She had long ago learned to calm her mind when calling forth the ability that lived just beneath. It wasn't a power to her—more of a second sight. For others, it was something unnatural, even frightening.

When she opened her eyes again, the world around her shifted. Colors bled into the air like an intricate tapestry, each hue telling a story.

The colors of their souls.

She let her gaze sweep over them, noting the subtle shades that vibrated in the space between. Cedar's soul burned with red and orange, the unmistakable signature of a Flame Summoner. Yet there was something different about her—an unusual spark of white flickered at the core of her, like a flame that burned with a purity Lyra hadn't seen in others of her kind.

Fin's soul, in contrast, was murky. His inner light was veiled, a soft, blurred purple that barely pushed through.

Bram's colors made Lyra pause. His deep blue soul was streaked with cracks of black, the cracks spreading quickly, as though something was trying to tear through the surface. A lighter blue flashed beneath, but the shadows swallowed it almost immediately. She frowned.

And then there was Sam. Her soul was a swirl of colors—greens, blues, purples—that shifted and blended into one another like water flowing in every direction at once. There was no distinct shape, no solid identity. It was as though she was caught in the in-between, neither here nor there.

Lyra's heart sank as she watched.

She blinked, pulling herself out of the haze of color.

"Lyra... your eyes," Cedar said softly, leaning forward, her voice thick with awe. "They were a salmon color like your hair, now they're- I don't know how to describe it." Cedar's mouth opened as the words tried to summon themselves.

Lyra laughed, but it came out a little too sharp. "Yeah, they do that," she said, brushing her hair back from her face. She didn't want to linger on the subject, not now. "Chrome. Nim has described the color as a rainbow chrome." She smiled again as she thought back to her grandmother.

The group stared at her for a beat longer, Cedar still entranced by the change in her eyes.

Fin cleared his throat, leaning in. "It's... incredible."

Lyra forced a smile, nodding. She could feel their eyes on her, but her mind kept wandering to what she had seen in their colors. To be lost like that, without any solid sense of self, had to be terrifying. She couldn't help but wonder what it was like for them.

"Are you okay?" Cedar asked, her voice suddenly gentle.

Lyra looked up, the moment of reflection broken. She nodded quickly, a little too quickly. "Yeah. I'm fine. Let's just... move on."

She focused on the others, pushing the unsettling feeling in her chest aside.

As she lifted herself, her eyes were immediately drawn back to the vast expanse of the sea. She could see the different currents, like roads inside the ocean.

"Here," she pointed out excitedly, "there is a current below. It is light green, and it goes back to Pearls Gate for a while, then takes a hard turn out to sea." She traced the visible current in the air as the group followed her finger. They looked on as she continued to detail the current they were riding on at the moment and the many others she could see around them.

Once Pearl's Gate was gone from view, her excitement dwindled and her energy slowly seeped out of her.

"I- I think I might go clean my spear and rest for a while." She could feel the weary smile on her face.

Sam nodded. Bram and Fin had already disappeared once the excitement of the new wore off. Cedar and Sam stayed, and they had told Lyra of the stories she had not yet heard from Sam.

Cedar stood and helped her up.

"If you need anything, let me know." She smiled sheepishly. "I'm somewhat of the group's medic."

"Thank you," Lyra nodded as her mind traveled away from the conversation.

"Go get some sleep. We will let you know if anything exciting happens."

"Thank you." She said again to the two, emphasizing that she meant for everything and not just for right then.

She hesitated, but drew them in for a hug as she tried to not prick them with the coral.

Sam gave her a knowing laugh and nodded towards the cabin. Lyra waved them off as the sun set on the horizon.

The moon stapled itself in dominance against the dark sky. Sideon sailed for the Guardian Mountains. He told them he could take them as far as the Sanctuary. After that, however, they were on their own.

Merrily, the ship floated along the coast. Cedar watched the water push into the land, giving to rivers then joining back to form the coast once again. Seaborne had many islands dotted throughout it. Unlike the Land where everything was connected by roots or moss, the connection here was the water. Whether it was ocean, rivers, waterfalls, or tiny streams, the water flowed, rejoining itself no matter where it went.

With each breath, her mind drifted back to the fight against the Sotrolden and the brief but powerful moment of connection she had grasped. She had burrowed into something much deeper than herself. Dipping her toe into a pool that held much more than she knew. When she channeled that power, she had almost lost control of the immensity of what she delved into. Goosebumps spread across her arms as she tried to remember what it felt like. The drape was cast though, it blocked her from seeing or feeling past it. Focused, she strained to reach for it, trying to recall what she had discovered in their time of need.

"You're gonna set Sideon's boat on fire if you're not careful," Fin commented behind her.

She opened her eyes to see her hair floating in a light flame around her like a torch. Fire licked her hands and arms that singed the railings black. She sucked her teeth.

"*Ugh,*" she groaned, whisking the flames away as she rubbed at the burnt wood. "Oops, you don't think he'll notice, do you?"

"I'm sure some spit and elbow grease will take it out." He laughed, then looking at the marks, he made a doubtful face.

With a dismissive shake of his head, he changed the subject and handed her a fresh apple. "So, how did I do during the battle? I came to the team's rescue, pretty dashing wasn't I?"

"I guess, I'd have to say you've done worse." Cedar weighed the fruit before taking a bite of it.

Her eyes brightened, and she held up a finger as she chewed and swallowed.

"I feel like I was more the star of that one. Did you see my column of heat slice through its tentacles?" She imitated the slicing motion with her hand.

He snorted. "I saw the tentacles floating around. It was definitely gross, so thanks for that. I think one touched me when we got down there." He made a face and shivered at the thought.

"Whatever." Cedar rolled her eyes.

"What are we chattin' about?" Sam strolled up and sat on a crate near them.

"We're comparing battle stories. You know, since we're seasoned warriors now."

"I have to say you came through today. I'm proud of you," Sam responded with a crooked smile.

"Thanks." He smiled goofily.

Cedar grunted at his response and took another bite of the apple.

"I was no help. I felt like a fish out of water, or- well... a dog in the ocean," Bram spoke up behind Cedar, startling her. She twirled on her heels, and her heart raced. He was sitting on the deck in the railing's shadow.

"Jeez, Bram, can you not sneak up like that? You scared me!" Cedar withered onto the railing as she calmed down.

"I might have to end up getting weapons if-" he broke off, his eyes dropping to the floor.

He struggled with the transformation still. Her eyes shot to Sam. She could see her shift her weight.

"I'm sorry, Bram." Cedar sat down next to him.

He sighed. "Mulling over it won't change the past. It's probably better this way. When I was the wolf, I never could control my self."

Fin sat next to Sam on the crate. "Ya, you were pretty rude."

Bram shot him a look, then turned toward the stars.

"Maybe I can find some answers in the Guardian Mountains."

At that, Cedar was reminded of what he told them in Vineke. She looked at Sam, who seemed upset about his comment, too. Fin gave no notion to what Bram said but Cedar knew that if he didn't have a snarky comment in response, then he was upset.

She could see glints of his hair and his eyes seeking the stars from the shadows he sat in. Longingly, he gazed up as if he searched for the answers to fall into his lap.

She sat down next to him.

"Yeah, maybe."

20

TO THE CUSP OF SEA & SKY

THEY SLEPT THROUGH THE night. The boat rocking them into a deep slumber of much needed rest from the battle they faced. As the sun rose, so did the life around them, rousing them from their sleep and ready to begin a new day. They moseyed about the ship, wandering around, waiting for their destination.

The sky and sun had worked together to create a morning of beauty. There was a pink haze all around them on that drizzly morning as the sun rose. Soon it settled itself into an orange that resembled the fresh fruit ready to be picked and eaten. Then, with a hint of clear yellow dappling the sky, it finally returned to normal, as if it had never happened. Once it did, the rain started.

They stayed in Sideon's cabin, talking, impatiently waiting for something to happen and as if they had called her forth. Nim appeared. Cedar spotted her first through the window that looked at the deck.

"What is that?" Cedar asked, her brows furrowed as she stood slowly. Her full attention turned to something that was happening outside.

Sam and the others followed her eyesight. The rain was soft. It piddled on the ship, but in a clear spot with no crates or ropes or items in the way. It fell, and then stopped. Floating. More rain collected itself, then water from the side of the ship crawled upwards to the now suspended puddle. More little streams joined until it was a swirling pillar the size of a human.

"Nim!" Lyra bounced to the small window. Her hands pressed against the door excitedly.

The others joined when it gradually morphed into human form. Finally, there stood Nim, the Lady in the Water, solid as if she had been there the whole time. She smiled at the group, lightly waving at them as she made her way to the cabin door.

"Sideon, please join us," her muffled voice called from outside.

A loud thump came from above, then smaller ones followed. He hopped down from the helm, giving her a welcoming smile, they entered the cabin together. Sideon mildly soaked from the drizzle. Nim completely dry.

Sideon shook his head like a dog and sprayed the fire warmed cabin with droplets of water, sending groans of disapproval out amongst the group. Simultaneously, he shook his jacket and stomped his feet as he unsuccessfully tried to get dry.

Nim chuckled, holding open her hand. The water from Sideons' playful rampage seeped from around the room and off of him into Nim's palm. After a moment, the room was no longer damp, and Sideon was as free from the rain as the rest of them were.

Lyra ran over to hug her. They embraced for a moment, then released to examine each other.

"It's been too long, Nim." Lyra sighed. Her smile radiant to see her, but her eyes hurt from the absence.

"Yes, my dear, it has been." Nim pecked her on the cheek and then turned to look over the rest of the group.

"You all look well, especially after a clash with the Sotrolden," she nodded content.

"It was rough, but Lyra came through just in the nick of time," Sam spoke up.

Fin coughed, Sam rolled her eyes.

"And Fin. Fin helped too, I guess."

Nim chuckled lightly again, warming the hearts of everyone in the room.

"I've come with questions, news, and information you might want." She clasped her hands together.

"But first, tell me all about it. Don't leave out a single detail."

Sideon pulled out a chair for her, and she sunk into it, nodding her thanks to him.

Lyra relaid the story of what happened at Pearls Gate to her. Pulling out the letter for her to read over. Sam and the others interjected at times with parts of the story that were their own. Once it was complete, Nim clapped.

"What an interesting time you have had in the Sea Realm." Her eyes laid on Sam. Sam raised her brow and nodded in agreement.

"You could say that again." She mumbled.

"First, Lyra, keep this." She folded the letter and handed it back. "You will present it to the Dowager Queen after your journey is over. We have long suspected something was stirring in the deep underbelly of the ocean. I know this is upsetting to hear, but for now... we would like you to play the part of traitor to the Queen." Nim stopped, waiting.

"But why Nim? You know that I am not *actually* guilty of this by now!" Lyra's eyes pleaded with her grandmother as she grasped her hands into her own.

"Darling, of course you aren't, but to keep these fish from scattering into the sea and disappearing forever we must play the part. There are many more than Akros and Barclay we have to worry about. We need them to think they are safe. And by playing as a traitor, they will think they're in the clear."

Lyra frowned, looking down at the floor.

"I understand..."

All could see the ache behind her eyes.

Nim cupped her face. "Once you bring the letter to the Dowager in the King's Realm, we will use it as the next step of completing our plan."

"Ok- I understand," Lyra repeated, she let out a deep breath as she put on a brave face.

Nim's eyes laid on Cedar after that. "Now that I have been brought up to date on what happened in Pearls Gate. I have a message for you from your father."

Cedar and Sam sat up straight, becoming alert.

"My father?" Cedar gestured to herself. Nim smiled.

"How?"

"After you left, I reached out and caught them up on your journey. They were happy to hear about you two. And he wanted me to pass along a message about your next destination."

"Next destination?" Sam thought out loud.

"The next realm on your journey to find a sky runner," Nim responded.

"The Guardian Mountains," Bram added.

Each of them had a far off look as they imagined what this new land offered.

"He wanted me to tell you that this realm can be isolating at times. During his travels across the mountains, he found it to be unforgiving and few friends were made across the realm."

"Jeez, this sounds fun." Fin leaned back on the bed against his elbows.

"I've not traveled into the Realm of Sky for a while. From what I have heard, the cities are well advancing, faster than land or sea, but the sky folk look down on others for their *primitive* ways," Nim said.

"I have also heard of small villages that have isolated themselves in tradition, away from the bigger cities. Keep an eye out for them as well. Maybe you will find someone to help you along your way there," Sideon added.

"I don't remember it just being snowy mountain ranges, though," Bram spoke up. "There were long stretches of green and lakes hidden in the valleys."

"I'm sure there is more than snow, but it would be wise to dress in thick furs and prepare for the cold," Nim responded, then turned to Lyra.

"You have not been out of the water much in your life, let alone above sea level. This... will be a challenge for you. Your lungs are not used to air like this. I would take a bag of aquabreaths." She gestured to Sideon. "He has a stash somewhere on this ship. He will provide them for you."

Sideon flared his nostrils, but accepted defeat. "Yes- I will give you a bunch of my super expensive aquabreaths to take on your trip."

Nim patted his arm in thanks.

Fin's stomach growled loudly, interrupting the conversation.

"Sorry."

Sam could feel her stomach grumbling for food as well.

"How 'bout we take a break and have breakfast? We can finish this conversation after," Sideon said as he opened the door, calling for food as he pulled out a thick prismatic glass of water and some glasses.

"So what's this *Edel Sanctuary* about?" Sam asked.

She found a comfortable spot next to Cedar. Their shoulders bumping gently.

The rain stopped a couple of hours ago and the wood dried in the sun as it peaked out from the scattered drifting clouds. Sam joined Cedar and Bram in the crow's nest when she was done dozing with Ajax.

"The *Edel Sanctuary* is what it sounds like," she mimicked Sam's voice. "A sanctuary for species of animals to live without fear of being hunted. They have been homing animals there since it was created." Cedar's eyes lit up with excitement.

"I heard it was a massive piece of land with each section of the realms touching it," Bram added.

Cedar nodded, her wavy hair jumping up and down, the sunlight bouncing in it, making it hue into a brighter red than normal.

"It has so many weird and rare creatures. Have you ever heard of a pangolin?"

They shook their heads.

"That's supposedly there and *really* weird looking." She made a face.

"How does a creature get put in there?" Bram asked.

"Every so often there is a committee that submits one animal from each realm, and they look over them and if there is no way to halt the hunting and near extinction of the animal, then it is placed in the Sanctuary," she explained.

"The First King spent most of his time there in his old age. They said Edel was created for his plumifera."

Sam stopped.

"A what?"

"A plumifera, you know, a furry dragon with feathered wings."

Sam blinked, confused.

Then, letting a frustrated breath escape her nose, she scratched the back of her head.

Dragons.

"Sam?" Cedar leaned in.

"I'm sorry." She said, shaking her head. "This is crazy. I never thought I'd hear that a dragon actually exists."

"Ya, of course they would. It's not that far out," Bram snorted.

"I guess not... what else is in there, Cedar?" She turned her attention back to where they were headed.

A new question popped into her head and before Cedar could answer the first one, she threw it out there. "Wait, wait, what does the Sanctuary look like?"

"Umm," Cedar tilted her head to the side as her eyes distanced themselves, concentrating on the image before her.

"Well, the books and drawings I've seen are gardens with exotic plants. There's a greenhouse placed somewhere in the Sanctuary. There are natural pools and in most of the drawings, there are the mountains in the background too." She pursed her lips. Sam looked up to the sky, joining her in the imagining of this land.

"Lakes that sit still and willow trees overlooking them, waterfalls in some parts, for the lake creatures," Cedar added.

"O! I almost forgot. I think you'll like this part, Sam." She grinned mischievously at her.

Sam leaned in. Cedar did too and whispered.

"The part that's connected to the Realm of Land- is forbidden, no faus can enter, only the creatures can enter. It's known to be magical and ancient. The trees there are from the old times before the wars and the making of the Realms. That's where Ajax is from, the old forest, and people say it holds many secrets to the life of the trees."

Sam sucked in a breath and leaned back. "Wow," she whispered, thinking back to the first time she had seen him as a small fawn.

He'd gotten big, she wondered if he thought about his family.

Sam chewed on her fingernail in thought. She could hear Cedar and Bram talking more about the Sanctuary, but her mind strayed to the forest and its many guardians that held their secrets.

Hours passed. The sun reached as high as it could and then sunk. With all the rain cleared off, the group grew antsy. Their voyage on the Agalon close to its end. They gathered their items and packed what they needed, Nim decided to bid them farewell.

"It's time for me to leave you." She approached Lyra, Sam, and Bram.

"You're leaving already?" Lyra frowned and put down her spear that she had been cleaning.

"Yes, my Song. I must deal with other business in the sea."

Lyra's disappointment saddened Nim's eyes.

"Will I see you in the King's Realm?" Lyra prompted.

A smile formed Nim's face. "I will be there awaiting your arrival. *And* looking forward to meeting your sky runner along with hearing interesting new tales from your travels." She hugged Lyra. They embraced tightly, feeling the warmth and comfort of each other's presence.

Afterwards, Nim thanked both Sam and Bram for helping Lyra escape.

"I will find the others and say goodbye as well." She turned and stopped for a moment.

"O, and Sam," she turned. Her deep brown eyes piercing through Sam as if she could read her thoughts. "we will have much to discuss the next time we see each other."

And with that, she left.

"Spooky," Bram said in a chilling voice.

Chills ran up Sam's back.

"Stop that," Sam teased.

But she had to admit, it did leave her questioning what she meant, and hope brewed inside her chest at the thought of learning more about her past.

Ajax bleated towards the door as a goodbye of sorts. Sam turned and tousled his soft fur.

"We'll see her again, Ajax."

The Qilin laid his head back down and dozed off as the three of them returned to their prior activities.

"Mask, staff, extra aquabreath, chest piece, extra clothes for the cold, and some food." Sam pursed her lips. "Am I missing anything Ajax?"

He bleated at her, "No, you will not fit on me or in my pack, sir." She rolled her eyes. Her hands searched anxiously, and finally, she felt the object she had been searching for, bringing a wave of relief.

"Haha!" She laughed triumphantly as she held up her lotus dagger and examined it proudly.

"Woah! Sam! Do you know what that is?!" Lyra stood and hovered over her as a bee would.

She raised an eyebrow. "It's a blade, with a lotus on it. It's my... Lotus Blade."

"It's one of the Lotus Dozen daggers!" She took it gently and examined the metal flower on the base of the blade. "Only members of an elite guild carry these, and sense, there are only twelve colors of the lotus plant, that means there are only twelve assassins at a time!"

Sam took the dagger back and held it longways in her hands, examining it in the new light of mystery.

"Where'd you get it?" she asked, intrigued.

"I- I found it." Before Sam could question herself to why she lied to the two of them. She stuffed it in the bag. She secured it by sandwiching it between two of her spare tops, guaranteeing its safety.

"That's a crazy find, then! I bet you the owner of that blade is looking for it," Lyra exclaimed.

Fright pinged in Sam's mind. She turned to her hastily. "What do you mean, looking for it? What would happen to the person who had the dagger?" The questions flew out as she thought of her tiny friend stuck in an inn across the realms.

Lyra put her hands up. "Woah, it's ok. They are for the Seaborne and sometimes are hired to protect the King and his family. They won't hurt you, at least, I don't think."

Bram chimed in, "What she means is keep *it* hidden."

Sam pursed her lips. "I think I am getting hungry. Does anyone want anything?" She tried to level her panic so that neither of them could pick up on the reason why she had freaked out so fast.

Lyra blinked a couple of times. "I'll- take an apple. Thanks."

"Same, I guess," Bram added.

Sam closed the door behind her, leaving the two of them there. She leaned against the door and heard Lyra's voice through the crack.

"Did I do something? It seemed like she was upset at something I said." Her voice was muffled, but Sam sensed the worry behind it.

"Nah, I wouldn't worry about her. She's pretty much an open book. If she doesn't like you... she'll let you know. Trust me."

"Alright," she replied, concern lacing her words. "I hope she's okay."

Sam smiled, laughing to herself at what Bram said and trotted off to find something to eat.

With food toppling out of her grasp, she made her way back to the cabin.

Good thing she brought extra, Cedar and Fin were back now,

She looked down at the bread she had all but crushed in her grip.

Something caught her the corner of her eye.

With a brief pause to readjust, she turned her attention to the boundless night that lay ahead. All was dark. The sun had fallen behind the horizon, the moon crescent and barely hanging in the sky. She squinted, staring off into the distance.

"Something wrong?" Cedar came out and grabbed some of the food from her. Fin followed, plucking up an apple and staring off into the vast void as well.

"No, I don't think so. I thought something caught my eye, that's all."

Lyra and Bram joined, and the five of them stood, eating by the railing, and wondering what it was that made the night sky seem strange.

"There's something wrong with the sky?" Bram said, unsure about his theory.

"Yea, it's like something is missing," Cedar added. "The stars just stop."

"That's it, the stars are weird," Fin said.

"The bottom half is gone." Sam saw that the line of stars jagged along and dropped off about halfway down from the moon.

From behind them, Sideon let out a light-hearted laugh that filled the air.

"It's the mountains. Welcome to the Realm of Sky."

And as if the image became clear in all of their minds at once, they saw what was truly in front of them. Mountains veiled with the night, standing so tall that they eclipsed all that lay behind them.

Daylight brought clarity. The group had fallen asleep talking about the fascinating stories they had heard of the mysterious and dangerous realm that lay before them. Sam had awoken in the morning light, stretching, she opened the door to find a marvelous sight.

To her left lay the mountains, tall and proud, beckoning the call of adventure.

To her right spread the vast sea, beautiful and strong, bidding her luck on the rest of her journey.

In the middle, she was met with the thick red sun rising on the cusp of sea and sky.

End of Book 2

INDEX

Acknowledgements

First and foremost, to God, the ultimate storyteller, thank You for the gift of imagination, the love of words, and the patience to see this journey through. Every story is a whisper of something greater, and I am endlessly grateful for the inspiration You provide.

To my dad, who filled my childhood with stories, and the belief that wonder is everywhere if you know where to look. Your unwavering support has been a light in the darkness and a compass when I've lost my way.

To Xander, my husband, you have stood by me through every battle with self-doubt, every late-night, and every plot twist (both on and off the page). Thank you for believing in me even when I struggled to believe in myself. I love you endlessly.

To my incredible beta readers, the brave souls who found their way into my world before it was fully formed. You are the heroes of this tale. Your insights, encouragement, and sharp eyes have helped shape this story into something stronger, something truer. I am forever grateful for your time and dedication.

To my editors, the skilled alchemists who transformed rough words into polished prose, you are the unsung wizards behind the scenes, and I am in awe of your magic. Thank you for your patience, your wisdom, and your willingness to walk this road with me.

And to you, dear reader—no matter how you arrived—thank you for stepping into this world. May you find adventure, wonder, and perhaps a bit of magic within these pages.

About the Author

Shelby Gragg is a fiction writer specializing in fantasy and science fiction, where she weaves stories that explore themes of sacrifice, adventure, family, perseverance, and identity.

With a bachelor's degree in Early Childhood Education, Shelby's work is often influenced by her passion for mythology and storytelling. When not writing or working as an elementary school teacher, she enjoys reading, video games, and exploring the outdoors with her family. Shelby is currently working on completing her *In-Between Chronicles*, continuing to bring her unique blend of of wonder and depth to life.

ALSO BY

S.J.GRAGG

The Four Realms Saga
Of Land – Book One